TAYLOR DELONG

For EMD,
Because I made you plot and plot and PLOT for this story and then I totally ignored everything we talked about and wrote an entirely different story. Which is why I'm not a plotter, but maybe you will be. And hey, I can be your plot coach. Or not.
I can't wait to read your published books, but more importantly, put them on the shelf in our offices. Never give up on your dreams!
I love you, more than you'll ever know.

a not so merry rescue playlist

Roller Coaster Luke Bryan
All of Me John Legend
What My World Spins Around Jordan Davis
Messed Up As Me Keith Urban
Bulletproof Nate Smith
Fix What You Didn't Break Nate Smith
Gonna Love You Parmalee
Worst Way Riley Green
Am I Okay? Megan Moroney
We Found Love Rihanna ft. Calvin Harris
Who You Love John Mayer ft. Katy Perry
Everything Has Changed Taylor Swift ft. Ed Sheeran
Wind Up Missin' You Tucker Wetmore
Anything But Mine Kenny Chesney
It's the Most Wonderful Time of the Year Kylie Minogue
Wrap Me Up Jimmy Fallon & Meghan Trainor
Santa Baby Madonna
Little St. Nick Beach Boys
The Christmas Blues Dean Martin
Holly Jolly Christmas Michael Bublé

1
willa

THE FLURRIES of the last hour swirl into bigger flakes, and the sky darkens as the setting sun creeps toward the horizon. Throughout the drive, the temperature's been steadily dropping, hovering at a crisp thirty-one degrees. The wipers work overtime as I twist the knob to give them more power, attempting to combat the steadily falling snow.

A peek at the GPS reveals I still have over an hour left to drive. At this speed, it will be more like two or three. Which puts me at the cabin closer to midnight than I'd like. Had I not hit all the traffic along Route 89, I could have made it before the snow began. But that's on me for leaving the packing to the last minute.

Then forgetting the car needed gas.

And of course, having to stop for road trip snacks.

The last one brings a stupid smile to my face. "You can't go on a road trip without snacks," his faraway voice echoes in my ear. A voice of another time.

Before.

Tears prick my eyes, but I refuse to let them fall. No more headspace for him tonight. Besides, it's hard enough to see where I am without my eyes leaking.

Like a beacon, a Christmas tree farm sign catches my eye. A red truck with a fir tree in its bed emblazons the left corner. It reminds me of my cousins' tree farm in Oregon. It's been a while since I've spoken with them, even longer since I visited Murrtham's Tree Farm.

Christmas trees. Another memory I immediately banish.

The road is devoid of people, the smart humans who listened to the weathermen and stayed at home, not braving the elements.

I didn't think to check the weather where I was passing through. Only my starting point and my destination. I was too eager to get on the road, to get to the cabin, to worry about such trivial things as snow.

Chalk it up to growing up in a place where snow isn't a thing. An adjustment I'm still making to snowy winters in Vermont. Which begin before December. Who knew?

A thump reverberates through the car, and the wheel jerks to the right. My heart thunders and waves of unease wash over me, the unfamiliar conditions winning a battle I didn't realize I was fighting.

Panic tightens my chest in a viselike grip, my eyes widening as the car veers to the right. White-knuckling it, I spin the wheel to the left to overcorrect, but it's too much.

It's too late.

The tires don't have traction on the snow-covered road, and the SUV swerves out of control. I close my eyes, speaking to a higher being to at least let me land safely. No matter the damage to the car, let me stay unharmed. The car is replaceable. I'm not.

The earlier tears spring to my eyes, my emotions all over the map. Praying I make it safely, as safe as can be, my car skids to the side of the road. As I brace for impact, there's a heavy thud when the front passenger side hits a tree, the car lurching forward, the seat belt keeping me from slamming into the steering wheel. If I was traveling at twenty, it was fast, but running something over or blowing a tire—much as I can surmise the issue is—coupled with the snowy conditions, lends itself to a host of problems.

I don't breathe until the car's stopped. Tears track down my cheeks, twin lines of heightened fear making the situation more dire. My brain works double time at what to do first.

Do I get out and assess the damage?

Do I call for help?

Do I hope my guardian angel caught the incident and is sending help as I ponder what to do?

Of the three, calling for help seems to be the wisest. I don't want to stand in the snow any longer than I have to. Let an expert assess the damage.

A chill runs through me. I blast the heat, but it's not the frigid temperatures causing the iciness.

Flipping on the overhead light, I dig into the glove box, frantically searching for the roadside assistance card I'm certain is in there. I haven't taken it out since the service guy put it in there when I bought the car a little over two years ago. I haven't needed it, but man am I glad for it now.

A few minutes of digging through the papers later, the card's been acquired. With fumbling fingers, I dial the number, holding my breath until a gruff, "Roadside assistance," answers.

"Oh, uh, hi. I'm stuck." I slap my head at the absurdity of my message. "I mean, I need some help. Please," I tack on. The utterance is watery to my ears, my meltdown rising to the surface.

"City or town?"

"Um . . ." I scroll back to the map, pinching the screen to zoom out from the route, hoping to provide a clue about my whereabouts. "I'm not exactly sure. I'm on my way to Lake Champlain, but I think I hit an animal or a tire blew, and I lost control of the car and skidded into the side." The more I ramble, the higher my voice pitches, anxiety having a field day on my nerves. "Is there any way I can send my location? Drop a pin or something?"

Isn't that what the kids say? "Drop me a pin of your location."

"Hold on." The man's voice is anything but soothing. There's a rustling on the line, the least bit reassuring as the seconds tick away and more time gets added to my destination.

Closing my eyes, I pinch my nose, delving deep for strength I don't possess. If only I had waited until tomorrow morning to get on the road. But no, I had to leave tonight, to not waste a paid night at the cabin.

"You there?" The deep baritone brings me back to the current situation.

"Yep." My attempt at peppiness falls flat. "Still here. Where here is, I don't know."

"You got an iPhone?"

"Yes."

"K. Can you share your location with this number?" He rattles off a string of numbers, but it's too fast to catch them.

"Wait. Too fast. I didn't even get the area code."

A heavy sigh tumbles over the line, ratcheting my panic. "Tell me when you're ready."

It takes a minute to catch on to what he means. Remembering I stashed it earlier, I snatch the pen from behind my ear and hold it over my palm. "Ready."

Slowly, he gives me the ten digits. I make sure not to smudge them before I can get them inputted into my phone.

Once I've shared my location, he confirms, "Gotcha. You're not far from the shop. Probably be like twenty minutes. Thirty at the most with the snow. Sit tight. Name's Beckett."

"I'll be here. Trying not to freeze to death."

The deep timbre of his chuckle radiates through me, bringing a sort of comfort unusual for the situation. And ironically, heat. "How much gas you got?"

I glance at the dash. "One hundred miles. Hope that means something to you."

"Keep it running. Not like you'll be driving it away from the scene."

I cringe, and a deep sigh expels. "Most likely not."

"K. I'll be there as soon as I can."

"Be safe." The declaration falls from my lips uninhibited. But seriously. If he's not safe, he won't be able to rescue me.

"I'll do my best, ma'am." The line goes dead.

At least he's courteous.

From the back seat, I grab my winter coat, slipping my arms into the sleeves and zipping it closed. It's confining and uncomfortable, two things I hate with a passion, but I'd rather be stifled than freezing.

With nothing but time to kill, I exit out of the Maps app and pull up the phone. My sister's probably done putting the kids to bed.

She answers on the second ring. "Taking a break on your road trip?" she guesses.

"Something like that." No doubt she'll hear the defeat in my voice. She knows me too well. Hazard of being a twin.

"Why so glum, Willafred?"

"Well, Clementine, which part of the bad news do you want first?"

"The worst. Duh."

Her words bring a grin to my lips. When you start with the worst, the top of the list never looks as dreary. I'm not sure it applies in this situation but can't hurt to try.

"My front bumper is currently making out with a tree on the side of the road."

"Eep. That's bad. How'd that happen?"

I regale her with the tale, starting from getting a late start to the snow to the animal sacrificing its life to cross the road in a blizzard. When I finish, I feel marginally better.

"Oh shit. I was expecting maybe the rest stop didn't have a vending machine or something. Do you have a plan? What can I do to help?"

I laugh humorlessly. "What exactly are you going to do from one thousand miles away?"

"I can't help my instinct to save you from your troubles. I can call AAA."

"Beckett's on his way."

"*Beckett*?" she poses incredulously. "How are you already on a first-name basis with . . . whoever this Beckett character is?"

I blow out a breath. "He mentioned his name when I called roadside assistance. I don't know him. He's probably some creepy guy in his fifties." I sit up straighter as the words come out. "Oh my gosh. What if he's creepy? And he has my phone number. And my location." Once I start, I can't stop the illogical questions or the nonsense streaming out. "What should I do? Try to move the car? Try to drive away? He could be a serial killer."

"Willa. Breathe," comes across the line. "I'm sure it's fine."

"But you can't know for sure. It's imperative you stay on the phone until he gets here to make sure I'm not abducted."

Clem's laugh resounds in my ear. "I thought you were going to dial back listening to the true crime podcasts."

"Did I say that?"

"Several times. Glad I didn't hold my breath. I'd be dead many times over by now."

My mouth opens to refute her, but it closes quickly. It's an obsession, one I've tried to curb over the years to no avail. I can't help what my mind wants to listen to. The kind of information it craves. Because for a variety of reasons, I'm holding on to it with everything I have.

Bright lights shine on the opposite side of the road.

"I think the serial killer is here," I whisper, as if I didn't, he could hear me.

"You better go deal with him. Call me once you know your plan. I'll have my phone next to me in case you need me." Like before, the line goes dead without a goodbye.

Nerves dance through me. I'm about ninety-five percent sure

he won't be a serial killer, but it's the pesky five percent worrying me the most.

I send up one last petition to the universe to keep me safe.

A week before Christmas is a bad time to kick the bucket.

2
beckett

THE DARK LEXUS SUV straddles the edge of the road, the front passenger bumper lodged into a tree. It's iffy if it's drivable, but with tonight's conditions and the way the driver sounded panicked on the phone, the best course of action is a tow to the shop so I can assess it in the garage in the daytime.

I drive past the car, turn the truck around, and point it back toward the car, backing it up into position to lower the flatbed when needed. Pulling on my hat and gloves, I exit the vehicle, bracing against the frosty elements. I don't bother with the driver's side, instead knocking on the passenger side window. When it lowers, a pair of terrified eyes glares at me. Though the overhead light is still on, I can't make out the color beyond dark.

"Beckett Nicholas." I point at the undamaged door. "Mind if I sit a minute while we discuss what happens next?" It's too cold to do both—make the plan and then execute it.

"Uh, yeah."

She's bundled in a zippered evergreen coat. Her round face is devoid of makeup, but a natural beauty radiates from her. Her chestnut hair is loosely secured in a messy bun, a few strands fallen in her haste to secure it or the stress of the current situation. A rosy glow stains the apples of her cheeks.

I jiggle the handle, but it's locked. "You might want to unlock it." I keep my tone level, steady. She's frightened enough. No need to make it worse. However, the longer the window is open, the more snow drifts in.

"Oh, right." Trembling fingers work the button. First, locking it again before she tsks and moves it the other way. Her cheeks flush a deeper shade of red, and her fingers rub the lobe of her right ear.

Once it's unlocked, I open the door, sliding onto the seat, pushing a bag of snacks out of the way. I close the window and remove my gloves, blowing into my hands to give them a little more heat.

"I can't assess all the damage until I have it on the lift, so I'll put it on the flatbed and deliver it to the garage. Can probably work it into the schedule tomorrow afternoon. Slow week with the holiday and all."

I'm trying to set her at ease, but her expression pains more.

"Okay." She tugs on the ends of her chestnut locks, entwining her finger and twisting the hair around it.

"Where did you say you were headed?"

She starts to answer, but her mouth clamps shut. Her head shakes and she articulates, "I'd rather not say."

So much for polite chitchat while I brace the elements before I load up her car. Too bad for her I remember it from the earlier phone call.

"You'll have to stay here for the night."

"*Here*?" she squeaks, worry lacing the one word.

"There's an inn in town. Happy to drop you off on the way."

"That's kind of you." She tucks her top teeth into her mouth, the action adorable. "Guess I was wrong."

"About what?" My curiosity piqued, the question pops out.

"You being a serial killer." Her shoulders rise in a shrug, as if she didn't just peg me as a murderer.

"Dramatic much?" My teenage niece's voice rings in my ears.

"I don't know where I am. I'm supposed to just trust you are who you say you are?" She pauses, her eyes widen with whatever else she must be thinking. "Even then, it's not like serial killers announce themselves as serial killers."

And I've got a crazy one on my hands.

She angles her body away from me, putting more space in between us.

"I guess you'll have to trust me when I say I'm not a serial killer."

"Which is what a serial killer would say!" Exasperated, she throws her hands in the air.

"So you'd rather not take a chance on me? What will you do? Stay here until someone you know can come rescue you rather than me loading up the car onto my truck and dropping you off at the inn that's about ten minutes up the road?" I cross my arms over my chest, not missing the way her eyes home in on the action. Her tongue peeks out the left corner of her mouth before she snaps it closed.

"Where are we exactly?"

"Winterberry Junction," I rattle off.

"That's . . . an interesting name for a town. Did you say Winterberry?"

"Yep. Named for the season"—I wave my hand in front of me toward the windshield—"and the berries that grow here, specifically winterberries." I repeat words I've heard all my life. Don't have much use for the berries, but the town? I love it.

Her eyes narrow. "It sounds made up. Winterberry." Her nose scrunches when she emphasizes the word.

"I assure you, it's a real place. Even have our own zip code."

Outside the warmth of the car, the snow continues to fall, picking up speed as the wind gusts whip around. The longer this takes, the more time it will be before I can retire for the night. After today's grueling workout, a steam shower is screaming my name.

"I'm googling it." Her phone is out before I can make another comment. One along the lines of let's get a move on. But sometimes there's no arguing with crazy . . .

While she looks up the town, I send a text to the Snowy Peaks Inn to inquire about their availability. Christmas is a popular time in Winterberry, and visitors flock from near and far. As it gets closer to the holiday, tourists outnumber locals. The Snowy Peaks Inn is less popular, as many guests like the appeal and ambience of the two local bed-and-breakfasts.

"Wait. What's your name?" I question as realization sets in. Why I didn't get it earlier evades me.

"Willa," she states, almost on autopilot. Then she slaps her forehead and peers over at me.

"It's not much to go on, *Willa*." I stress her name, trying to further set her at ease. "It's not like I have a last name to go with it, and Willa is more common than other names." I'm not sure that's true. I wrack my brain if I've ever known a Willa before. Is it a nickname? Hopefully not pushing my luck, I guess, "Short for Wilhelmina?"

Her nose scrunches again, the action more adorable than the first time. "Ew. No. That's an old person's name."

"Don't let my sister-in-law hear you say that. It tops her list of baby names." Where the notion comes from, I don't know. Setting Willa "at ease" apparently involves riling her up with false information my brain conjures up.

A horrified expression jumps on her face. It takes all my willpower not to laugh or give myself away. "Seriously?"

I break easily. "Yeah, no. I don't have a pregnant sister-in-law."

Willa's arm reaches across the space, but I dart out of reach. "That wasn't nice. And also, now you've just lied to me, so I'm back to believing you could be a serial killer."

Much as I want to, I refrain from rolling my eyes, but I poke the bear a little more. "Come to think of it, there are a lot of spots around Winterberry to hide bodies. Probably wouldn't even have to kill you first. Just leave you outside in a remote location and let the elements take care of the rest."

Never predicted I'd be thinking of hiding bodies when my day started.

Never crossed my mind to ever consider it.

Neither did I imagine coming in contact with this beautiful woman beside me.

Must be my lucky day.

I wait patiently for Willa's reaction to my comments, but all I get is her mouth opening and closing several times. What a disappointment.

"Come on. Not even a snarky comeback? Did you not hear my plan to—"

She cuts me off. "I heard you. I've decided you're most likely not a murderer. And if you are, it wouldn't be wise to give up your plan to your victims." Her comments expressed, she shrugs and reverts back to her phone.

Letdown, I go back to my unsent text.

> Got a wayward traveler. You got any rooms for the night?

SNOWY PEAKS INN

> Wish I could say yes, but we're slammed. Between the snow and Christmas, we're booked up.

"Oh, shit."

That gets Willa's attention.

"I'm sensing there's a problem."

I look up to find her wary countenance aimed my way. "No rooms at the inn."

She flashes her phone. "How about one of the bed-and-breakfasts?"

"I'll check, but they usually book up faster than the inn."

I shoot a text to my brother-in-law, but his response is as I feared.

"Sold out."

"Both of them?" Her voice elevates in frequency, anxiety settling back in.

"Yep. Unfortunately." I scratch my head, pondering her options.

The next town over is a good fifteen miles. Any night it wasn't snowing, I'd offer to bring her there, but that's not happening tonight.

"Okay, but what am I going to do? Where am I going to stay?" Near hysteria grips every syllable, and concern blankets her expression.

Nervous energy palpitates the car, and her panic stirs something within me. It's the only explanation for the words spewing from my mouth.

"You'll come home with me."

3
willa

"I most certainly won't be *coming home with you*," I all but squeal.

Somehow my brain deciphered his words and sent the message to my mouth.

Because in what world does this man think I'm going home with him?

His eyes go wide at the sound of my voice. Whether it's the words or the tone, I can't ascertain. Not that I care which it is. I'm glad he's affected.

"Oh, shit. I didn't mean come home with me."

"Then why did you say 'you'll come home with me'?" My voice is tinny and pitched high, and my body shudders, the thought beyond ludicrous.

He holds up his hands, palms facing me. If it's to get me to calm down or change my tune, I don't know. "Hear me out."

The adrenaline from earlier returns, my heart rate accelerating as if I've been running or doing a HIIT workout. And since I like neither of those and avoid them at all costs, it's not a good feeling.

A stare-down ensues, the only sounds the wind gusts outside and our labored breaths. I'm hoping only I can hear the pounding of my heart.

When he doesn't speak for several minutes, I prod, "Well? I'm listening."

Beckett shoves his fingers through his brown hair, mussing up the medium-length strands. If I was certain he wasn't a serial killer, I'd find him attractive.

Hell, no matter his side profession, the man's an eleven on the attraction scale.

Dark, wavy, thick hair. Not curly, but wavy. Like girls would kill to have those kinds of waves.

Long lashes surrounding the bluest of eyes. Lakes of enchanting cerulean to get lost in if one stared too long.

Under a layer of stubble, one dimple on his left cheek, a divot I'd like to poke the tip of my finger in.

And the quirkiest crooked smile. I've only seen it once, but damn did my lady parts sing.

This is exactly why I'd be taken by a kidnapper if approached. If I've learned anything from the podcasts and documentaries to protect myself against predators, it's that I've learned nothing.

One look at this stranger and I'm all like "have my babies."

Wait. That doesn't make sense.

He can't have *my* babies.

It's more like "let me have *your* babies."

My mind diverges down a path it shouldn't, and when I clue in, his mouth is moving. I force my ears to listen.

"I have a rental property. You could stay there. That's what I meant by 'home.'"

"Like an Airbnb?" I state incredulously. He nods, like the information isn't the best piece of news I've heard all day. "Why didn't you say that like ten minutes ago? Instead of texting people about the inn and the bed-and-breakfasts?" I swat his chest. Even under his sweatshirt, it's well-defined.

Add that to the list of his incredible qualities.

"It's a bit of a construction zone with renovations and not quite ready for occupancy, but you can stay at my house and I'll stay at the rental. It's one night, two at most. I'll sacrifice for you, Willa."

The way he speaks my name has me wanting him to never stop saying it. The last syllable is "la" instead of the "uh" sound most people use.

What the heck is in the air tonight that has me thinking these thoughts?

"That's . . . generous of you." Too enthralled with his pronunciation of my name, the rest of his statement penetrates slowly, not fully sticking all at once. "Wait. Did you say I could stay at your house?"

"Yeah, but don't worry. I won't be there. You'll be safe from the likes of all predators. Me included." He flashes that damned crooked smile, causing my ovaries to wave the white flag. *Traitors.*

"Just so I understand correctly. You'll hole up at some random rental you've forgotten about, and I'll stay at your house?" Between the car predicament and Beckett's hotness, my mind's all foggy. Hence why I have to confirm.

He exhales, his breath mixing with the hot air blowing from the vents. "I'd say it's your best option."

"It's kinda my only option," I blurt.

Not that I'm on board or completely comfortable with it yet, but what choice do I have?

None, that's what.

He claps his hands together, giddiness wafting off him. "Great. Shall I get your car loaded on my truck so we can be on our way to my house?" I go to speak, but he cuts me off. "Where you will stay by yourself. I will grab some clothes and toiletries and be on my way to the rental. By myself," he adds for good measure. Probably because he sees I'm still freaking out a tad.

"Guess it's our only plan, so yes. Let's do that."

Hope I know what I'm getting into.

While Beckett collects my suitcase and stows it in his truck, I peek at the damage to my car and cringe. The front side panel smooshes against the tree, and the tire is definitely blown.

He doesn't seem too fazed by the damage, but towing banged up vehicles is his specialty. No doubt he's seen worse. Completely totaled cars, if I had to guess.

Beckett's kind enough to start his truck, blasting the heat so I won't freeze. The irony isn't lost on me how he's battling the elements to secure my car on the flatbed but made sure I'm taken care of. His kindness is genuine, exuding off him in waves. He can't *not* help to make sure I'm comfortable.

I shoot my sister a text while I watch him load up my vehicle.

> Call me in twenty minutes. If I don't answer, call
> the cops. Winterberry Junction, Vermont. Tell
> them I was last seen with Beckett Nicholas.
> Hopefully they'll know where to find my body.

I can't help the dramatics. My imagination's always been overactive. Comes in handy for my bestselling children's books series. My main character, AJ Hart, is a combination of Sammy Keyes, Cam Jansen, and Nancy Drew. Given our technical advances, she's a lot more tech-savvy than the others, solving crimes in her small town with her kickass sidekicks, Penelope and Ellis Wooten.

What started as a short story for a senior seminar quickly morphed into kids everywhere clamoring for my autograph. My agent's hounding me to get back out on tour next year, but I've had the worst writer's block the past two years. Part of the reason I booked the week at the cabin.

Well, and to avoid Christmas. Last year was . . . too much. The thought makes me twitch. Thankfully, Beckett's loaded my SUV onto his flatbed.

The driver's side door creaks open, and Beckett climbs up into the seat. He removes his cap and gloves, holding his bare hands to the vents.

"How far away is your house from here?"

"About five miles north." Once his hands are warmer, he clicks his seat belt. "Might take a little while with the snow. It's coming down harder. It's too bad we aren't closer to Christmas with the snow they're predicting overnight. Perfect conditions for a Christmas whiteout."

"Nothing perfect about a whiteout," I mumble. "Especially on Christmas."

I shift my body to face the windshield, away from Beckett's curious eyes. I suppose he'll have to focus on the road once we're on the way, but I like to be the first one to look away. Gives me some semblance of control over an out-of-control situation.

His deep chuckle rumbles through the cab. "The folks of Winterberry Junction would politely disagree with you. Any snow the week leading up to Christmas is a cause for celebration."

"Is that so?"

"You'll see."

I chance a gander his way, the crooked smile splayed on his lips. If possible, it's even bigger than before.

My phone vibrates in my hand, eliciting a rise in me. I'd all but forgotten I texted my sister.

For once in our life, I can't tell if you're joking.
Guess I'll find out when I call you.

In case I don't answer, I love you. You're the best sister I could ever ask for.

Tell the boys I love them.

and Mom and Dad too. Hope this won't ruin anyone's Christmas

I really hope you're kidding.

. . .

"Everything okay over there?" Beckett's rasp hits me like an arrow, square in the chest. This strange yet kind man who's letting me stay at his place.

Who does that? Is this typical of all Winterberry Junction residents? Or did I come across a nice one?

"Uh, ye-yeah. Yep. All good. Ready for your house." I'm lying through my teeth. I'm in no way ready for his house.

"Prepare yourself. It's less of a house and more like a cabin."

"No problem. A cabin, condo, apartment. If it has four walls, a roof, a bed, heat, and some running water, I'm good. Better than sleeping in my car."

He grunts. "That was never happening."

"Well, I appreciate it. Thank you for coming to my rescue. With the car and the place to stay."

I should say more, but if I continue, I'll probably ramble, giving up my secrets he's not privy to. Some secrets are best kept hidden.

The rest of the drive to the auto body shop is quiet, save for the wind outside. The snow continues to fall, harder now, like streaks of white dropping from the sky. I'm relieved I don't have to drive in it. I wouldn't have minded if it had stormed after I got to the cabin because I wasn't planning on leaving there for a week. But this hiccup isn't pleasant.

As we creep closer to what I assume is the center of Winterberry, white streetlamps illuminate the snow. Upon closer inspection, the poles are adorned with green garland. And not just a few of them.

All of them.

Up ahead a little way appear more lights. Even with the snow, it's like it's lit up with the power of a million watts. I wish I were exaggerating.

"What the heck . . ." I trail off, bewitched as Beckett makes the turn onto a street I can only describe as Christmas vomit.

Colored lights galore.

Every building covered in strings of different colors.

Both sides of the street distastefully decorated with bright lights.

My stomach lurches, and I close my eyes, squeezing them shut to prevent being blinded by the lights.

And not like in the song.

Oh, no. This is so much worse.

Despite my closed lids, light beams into my eyes. Like it has nowhere to go, nothing to do but shine, and my eyelids can't keep it out.

"Make it stop," I groan. "Why so fucking bright?"

From my left, Beckett chuckles. "Is this not what your town does for the holiday?"

"No. Not like this. And I thought Havenwood was over the top. There's a Main Street display, which I avoid at all costs." I shove my palms into my eyes, blocking the audacious beaming attempting to render me sightless. "Why? Why? *Why?*" I stress the last repeated word. I can't understand why any of this is necessary.

"Gotta keep up our reputation."

"The reputation as Whoville's competition?" I snark, feeling much like a grinch. Unlike him, my heart wasn't always this small and frigid.

"The reputation of the most decorated small town in the US. We lost three years ago, and no one in town wants to lose again."

"That's a real thing?" I blink one eye open, looking for clues he's serious.

"Oh, yeah. There's a plaque and all. Housed in our town hall."

"You're lying."

For a few beats, his expression remains stoic, and I think maybe he's serious. But then his armor cracks.

"No, I'm kidding. Some travel guru created a website listing the top ten most decorated towns, and when Winterberry wasn't the first on the list three years ago, there was a riot."

I'm so invested in the story—how serious he is—I forget

about the obscuring lights and open both eyes. A playful smirk dances on Beckett's lips, but I'm not well enough acquainted with him to decipher it.

A shrilling noise rings out around us, and I take way too long to realize it's my phone blaring with an incoming call. Clem's name and face light up the screen, and I swipe to answer before recognition dawns on where I am and who I'm with.

"'Lo?"

"Are you alive?"

I roll my eyes at the dramatic question. "I'm answering. And not from the dead."

"Are you hurt?"

"Just my eyes at the moment. So many freaking bright lights."

"Bright lights like at the hospital?" Before I can get my answer in, she gasps. "Or bright lights like it's calling you home? Do not go toward it, Willafred. Do not go near the light!" Her panic shrills in my ear, and I have to move the phone away unless I want to go deaf. She's still screaming nonsense, but I can only make out every third word.

"I'm fine, Clementine. Calm down." Even though she can't see, I pinch my nose in annoyance. Though, her point is valid.

"Calm down? You told me to call you and hope you weren't dead. How am I supposed to not react?"

"Relax. I'm fine. Beckett's driving me to his house because all the rental options are occupied." I voice the words, hearing how they sound. If roles were reversed, I'd have a lot of questions. More than she probably will. It's my nature.

"Who the hell is Beckett?" Another screech, a little louder this time.

"The tow truck driver."

"Oh, the serial killer?" Damn, she's been paying close attention to everything I've said today. That's not usually her MO.

"I confirmed he's not one."

"Oh, you *confirmed* it, did you? How'd you do that, Willafred?"

I hate when our personalities do a switcheroo. Right now, I need her to be the calm one, not the hysterical one.

"Hold on." I tap the speakerphone button, her winded breath coming over the line. "Beckett, can you kindly tell my sister you're not a serial killer?"

"As if a serial killer would say such a thing," comes Clem's exasperated tone.

"Clementine, is it?" Beckett inquires, his tone light and jovial. Clearly at our expense.

"Clem," she corrects.

He glances my way. "My mistake, sorry. Can I ask you a question?"

"Soon as I determine you don't have nefarious plans to take my sister out or force her to be your sex slave."

Beckett guffaws as I shriek, "Clementine!"

"I assure you, she's safe."

In a different situation, I could get lost in his voice. The clarity. The robustness. The confidence.

"Oh, well if you assure me she's safe, I'm totes reassured. How do I know she's even where she says she is?"

"Check my location," I mutter.

"Why didn't I think of that?" There's rustling over the line. "Hmm. Winterberry Junction, south of Lake Champlain. At least he wasn't lying about that."

"Can I ask my question yet?"

"I suppose," comes Clem's snarky response.

My eyes roll again. At least this conversation has distracted me from the eyesore that is Main Street. How long is this damn street? Exactly how many lights do they use to illuminate it so brightly?

I shake my head to ward off any more wayward thoughts.

"What's your sister got against Christmas lights?"

I choke on my saliva. How dare he?

"Um, that answer would require a full dissertation. Is she freaked about them?"

"Totes. Like they're the ones trying to bring death upon her."

I swat his arm, my hand hitting a solid mass. *Damn.*

"Ha. That's a good one. You're kinda funny, Beckett. Can I call you Beckett?"

"Sure, seeing as it's my name."

After what seems like forever, he directs the car left, and the luminescence fades from view. *Thank goodness.* Thought I might start seizing with all the flashing.

"So what's the plan with Willa? 'Cause I got some kids here that I can't leave until their father gets home, and I'm not sure how long that will be. And then it's a solid twelve hours or more to get to this Winterberry Junction from North Carolina. Even if I could get a flight, not sure it would be much faster."

"And definitely longer with the storm," he butts in. It's yet to be determined whether it's helpful.

"Right. Good point. Forgot about the snow."

"I'm going to get her set up in my cabin—"

Clem cuts him off. "Tell me you're not taking her to a cabin in the woods. Because I might have to find a way to get up there sooner."

"It's on the edge of the woods, does that make it better?" It's not really a question, but for Clem's sake, he makes it one.

"Where's the nearest house?"

"There are two cabins on the road, so directly across the street."

"And who lives in the other one?"

"My neighbor."

I crack a laugh. "Good one." Though it's probably not funny or wise to encourage this behavior. But I've relaxed more since he's been driving. Call me naive, but I think I'm safe.

Which is probably what all the abductees say right before they're kidnapped or murdered.

"Willa, much as I can't make heads or tails of what's going

on, you got yourself into this mess, and it's on you to get your-self out. Be as safe as you can. I love you. Keep me updated." Clem's voice cuts off, the call ending.

"Rude."

"Guess she figures there's no real threat here."

"Is there an actual threat here, Beckett Nicholas?" I narrow my eyes his way, but his composure doesn't break. Neither does his sight on the road. Which I appreciate considering the weather.

"None that I can see, Willafred."

"Ugh. You heard that, did ya?"

"Kinda hard to miss." His lips form a smile, and my lady parts take notice without my permission.

I may be physically "safe," but I get the sense I'm not leaving Winterberry Junction unscathed.

4
beckett

WHY I DECIDE to drop her car off at the shop before bringing Willa to the cabin is beyond me. I'm setting myself up for torture of my own doing. But there's something about her.

Maybe it's the way she seems so concerned with me being a serial killer, but then not.

Or maybe it's because she can't stand Christmas lights, and the desire to understand why burns brighter than all of Main Street. And with every building adorned with thousands of lights, the brilliance is off the charts.

"Stay here until I unload the car." I leave the truck running, confident she won't try anything stupid. How I know is another mystery yearning to be solved.

Ten minutes later, I've got the SUV off the flatbed and pulled into the garage. Sliding into the truck, I kill the engine. "Come on. Let's get you to your home for the night." She gathers her bags and climbs down, the snow swiftly clinging to her hair. "My truck's over here." I lead the way to my truck, wishing I had the SUV with me today instead. It's a short ride to the cabin, but the heat takes forever to kick on and there aren't seat warmers. It's a bitter contrast to the warmth she's been used to the past several hours. "It's going to be cold." I point to the truck.

"Uh, yeah. It's snowing. In December. But thanks for the heads up."

Don't think my cock doesn't take notice of the snark in her tone or the way her ass sashays from side to side. Definitely not on purpose or for my benefit, but that's a guess.

"Don't say I didn't warn you," I mutter, keeping my voice low so she won't hear.

I unlock the doors, opening the back door for her to unload her bags. Once stuffed in the back seat, she yanks her door open. I'd advise her not to pull so hard, but it's kinda the only way to get the door open.

"Hey, any chance you know an auto body technician? 'Cause this door needs some work." She delivers the barb straight-laced and straight-faced. It's not until she pulls her bottom lip into her mouth to try and hide her smile does she give herself away.

"You know what they say. Doctors make the worst patients. Same for auto body repair."

Pondering my statement, she stops her entry into the truck. "You're not just the tow truck driver?"

I wave my hand behind me. "Proud co-owner and operator of Frostline Auto Garage for seven years."

"Huh. When you said you'd take the car to the shop, I didn't realize it was *your* shop."

"Weird assumption to make."

I turn the key, tapping the dash to encourage the engine to turn over, cursing myself again for not taking the SUV when I went out earlier. Then I'd have it instead of this old thing.

"Is this thing safe? Maybe you want to have it looked at. Fix it yourself, even. Seeing as that's what you do. Fix cars and all. Or maybe not trucks?"

She's rambling again, at my expense this time. But at least she's let down some of her barriers and seems to have dropped the whole "serial killer" theory.

"I prefer the exterior of cars and trucks. I'm not so great under the hood." At least, not yet.

The engine purrs to life. Or it would "purr" had it been a new engine. This is more like a rumble and a stuttering start. But it's a win it started.

"What is it with this town and unnecessary lights?"

I'm momentarily confused by what she means until she points to the dash. Almost every warning indicator is lit up, but I use her question to get an answer of my own.

Once out of the lot and on the road, I ask, "Why are Christmas lights unnecessary?"

Her body quivers, one long shudder from head-to-toe

"Wasted electricity on something too bright."

"You got sensitive eyes?"

"No."

"You into conserving the world's energy?"

"Nope." She pops the p. The struggle is real to stay on this side of the center console.

"Weak argument," I mutter, all prepared to go to battle to defend the need for Christmas lights and decorations.

I sneak a peek at her. Her arms cross over her chest. "My opinion is valid since it's *mine*."

"Not when it's wrong," I mumble under my breath, hoping she doesn't hear me. I divert my attention back to the road, but the sounds of her huffs and sighs intrigue me, leaving me wondering what other nonsense she's prepared to unleash.

Do I mind getting her riled? Not in the slightest.

Am I doing it on purpose? Yep.

She's at my beck—no pun intended—and call because she can't drive her car in the shape it's in. She can't even get out of Winterberry, let alone wherever she's headed.

"What do you like about Christmas lights?" Her voice is softer, more inquisitive.

"The joy it brings to the people in town. The ambience it sets for the surrounding area. The ways the different color lights create a magical atmosphere. The vivid colors. Shall I keep going?"

"Nope, nauseated enough."

I appreciate how she's not afraid to give her opinions, wrong as they may be. She's got gusto, a trait I admire.

We've reached my road, and I anticipate the jabs as we get closer to my house.

"No. Nuh-uh. No, Beckett. I can't stay here. Nope, not happening."

"Relax, Bundy. A flip of a switch will turn them off."

The truck in park, I glance her way. A wave of horror coats her face.

"Did you just . . . call me . . . Bundy? As in *Ted* Bundy?"

I shrug, keeping my emotions in check and my tone steady. "Seems apropos, no?" I fully admit the name is off the cuff, but once it spilled from my mouth, I'm not taking it back or apologizing.

Her eyes become slits.

Her hands clam into fists.

Her nostrils flare with annoyance.

I almost expect her head to explode, steam billowing into the truck.

Her mouth opens but nothing comes out except a small squeak.

"Seems I've rendered you speechless."

Without waiting for her response, I open my door, only bothering to turn off the truck and take the key because the SUV will be better equipped to handle the snow. I fetch her bags and head for the front door.

The cabin's lit up with hundreds of lights, though I went less than in prior years. Much as I love the holiday, there's something off about this year. Wish I could pinpoint what it was exactly.

Something twinges in my chest, and I rub the spot with my palm, coaxing away the weird jolt.

I unlock the door, depositing her bags inside. Holding the door open with my foot, I twist to watch Willa taking it all in. Her lips are moving, like she's grumbling to herself, but it's too quiet for me to hear any of it. Her head moves from side to side, her eyes squeezing shut to block out the view. Except with the snow and the unfamiliar terrain, she can't get to the porch without sight. One last shake of her head, she opens her eyes, casting them down to forge a path.

"Put a little pep in your step. I'm not planning on heating the neighborhood."

I should have kept my mouth shut. My comments elicit her to stop all movement, her narrowed gaze seeking mine. Her head tilts to the side. "Do two cabins make a neighborhood?" she contemplates, serious as can be.

Why her mind fixates on that part of the comment, I'll never know.

"Come inside and we'll google it."

Defiance eclipses her expression, and for a hot minute, I think she's going to move slower. But the falling snow fixes her ass in gear, and she rushes inside, flinging her coat off the second she breaches the threshold. Both the action of jerking out of it and slinging it to the floor are odd. But then, so is she.

"What did that coat do to you?"

She looks down at it. Not with a sense of shame for her actions, but as if the coat maimed her. "It's a straitjacket."

I'm confused by her use of "straight," until the metaphor dawns on me. "Too confining."

The enigma is strong with this one.

I shake it away. I've got better things to use my brain cells for.

"Welcome to Evergreen Hideaway, your home for the night or two."

She stands in front of the closed door, soaking it all in. I follow her eyes as they travel to the small kitchen on the left, passing over the hallway leading to the bathroom and bedroom, moving to the fireplace, and ending on the too-large Christmas tree in the corner of the living room. The lights aren't on, but damn how I wish they were. Her reaction would be priceless.

I'm not foolish enough to turn them on. My mother raised me

to be a gentleman. I never start trouble, but provoking it when it's in motion isn't out of my wheelhouse.

She glances around again, this time at the wall behind her, locates the light switch, and immediately flicks each one until the front yard goes dark.

Willa slumps against the door, a huge sigh drawing from her. "Oh my god. I can breathe. Hopefully, the dots in my vision don't last too long." She blinks her eyes, probably trying to clear the aforementioned dots. "It's cozy in here. Besides for the abomination in the corner."

I don't have to ask to confirm she means the Christmas tree.

"It's not even lit. Or do you have an issue with everything related to the holiday?" The thought makes me queasy. I'll forgive the lights thing, but who doesn't enjoy the best holiday of the year?

She's quiet for longer than necessary, and I have my answer.

"What?" The question shoots from my mouth. Except I'm not sure I want to know how deep her hatred goes. How she can be so bothered by a tree or something as magical as Christmas. It's inconceivable.

Unimaginable.

Incomprehensible.

"Nope. Never mind. I'm gonna pack a few things and be on my merry way." I can't help the dig. One, because it's part of my nature. And two, because of her attitude.

Toeing out of my boots, I stomp to the hallway and into my bedroom, opening the drawers of my dresser a little too hard.

"Calm down, Beckett. So she doesn't like Christmas. It's not like it's the best holiday ever." My gentleman ways out the window, I shout the last part of my rant, hoping she can hear me. "It's not like she's forcing you to not like it. But when she turned off the outdoor lights, she killed the joy in the yard." I yell that part, too. Exasperated, I'm not sure what I'm packing, tossing articles of clothing haphazardly into a duffle. Long as I have boxers, a T-shirt, jeans, and a hoodie, I can get the rest tomorrow.

"I can hear you," comes her reply from the living room.

"Good. And if I were a murderer, before I killed you, I'd torture you with Christmas music and lights and movies and eggnog and anything else I could think of. Because who hates Christmas?"

I'm practically out of breath when I finish, my lips foaming with frustration. I trod back to the living room, my trek halted at the end of the hallway where Willa stands, hands crossed over her chest, a different fire blazing in her eyes.

"I have reasons, okay?" she shouts at the same decibel I used. "But I don't have to tell them to you. You wouldn't understand."

"Try me." I can't imagine what "reasons" she could have that would be valid, but damn if I'm not invested.

You don't grow up in a place like Winterberry Junction and not become obsessed with Christmas. The magic, the splendor, the festivities. Every year, the town's celebration gets bigger, and in my humble opinion, better. The holiday is commercialized to the nth degree, the true meaning of the day commemorated only by the smallest manger on the church's lawn. I can't fathom hating it even a sliver.

Willa shuffles from one foot to the other, her body fidgety. "It's . . ." She shakes her head and drops her gaze to the floor. "Reasons, okay?"

"Yeah, sure. You don't owe me an explanation or anything. I only saved your ass." I blow out an irate breath. I don't mean for the comment to sound so trite, so impending, but I'm worked up, a frantic energy best spent by running or tinkering in the garage. However, I'm a little afraid of what I might break instead of fix.

Our gazes lock, the brightness in her eyes of moments ago now dimmed.

"Thank you. I'm truly grateful for your help with my car and for letting me stay here. I'm sorry we don't share the same thoughts about the holiday—"

I cut her off with an incredulous laugh, but it doesn't stop her from continuing.

"But as soon as my car is fixed and the roads are clear, I'll be out of your way. Plenty of time for each of us to observe the holiday any way we choose."

She pauses, giving me time to compose a comeback. But the only thing I can say is "Bedroom and bathroom are down the hall. Sheets are clean. Make yourself comfortable. Help yourself to anything in the fridge. There's coffee for the morning. I have your number. I'll be in touch."

Ripping my duffle from where it dropped during my tirade, instead of walking out the front door, I step into boots at the back door, needing to get this pent-up energy out of my system.

5
willa

"WELL, that was rude and uncalled for," I say to the empty room once Beckett slams the door behind him and disappears into the night. "What's his problem, anyway? What's it to him if *I* don't like Christmas? He's acting like a toddler who lost his favorite toy."

I spin around where I'm standing, taking in the quaint cabin.

Besides the hideous decorations, it's cozy. Especially for a guy who appears to live alone. If there was a woman in his life, I can't imagine she'd be okay with me staying here, so I'll go out on a limb and say he's unattached.

Why does my stomach flutter with that presumption?

The dark couch has seen better days, the cushions sunken in where Beckett must usually sit, but it looks super comfy. It's positioned directly in front of the fireplace, a TV mounted on the wall above. My thoughts drift to a prone Beckett watching TV in front of the fire.

Nope. No thanks.

I stride to the kitchen, not hungry but curious about what he has in the fridge. I'm shocked to find it stocked with ingredients and a few containers of homemade leftovers. A box with a half-eaten pizza takes up most of one shelf. For funsies, I poke my head in the freezer, finding it piled with meats and more containers of food. I didn't peg him for a guy who cooked, but then again, I haven't given too much thought to who he is beyond his striking appearance.

Why does a man who looks like him have to be so into Christmas?

As if when I leave here, I'll ever see him again.

As if I'm in the market for a man in my life.

I've told you, you should be . . .

His voice hits from out of the blue, so loud and real, I'm forced to catch myself on the counter and find my footing when I almost stumble.

I check in with my mom. She's already spoken to Clem and knows the situation. Her concern about my predicament hardly mirrors Clem's. She seems more worried about being in a snowstorm than being stranded at a stranger's house without a car, a very fitting reaction for my mother. She asks if she should put my dad on a plane to Vermont, but I turn down the offer. My dad's not the best man in a crisis, and I'm sure his anxiety would make the situation worse.

If that's possible.

Deciding it's time to end this horrendous day, I swipe my bags from where Beckett left them by the door and search out his bedroom.

It's a little weird to be in this stranger's space, to be sleeping in his bed, when I know so little about him. But I guess it's no different from the cabin I've rented for my stay. Except I won't have to deal with the host unless there's an issue. I've stayed at Airbnbs before and I've never once thought about the person who owns the place. Good thing I'm good at pretending.

The wood paneling from the living room continues into Beckett's bedroom. It's not too big, but it's organized. Only a few trinkets and photos on the dresser, a pile of books and a lamp on the nightstand, the bed in the center of the room neatly made. I can't decide if this fits with the man I've spent the last couple of hours with or not.

Even with writer's block, my brain works overtime to decipher what makes people tick, what quirks I can use for future characters. I'm not sure I'll take anything from Beckett. He seems too . . . complex, for lack of a better term. Honestly, I wouldn't mind unraveling some of his layers, getting to the core of who he is. If he'd let me.

Most likely not. I'll be lucky to get him to fix my SUV tomorrow and not charge me an arm and a leg.

I fall onto my back on the mattress, my arms and legs starfishing, my eyes getting a good view of the ceiling. This is the view Beckett sees every night before he goes to sleep.

It's the last thought I have before my lids lower, the comfort of the bed lulling me to dreamland.

I'm awoken by a slamming door.

The fuzzy room comes into view as my eyes adjust to the light. My heart pounds in my chest as I decipher where I am. It takes a few minutes to remember: Beckett's cabin. I fell asleep with my clothes on, my teeth unbrushed, my contacts still in.

Sitting up on the bed, the sound of running water kicks my heart rate faster.

Fuck. There's someone else in the cabin!

Adrenaline courses through me, the possibilities endless of who could be on the other side of the door.

A genuine serial killer.

A rapist.

A burglar.

My overactive imagination runs haywire with options.

I scan the room for a weapon to protect myself from whoever it might be. At the very least, I should call Beckett. Or maybe 9-1-1.

Searching for my phone, it's nowhere to be found, meaning I must have left it out in the kitchen or living room. Right, after my call to Mom to assure her I was safe and sound at my destination.

Not having my phone ratchets my anxiety. I can't let the memories of last time get the better of me . . .

"Shit." I keep my voice low, not wanting whoever's out there to know I'm here. Maybe they'll just take what they came for and be on their way and not realize I'm even here.

Wishful thinking.

Hardly unlikely, especially if it's someone who wants something from Beckett.

I still my breathing, making myself into a ball as I ponder what to do, how to keep myself safe in this situation. I will myself to keep calm, my thoughts not to spiral out of control, my breathing to remain steady.

Who am I kidding? That's an impossible task. Each one of them by themselves. But together? Yeah, not happening.

A loud thump echoes beyond the door. "Ow. Fuck." A man's deep timbre penetrates my brain. It sounds somewhat familiar, like I've heard it before.

I test it out. "Beckett?" I say it just loud enough to be heard in the other room, fearful I'm wrong.

"Yeah, it's me. Sorry." A soft knock comes on the door. "Can I come in? Or you come out?"

"You can come in." I move against the headboard, tucking my knees into my chest and wrapping my arms around them, willing my heart rate to return to normal.

It's just Beckett.

Who's still very much a stranger, but at least he's not completely unfamiliar.

The door opens, and he pokes his head in. His hair's more disheveled, like he's been tugging on the ends of it. "Uh, sorry. Did I wake you?"

"I didn't mean to fall asleep, but I need to take out my

contacts. What time is it? Why are you here?" The last question is rude considering the man owns the place, but hell if I can stop it.

"Almost midnight. The snow's pretty bad, probably not safe to drive to the rental."

"But you left hours ago. How did you get back if the roads are bad?"

"I was in the garage taking out my aggression and working on . . . something."

I don't miss the way he exaggerates *aggression* nor how he doesn't tell me what he's working on. Not that it's my business.

"Oh, okay. So, do you need your bed?"

"Nah. I'll sleep on the couch. I didn't want you to think it was someone else in the cabin. A predator or such." One side of his mouth curls up, and heat inflames my cheeks.

"I didn't think . . ." He raises an eyebrow. In any other situation, it would be sexy, but given my current predicament, I shove it away. My shoulders drop from where they crept to my ears. "Okay, I totally went there. Didn't even think it could be you. What's wrong with me?"

"You seriously want me to answer that question?"

"Uh, nope." A nervous laugh spills out. "I can take the couch." The comment escapes with no prior thought. While it appears comfy, not for a night of sleep. And this bed is way comfier than I expected as evidenced by my deep slumber. I don't know if I want to give it up. I stand up, halted in place when Beckett pushes the door open wider.

"Nonsense. The bed is way more comfortable."

I won't argue with him if he's offering his bed. "Um, okay. Thanks." He doesn't move from the doorway, but now that I'm awake, a need to empty my bladder comes over me. "I, uh, need to use the bathroom."

He stares down at me for a few beats, his mind working through something he's not sharing. The way he's studying me, eyeing me intently, it's almost like he didn't hear me.

"Oh, shit. Sorry." He moves out of the way, and I hurry across to the bathroom.

I do my business and wash up, not letting anything in the room grab my attention. Least of all his shower curtain. His *Christmas* shower curtain. A shudder ripples through me.

I won't always be so affected, right?

Shoving the notion away, I exit the bathroom, Beckett standing outside the door.

"Should I add creeper to your list of possible professions?"

He cackles, and it rumbles his entire torso, now covered only by a T-shirt. Pulled taut across his chest, his biceps bulge. It's a sight. Coupled with his black joggers, the man is the epitome of attractive.

"You hungry? I can make snacks."

I consider his expression. It's not exactly gleeful but gone is the angry man who stormed out earlier, resembling more of the man I first met. "Figured you were mad at me."

"I was." He shakes his head, a scowl trying to slip on his lips. "Nope, can't go there yet. But I'm kinda hungry, and what kind of host would I be if I didn't offer you some?"

"Do you often cook snacks for your guests this late at night?"

"If I had some and we were hungry, I suppose I would."

Interesting.

"What did you have in mind? I didn't get to eat many road trip snacks today for obvious reasons."

"I'm kinda craving something chocolate. Brownies? Double fudge cookies? Chocolate lava cake?"

The last one breaks the resolve I'm trying hard to hold on to. "You're going to eat chocolate lava cake in the middle of the night?"

"Hmm. I suppose it would be late by the time it was cooked and we were eating it. Brownies it is." With his decision made, he turns on his bare feet and pads toward the kitchen.

I trail behind. "Why not something premade? A candy bar?

Ice cream, maybe? What's the obsession with cooking something?"

He turns around, not expecting I'm following so close. He steadies me by my shoulders so I don't topple over, and electricity buzzes around us. Can he feel it, too?

"It's gotta be something warm. Brownies take less than thirty minutes. Unless you're too tired and want to head back to bed…"

He dangles the threat in front of me. Not so much a threat as an invitation.

"Ironically, when I can't sleep, I bake, too."

His eyes widen. "No shit?"

"No." I don't resist the urge to roll my eyes. "When I can't sleep, I stay in my bed, like normal people. Watch TV. Read." *Furiously write chapters and get lost in a book,* I don't admit aloud. It feels like forever since I've done that. I kinda miss it. Maybe tonight's brownies will kick-start something in me, unlock a piece of the writer's block mystery.

His eyes narrow into slits. "Just for that, no brownies for you. You're dismissed." He waves a hand in my direction before heading back to the kitchen. His tone implies anything but, and the way he spoke "you're dismissed," beckons me toward the kitchen.

He's got the pantry door open, which isn't so much more than a bunch of neatly organized shelves of food. He pulls out flour, cocoa, and other ingredients, lining them up on the counter. Next, he moves to the fridge, grabbing out the eggs. Lastly, he reaches into a high cabinet for a few more items. My feet rooted to the ground beneath them, I'm shocked.

"You're making them from scratch?" Not only is he baking in the middle of the night, he's not using a box mix?

"Only cheaters use a box mix, Willafred." How he reads my mind and his use of my full name stir something in my chest, the three syllables conjuring up feelings long ago buried. His eyes blink rapidly a few times. "Are you a cheater?"

Another taunt, this time, raspier, more implication of other things.

Hell if I can figure out why I answer, "No."

Which is a lie if we're talking about brownies. I only use a box. When the occasion calls for me to make brownies, which is rare. I'm partial to Ghirardelli, a little more upscale than the other ones.

He nods, accepting my answer as if it's gospel. "You wanna help?"

"I'll certainly help eat them. *After* they're baked."

He reflects on my answer for a moment before his top lip quirks up. "Ah. You're one of those." He doesn't indicate what "those" implies, but I'm guessing he's probably not wrong. No doubt I've been accused of worse.

One shoulder rises. "You're better off. Especially if you want them to be good."

"Seems like there's a dare in that statement," the sexy man goads.

"In no way did I imply any such thing." I cross my arms over my chest, grateful to still be wearing a bra.

Why my mind goes there is surprising.

Probably because I can't reconcile the different parts of Beckett's personality I've gleaned in the few hours since he came to rescue me. Most importantly, his sexiness.

Beckett moves from where he stands behind the counter, sauntering to where I stand at the edge of the kitchen, a mask of emotions on his face. I'm not so much scared as intrigued.

Wondering what he's going to do.

Contemplating how I'm going to react.

My breath hitches the closer he gets, temptation exuding off him.

So much temptation.

What is it about this man getting me hot and bothered? Beyond his external attraction, there's so much more.

Perhaps being stuck in this middle of nowhere cabin with a stranger has appeal.

6
beckett

ABORT MISSION, my brain yells.

Because I'm asking for trouble if I pursue whatever it is I'm doing.

She hates Christmas jabs from the deep recesses of my mind.

Even that's not enough to stop this tirade I'm on.

And for what?

What's my goal here? A severe case of blue balls? Because that's about all I'm getting out of tonight's interaction.

I stop two feet from her, her chest hitching with my movements, her eyes not quite wide, but intrigued.

Wondering.

Skeptical.

Captivated.

The last one may be my imagination, an expectation she's as affected by me as I am by her.

"It wasn't a dare," she murmurs, laced with sultry undertones. She steps back, as if physical distance will stop the emotional torment.

"Sounded like it to me. Why don't we try it out? I gather you can read?"

My question catches her off guard, like she anticipated something else. "I can read."

"Great. Tell me what to do when."

I don't know what makes me do it, but once my finger is in the air, hell if I can stop it from moving toward her nose and booping it. Like I used to do with Shania when she was younger and her sass was out in full force.

I spin around, needing more of a separation between us, and grab the recipe from the cookbook in the pantry, making a quick adjustment in my pants.

"She hates *Christmas*," I mutter incoherently.

Perhaps that's why she's so compelling. Because I need to know why she hates my favorite holiday. What her "reasons" are.

I hand her the tattered paper. Her eyes scan up and down before locking with mine, a hint of question lingering in the intense blue color. Dark, like the current midnight sky.

"Okay, first up?"

She glances back at the paper and up at me. She fists her hips. "I'm to assume you need my help reading the recipe given the state of this piece of paper?"

The woman's astute, I'll give her that. "Not much gets by you, does it?"

"It helps—" Her mouth clamps shut, as if she's going to divulge a secret. Instead, she hops up on the counter next to where I've placed the ingredients. "You also mentioned you do this often."

"I don't recall saying often." I measure out the flour, leveling it with a knife before adding it to the mixing bowl. I may have said often, which wouldn't be a lie, but I've also been making brownies from scratch since I was a kid alongside my grandmother in her kitchen. We'd get fancy for the holidays—adding sprinkles or green and red M&M's—but that might shove Willa right over the edge and straight into the land of crazy.

What I wouldn't give to see her all agitated again.

No. She's your guest. No riling up the guests.

I work in awkward silence for a few minutes, measuring and adding ingredients, turning on the oven, sneaking peeks at Willa as she intently watches from her perch on the counter. When I can't take the quiet, I blurt, "What do you do for a living?"

She's taken by surprise by my question. Either the question itself or me speaking in general.

"Uh, I'm an author."

My hand halts with oil in the teaspoon poised above the mixing bowl. "Seriously?"

"Yeah."

"That's cool. Are your books 'BookTok famous'?"

She giggles, the sound incongruent with what I've learned about her. "Didn't peg you for a guy on BookTok. Are you?"

"No, but my sister and my niece are all over that shit. Big readers. What's your pen name? Maybe they've read you?"

"How old is your niece?"

"Thirteen going on thirty."

She laughs again, and tension rolls off her shoulders. Good. She needs to relax. "Like the movie?"

"She wishes." I hand over the can of cooking spray and a foil tin. "Spray this for me. Please," I tack on, not wanting to sound rude or disturb this little slice of peace we've got going on. Her eyes widen, but I give her no choice but to take the spray and lay the tin across her lap. "She'd like to skip high school at the least and go directly to college."

"What's her rush? Adulting isn't all it's cracked up to be." With shaky fingers, she removes the cap, setting it beside her thigh.

"I tell her that multiple times a week. Though if I had my way, she'd still be little enough for me to cuddle against my chest or ride on my shoulders."

"They grow up fast."

"Do you have nieces or nephews?"

"Two nephews. My sister's kids. They're three and six."

"Clem's kids she mentioned on the phone earlier?" She seems startled by my comment, her hackles rising. I can't help if I pay attention to details. Especially about strangers I want to know better.

"Right. You spoke to her. Yes, her underlings."

"Is she older or younger?"

"Older, ugh. As if making her way out of the womb ten minutes before me gives her 'older sister' status."

"Ah, twins. Is it only the two of you?" I grab the wooden spoon from the utensil caddy and offer it to Willa. She grunts her objection, so I mix the wet and dry ingredients.

"Fortunately, yes. You?"

"The youngest of four. Two sisters, one brother. He's got fifteen months on me, but you'd think it was fifteen years."

"Four kids is . . . a lot." A shudder passes through her, not quite as big as the few earlier. "Do the others have children?"

I test the batter for lumps, having lost count of strokes. Nana's way is far superior to counting.

"No, just Shania. For now. Heidi got married two years ago, and Mom's itching for her to be knocked up. Dax is the ultimate bachelor."

"Unlike you."

I frown, not understanding how she's deduced the information in such a short amount of time. Or at all. "Unlike me how?" After pouring the batter into the tin, I slip them into the preheated oven, setting a timer. I like them a little undercooked, so I always shave off a few minutes per the recipe.

"You're very un-bachelor-like."

"How so?" I lean back against the counter opposite her, arms folded across my chest. It doesn't escape my notice how the movement draws her eyes.

"Your place is spic and span. Not a typical bachelor pad. Even the way you stacked the dirty dishes in the sink is neat." She waves to the area next to me.

"A bachelor can't be tidy?"

"Not in my world."

"Glad I don't live in your world." It's a little harsh, but her comments feel judgmental.

There goes the little thread of peace we had.

In an unexpected move, Willa hops down, standing directly in front of me. I've got a good eight inches on her, and though her expression is penitent, she stands her ground. "I didn't mean that. Or maybe I didn't mean it as poorly as it came out. You're an enigma, Beckett. Between the snow, the car crash, and you, I'm all out of sorts."

"So, this isn't your true personality?" I fire back, my comment having zero lead time to process.

She pulls her bottom lip into her mouth. My fingers itch to pull it out. And she says *I'm* the enigma. Maybe I agree with her.

"I'd be lying if I said no. Well, at least currently. Before . . ." She shakes her head, her statements trailing off.

Standing so close to her, I notice the pain in her eyes, the murky storms swirling in her irises.

"Did someone hurt you, Willa?" I temper my voice, wanting her to know it's okay to open up. Because clearly, we're at this stage now. I roll my eyes at the idiocy of the notion.

To say I'm shocked when she answers, "Not on purpose," is an understatement.

I hide away my shock, not letting her see I'm affected. I want to know more, ask more about what she means, but she steps back, putting up a wall of defense between us. Seems for every sliver of weakness, a concrete barricade is soon to follow.

"I have a question about your brother."

"Shoot."

"Does he have a cabin nestled in the woods to lure in his prey?" There's not even a crack in her armor, not the tiniest chink. Her tone remains steady, with no traces of sarcasm or humor. It's exactly the thing we need to slice the tension.

A hearty chuckle releases, and it frees up some of the bad juju in the room. At least for the time being.

"No cabin. But he lives in the basement of my parents' house, which is super creepy if you ask me. Perhaps even more than a cabin."

She lifts her hands in the air, raising and lowering them in rhythm. "Definitely a toss-up. Does he also decorate for the holiday?" She gags, almost choking on the words coming from her mouth.

"You think this is bad? His place is way worse. And he's got more square footage. He's been known to put up *two* trees."

It was only once, but Willa doesn't need to know that.

"Those poor trees. Having to live inside, drying up from the heat, the heavy ornaments on their branches . . . such disrespect."

"Says you. Plenty of people disagree." The room is stifling, the heat almost suffocating. I push from the counter, suddenly parched. "You want something to drink? Coffee? Tea? Eggnog?"

Willa's face pales. "Ew, gross. It's a little late for caffeine, unless you've got some herbal tea."

"Let me check. Sometimes my sister leaves a few bags here." I search the pantry, pulling out a box of assorted flavors. Handing it to Willa, I encourage, "Check the expiration date. Autumn hasn't crashed here in a while."

She takes the box from my hands, examining the bottom. "Looks good. I'll have this one." She pulls out a lemon packet and sets the box on the counter. "How is it after midnight, and I'm not the least bit tired?"

"You did nap, and your body's probably running on adrenaline. Plus, I'm here, entertaining you."

"You are entertaining," she confirms, much to my pleasure.

While the brownies bake, I boil water for her and pop open a beer for myself. She turns her nose up at the flavor: Winter Warmer Holiday Ale.

She's all in on this hating Christmas thing.

After cooking, we let the brownies cool for ten minutes. I start on the dishes while Willa disappears from the kitchen. She returns in a pair of black-rimmed glasses. The frames are a bit oversized, but they only enhance her beauty.

As if I wasn't already in trouble.

Hoping not to let her see me ogling her, I motion to the table, placing a plate with a brownie in front of each of us. "Tea and beer aren't the best combination for brownies. Want a glass of milk?"

"Sure." She nibbles a bite of the brownie, like the smallest bite ever. Like I added poison to the batter or something, yet she scrutinized me as I added every ingredient. I'm about to ask her how she likes it, but she goes back for more. A much bigger bite this time. Before it's even down her throat, she moans. "Goodness," she exclaims after swallowing. "Ah-may-zing." She chomps again, exaggerating the moan.

As if I'm not turned on enough.

"So, no more doubts about my baking skills?"

"Did I doubt you? I don't remember doing any such thing. Can I get that milk now?" She shoves the rest of it in her mouth. I chuckle, happy she's enjoying it but glad she's finished. Her noises are too much.

I set a glass of milk in front of her, which she immediately chugs.

"Can I, uh, have another brownie? Or is that too much?"

I'm already sitting, but I wave my hands in the direction of the brownies. "Have at it. Glad you're enjoying them."

She pops out of her seat and shimmies her way to the pan.

Yes, shimmies.

I can see the headlines now: *Death by cute and adorable female.* She'll probably get off on a technicality.

SHE HATES CHRISTMAS! my mind supplies, the voice loud and demanding me to stop whatever this instant attraction is.

And it's nothing more than attraction.

Surface-level stuff.

Stuff that leads nowhere.

It's helpful to remember she's only here until I fix her car, then she'll be on her way to her destination and a memory in my rearview mirror.

I'm so caught up in my thoughts, her presence across the table startles me. She's got two brownies stacked on her plate. Not sure where she'll hide these calories away on her lithe body.

"Hats off to you, chef Beckett. I can't remember the last time I enjoyed a brownie so delicious." She shovels half a brownie into her mouth, licking the bits of chocolate left on her fingers.

I rip my focus away, inhaling my brownie. "See what happens when you make them from scratch instead of cheating with a box mix?" I offer after swallowing. "Makes all the difference."

"I agree. I'm going to have to find someone back at home to make these regularly. Can I get the recipe?"

Intentionally ignoring her request, I return to our earlier conversation. "What type of books do you write?"

"Children's mystery chapter books."

Huh. Was not quite expecting that. Except it's fair to say I don't know what I was expecting. This girl's certainly surprising me at every turn.

"That's cool. Anything I'd know?"

Her brows jump to her hairline. "Do you often read children's mystery books?"

"Often might be a stretch, but sometimes. At least when Shania was little. She loved the alphabet ones when she was in early elementary. And Nancy Drew. I'm not ashamed to admit that one night after she went to bed, I finished reading the book to find out how Nancy solved the mystery."

"You continue to astonish me. I'm sorry I ever pegged you as a serial killer."

"Stop it with the serial killer nonsense. Though now that I know what you do, it makes a little more sense."

"Does it though? I write mystery books. For *children*." She stresses the last word.

I shrug a shoulder. "It's not a stretch for you, an adult, to make the leap."

I'm not sure that's true, but once it's out there, I'm not taking it back.

"How did you get into writing?"

"My mom says I've been penning tales since I could talk. I'd take her phone and record ideas and notes and eventually, dictate 'stories' all before I could write. One year for my birthday, she typed up my garbled mess and had it published into a 'book.' I couldn't even read, but I was so proud to see my words in print. I chased that high until my first mystery book was published six years ago. It never gets old seeing my books on the shelf of the bookstores or kids' shelves. It amazes me every day kids read words I've created."

Passion leaks out of her, her zeal for her craft evident in every word she speaks.

"Do you still have that first book?"

She nods. "Want to see it?"

I roll my eyes. "Duh."

She takes another bite of brownie and exits the kitchen, returning a few minutes later with her phone. She points it in my direction, and a photo of a bookshelf stares back at me. Front and center is a handmade printed copy of a book called "Sammy's Superhero Cape" propped up by some sort of small stand. It's well-loved, wrinkles on the front, and the corners creased. I barely have a chance to peruse the titles of the books before she removes the phone.

"That's really cool, Willa. I've never met a published author before. Now I can tell people I know you. That you slept at my house. Do you write under your real name?"

"No." I wait for her to give more, but when she doesn't, I don't push her for it. If she wanted me to know, she'd tell me. I'll respect her privacy.

Her mouth stretches wide in a yawn. "Shit. I'm crashing."

"Even with the sugar rush?" I point to the sliver of brownie remaining on her plate.

"Tea always makes me sleepy."

"You have everything you need for the night?"

"I think so. Thanks for the delicious brownies and middle of the night drinks. An unexpected delight, definitely the yummy brownies."

"Now you'll know not to doubt me again." Before she can refute my claim, I add, "I'll probably be out early in the morning to plow. I apologize in advance if I wake you."

She stares at me, her eyes like saucers. "You plow too? Is there anything you don't do?"

"Wouldn't you like to know."

Can't tell you why those words rush from my mouth, but soon as they're out, I stand up and clean up the dishes, hoping she takes the hint not to push me.

If I've learned anything about this girl in the last several hours, it's I doubt that will happen.

7
willa

THE SMELL of bacon rouses me from a deep slumber. My mind struggles to make sense of why there would be bacon cooking in my house. More importantly, who would be cooking it.

I blink my eyes open, noting the unfamiliar room. Coupled with the distinctive—but not unpleasant—fresh scent of linen and masculinity, I recollect where I am.

Beckett's bedroom in his cabin.

What is it about this room causing me to lose my sense of where I am? It's happened twice now.

Another aroma filters in—the smell of strong coffee. If it weren't for the need to relieve the pressure in my bladder, I'd cocoon myself in the sheets and blanket, taking comfort in a space that should be the opposite.

With my glasses on, I take care of business in the bathroom and go in search of liquid sustenance. I'm met with the gorgeous sight of Beckett's backside standing in front of the stove. I stare for way longer than appropriate.

Still in the same T-shirt as he wore in the middle of the night, he wears holiday PJ pants, and his brown hair is tousled with sleep. His arm moves, making his bicep stretch the material around it, and veins pop in his forearm. I'm at a vantage point to be front and center of what my sister refers to as "arm porn." I did not think it was real. But here's this real-life, living and breathing man proving me wrong.

"Morning." Beckett's croaky greeting makes me jump.

"Uh, hey. Did you go plowing already?" I recall him mentioning that last night.

He spins around, his smile bright. Of course, he's a morning person.

His eyes linger on my glasses for longer than necessary, but instead of pulling away, his eyes move down me, checking out the T-shirt and flannel pants I changed into after our midnight snack. I kinda wish I had the forethought to put on my bra before I ventured into the kitchen. I cross my arms over my chest, hiding my breasts from his view.

"Only drawing more attention to them," he drawls, his vision on my chest.

"Perv," I spit, hugging my arms tighter around me.

"Nice frames. They suit you." He turns back to his task of cooking the bacon, his approval igniting a spark in the defunct organ in my chest. It feels like it's been forever, I almost don't recognize it for what it is.

"Thanks?" I say in response to his compliment.

"Hungry?"

"Famished. Bacon is my weakness."

He looks over his shoulder. "Mine too."

Imagine that.

I ignore the connection, making my way farther into the kitchen. "Mind if I grab some coffee?"

He reaches into a cupboard on his right, grabbing out a mug. It isn't until he pushes it into my hands do I wince at the image of the Grinch. Out of my control, my body spasms, something Beckett makes a note of with a tsking sound.

"The Grinch, huh?" The words are bitter on my tongue, and the irony hits a little too close.

"Family joke, but for you, most fitting. My other mugs are put away for the season. If you want coffee, that's what I've got."

I swallow down the nasty retort on my tongue, not giving him the satisfaction. "I want coffee," I mumble, ambling to the coffee maker and filling the mug, only leaving room for a splash of milk.

"Help yourself to milk or creamer in the fridge. Need sugar?"

"Milk will do it." I add a bit to the top, giving it a stir with the spoon Beckett produces out of thin air. "How are the roads?" I sit at the table, curling my fingers around the mug to warm them up and allowing the steam to do the same.

"Haven't been out yet. Got more snow than predicted. A hearty meal will keep me full longer than the granola bar I planned on. I'll probably head out in an hour, be gone most of the day. Not sure I'll get to your car today. Depends on how many guys come to help with the cleanup." There's apology in his tone layered with disappointment.

Or I'm imagining that. I'm good at making shit up. I do it for a living.

"Oh. So I'm stuck here another night?" The thought isn't quite as daunting as it would have been yesterday. Now that I've gotten to know Beckett a little more and trust he won't hurt me, his company is kinda nice.

"Don't sound so dismayed. You can gorge on brownies."

Piece by piece, he lifts the bacon from the pan, laying the slices on the paper towel on the counter. It's such a simple task, but I'm mesmerized.

More like jealous.

"Quiche will be ready in about five minutes. Wasn't sure if you like veggies or not, so I left them out. Hope you're okay with American."

"Did you even sleep last night?"

All the bowls and utensils he used last night are put away, and foil covers the brownies. There are a few items in the sink, but I'm guessing they're from breakfast.

"Got a few hours. Couch isn't as comfortable as I remember."

I kinda feel bad. I had a great night's sleep in his uber-comfortable bed, and he suffered on the couch.

"I'm so—"

"Don't apologize. Not your fault."

I can't help feeling it *is* my fault. If I hadn't crashed my car, he wouldn't have had to rescue me nor have to give up his bed to me as his guest.

With practiced precision, he moves the pan to a back burner, flicks the knob off, and joins me at the table. His mug is red and festive with Christmas lights spelling out the words "Holly Jolly Christmas."

Gag me.

"Coffee's good. What's the flavor?"

He smirks behind his mug. "You don't want to know."

I'm ashamed to admit how much I'm enjoying it. One, because I didn't have to make it. Two, because he made it. But three, because it's tasty and has a unique flavor. Yet I'm frustrated because I'm sure it has something to do with the upcoming holiday.

An internal war begins—finish it because it's so delicious or pour it down the drain on principle.

The latter isn't a logical choice because I don't want him to think I'm wasteful or not appreciative of his help.

"I'm going to pretend it's not what you imply."

"Suit yourself. There's plenty more."

"Who taught you all these kitchen skills?"

"My grandmother. Her father owned the first restaurant in Winterberry, but they had to sell it when the recession hit. Her dream was to reopen it, but life happened, she got married, had babies and grandbabies, and the dream got pushed to the back burner."

"And now she's too old?" I surmise.

"She passed about three years ago." A smattering of melancholy clings to his words, the grief of her passing still felt deeply.

I swallow, not allowing myself to take on the emotion of his loss. "I'm sorry."

The timer buzzes, and Beckett hops up and removes the quiche from the oven. "White, wheat, or rye toast?"

"Rye, please. With butter."

I feel pampered. The comfy bed. Ready-made coffee. A nutritious breakfast. I could get used to this.

As if goading me, my eyes snag on the tree.

Or not.

Beckett's not too chatty during breakfast, but I'm glad for the reprieve of having to answer his questions. He wants to ask—to *know*—what I have against Christmas. I can't tell him. It's not for him to know or understand because it's not his life. What and how I choose to live my life has no impact on others, specifically a stranger I'll never see again once my car is fixed.

I offer to clean up, and with some hesitation, he agrees. While he prepares to head out for a day of plowing, I load the dishwasher, hand-wash the pans, and wipe down the counters, leaving it as I found it yesterday. Or to the best of my ability.

Dressed in a heavy sweatshirt, track pants, a hat, and gloves, Beckett grabs snow boots from the closet. "Make yourself whatever you can find for lunch. Remotes are in the ottoman. I'm not sure when I'll be back. I can text you?" He asks it as a question, like he's not sure I'll agree, but there's a morsel of hope embedded in it.

I can't be the one who bursts his bubble.

"Sure. Do you have my number?"

He produces his phone from his pocket and waves it. "Got it, Bundy." He flashes a sinister smile.

It should be nefarious or irk me in every way.

Except there's no hatred found.

Why has this guy got me all tangled in knots?

Why am I so enamored by him?

I don't want him to know how much the name affects me, so I school my features. "Be safe out there. Text me."

"Happy writing." His salutation given, he trudges out the back door. I watch through the window as he fights the still falling snow to the garage. He slides in through a side door, and one of the three—I swear there's more square footage in the garage than the cabin, probably space for more than three cars—doors opens. There's a plow attached to a truck in the bay, the headlights illuminating the snow.

Within a minute, he pulls out, the door closes, and the taillights of an unfamiliar truck disappear down the driveway.

"Happy writing," I mumble, pouring myself another mug of coffee, daring myself to stay out of the pantry to determine what flavor is tantalizing my taste buds. It's piping hot thanks to Beckett brewing a full pot before he set out on his way. He took two to-go mugs and left the rest for me.

If he ever decides the bachelor life isn't for him, he's going to make some special woman very happy.

He cooks, cleans, is neat, considerate, and charming, even to strangers. The only flaw is his staunchness for Christmas.

Ugh.

Dealbreaker.

It doesn't have to be, a voice from beyond whispers. *Give him a chance.*

"I'm not here looking for love," I shout to the empty room.

This week is about getting my writing mojo back.

My skin crawls at the mere thought of staring at a blank page.

At having to come up with a plot.

Of having to type cohesive sentences and paragraphs.

Of editing.

Forget the first draft.

It's the round of revisions I'm dreading the most. It's what's causing the writer's block. I'm one hundred percent convinced.

For shits and giggles, I dig out my laptop and make myself comfortable at the kitchen table. It's not my desk at home—or the coffee shop I work at on occasion—but it'll do. At least for this test of sorts.

Ignoring emails and social media, I start a blank document and type "Chapter One."

My fingers hover over the keys, frozen in place, the words of the story locked in a part of my brain I don't have the key to. The one Elias took with him . . .

Slamming down the top of the laptop—thank goodness it's only a travel one—I push it away, frustration rolling off in waves.

Waves that knock a person down, the undertow so strong, the person is swept away.

"Ahhhh!" I yell, trying to clear the tension, the anger, the huge emotions dragging me down, attempting to sweep me away with the current.

This is possibly the worst writer's retreat slash vacation slash escape I've ever had.

First, the accident.

Next, stranded in a town of the North Pole's vomit.

Third, being stuck in this cabin alone, being mocked by the tree and ornaments in the corner.

My eyesight catches on the half-full mug, the Grinch staring back at me.

I didn't always feel like him.

Before.

Before, I loved Christmas, the lights, the festivities, the presents, the joy.

It was all stolen that fateful day.

8
beckett

IT'S BEEN A DAY.

The town plowing crews couldn't keep up with the storm, so they called in private plows for the smaller areas. My straight plow works great for driveways and small lots, but it can't compete with the V-plows or the commercial ones the town owns. On a day like today, I'm thankful for any plow, to do my part however I can, but a bigger one would allow me to help more and in less time.

I didn't get a chance to text Willa until late in the afternoon. Her reply was interesting. Concerning, yet intriguing.

BUNDY

I didn't burn down the house. The tree is still standing. You're welcome

> I'm too tired to cook dinner. Shall I bring something home for us?

Pepperoni pizza would hit the spot

> Might take a while

I've got nowhere else to be

"likes a message"

I call in the order and am given a wait time of forty-five minutes.

The snow finally stopped a couple of hours ago, so the cleanup efforts can make some headway. While I wait, I tackle a few more driveways on the way to my parents' house.

Dad or Dax already took care of the driveway, the walkway, and the cars.

Inside the back door, I shake the snow off in the mudroom, toeing out of my boots and gear, and hang it in my cubby, a childhood habit I can't break. I appreciate how my folks leave the kids' ones empty for us. It's a welcome home, something Mom's very much in favor of.

"Beck, that you?" Mom's voice drifts to me.

"Yeah. Waiting out my pizza pickup time." I greet her in the kitchen with a kiss on her cheek. "Everyone holding up okay in here?"

"We're fine. Gives me an excuse to stay in and bake all day."

"I thought your holiday baking was done?"

She hands me a steaming mug of coffee doctored exactly how I like it. "Is it ever really done? Can we ever have too many Christmas cookies or desserts?"

I can't stop the laugh bubbling at how Willa would react.

With the monotony of the day, my thoughts wandered to the pixie more than they should have. I wondered how she spent the day, what she scrounged up for lunch, if she got any work done.

When things were boring, thoughts of her naked in my shower and my bed crept in. Why my brain conjured her naked in my bed is a mystery, but I didn't mind.

It was the highlight of my day.

Standing in the kitchen with my mother, I shut these thoughts down.

"Nope. Not when they're coming from your kitchen."

I peek at the cookies cooling on the racks.

"Mind if I swipe a few?" Snowballs are my weakness, and I'll go out on a limb and say Willa would prefer those over candy canes or gingerbread.

Mom does me one better, handing over a paper plate covered with foil. "Knew you'd be by eventually. I've got chicken noodle soup, too. Oh, and some mac and cheese." She raises her brow, like she knows something she's not willing to share. It's the same look she's given us kids all our lives. Though her hair's grayer now, her wrinkles more distinguished, and I tower over her, the look is the same from my childhood.

Though I'm not sure how she could know about Willa. I didn't mention her to anyone.

"Heard you've got a houseguest."

"How did you—"

"Child, you must have forgotten your sister owns two of the three lodging places in town. Did you think word wouldn't get around?"

"The pitfall of small-town living rears its ugly head."

"Nonsense. You love our town, small and nosy as it is."

I'm not sure I'd survive a week in a big city. Which is a gross exaggeration, though I'm not prepared to try it out. For all its drawbacks, Winterberry has been an awesome place to grow up, build a business, and support the community. My family's all here. Why would I leave? Where would I go?

"Is she staying long?"

"Until I'm able to fix her car. Probably tomorrow if I get all the necessary parts. If not, when it's done."

"It's too bad she won't be here for Christmas. Show her the best of our town . . ." My expression morphs into one Mom reads well. She waves away the disappointment trying to settle in. "She's probably got family to celebrate with. Makes sense."

My alarm blares from my pocket, saving me from elaborating further.

"She does." Hey, it's not a lie. She has a family. Whether she celebrates, Mom doesn't need to know. I hold up my mug. "Can I get this to go?"

Mom grabs a Styrofoam cup from the top of the stack and pours the liquid in it. She covers it with a lid and sends me on my way. "Don't forget your cookies and meals. Hope . . . your guest likes them. What's her name?"

"Willa. I'll keep you posted."

Not. A sudden urge not to share her with anyone overcomes me. Even if it won't ever be a possibility for them to meet.

I hurry into my boots and coat, forgoing the hat and gloves.

Fifteen minutes later, I'm pulling down the snow-covered driveway to the cabin. I'll plow what remains after we eat dinner.

I don't miss how the front yard is dark. I swear I flipped the switch back on last night, but Willa must have turned it off. I can't help but notice the blinds are drawn, too.

Inside, Willa sits at the kitchen table, her laptop open in front of her. A different pair of glasses perches over her eyes, the colorful frames accentuating the deep blue.

Damn, she's beautiful. If not for her idiotic hatred of Christmas, she could be someone I fell for. Though her beauty's the last on the list of admirable traits.

She's quick-witted and funny, has a flair for the dramatic, and isn't afraid to share her opinions. She'd be an avid opponent in any sort of challenge and, most likely, fun in bed.

"That smells delish. I'm starving."

Her statement snaps me out of the hold she has over me. I step out of my boots and deposit the pizza, bag, and coffee on the counter.

"Did you not eat?"

"I did. Well, actually. Kudos to the chef on the pork. Restaurant quality."

"What makes you think it wasn't me?"

"Kudos to you, chef. Bon appétit. Muy bueno. Delicioso." She kisses her fingers, opening them up in what Shania calls a "chef's kiss" action.

"Thank you. I'm glad you enjoyed it. It's better leftover."

She closes her laptop, sliding it out of the way. She sets the table with the two plates, napkins, and utensils already set out.

I nod to her laptop. "Get some writing done?"

Her face turns crimson. "Nope. Had to catch up on some emails and marketing tasks. Scheduled a few social media posts."

Her answer seems genuine. I wonder what she's ashamed about.

I sit down, plating a piece of pizza for both of us. "The lights too much?"

She's not fazed by my left-field question. "I nearly had a heart attack and went blind when they all turned on. Give a girl some warning."

"Sorry." I'm anything but. I forget they're on a timer since I love them. When they turn on each night, it warms my heart.

"Right. Sure you are." She calls my bluff. She bites into the pizza, a moan escaping. Not as tempting as the brownies or breakfast, but enough for my dick to press against my zipper. "Exactly what I needed. Thanks for indulging me."

"You're welcome. Once you mentioned it, pizza sounded like a superb choice."

We chat about our day as we eat the rest of the meal. She seems a little less hesitant to answer my questions about her job tonight, but I stick to easy topics.

What's her process?

Does she have an agent, editor, publisher?

How long has she been published?

Nothing too personal or revealing of intimate information.

"As long as I can get all the parts for your car, it should be done tomorrow."

The news has her meeting my gaze. "Oh, that's great. Thanks. Do you think you'll have trouble getting the parts?"

"I can't say. Between the storm and the holiday, it's uncertain. But I'll certainly try."

"I appreciate it, Beckett."

There's a hint of something I can't decipher about how she says my name. I don't dislike it.

"Are you done with work for the day? I thought I'd build a fire, and we could watch a movie. Make hot cocoa and popcorn."

"Brownies, too," she adds.

"My mom also sent cookies. She says hope you're enjoying your stay."

Her brows furrow. "You told your mom about me?"

"Only when she asked. Remember when I called around to the B and B's?" Willa nods. "My sister and brother-in-law own them. Guess it was easy enough to put two and two together."

"Oh."

"I didn't give her anything about you specifically, only that I have a guest here until her car is fixed."

"I'm not upset. Just perplexed." She grabs another slice of pizza. "Add whatever costs for food to my repair bill."

"I'm not doing that," I state, getting a beer from the fridge. "Beer? Wine? Eggnog? Holiday spritzer?" I'm not usually this antagonistic toward other people, but it's so easy with her. I adore getting a rise out of her, watching her get all worked up. It's like I can't help it.

She turns her nose up. "Beer is great, thanks."

"Lager? Ale? Stout?"

"Any of them. I'm easy."

She makes it too effortless sometimes.

"Are you? Pegged you differently. As someone who wouldn't give away the farm. Not immediately, anyway." I'm rambling, but the more I say, the rosier her cheeks flush. Her neck, too. Like Rudolph's nose, all shiny and bright.

"Walked myself into that one. Lager. Nothing holiday related."

I grab two, opening them up on the bottle opener screwed to the wall. "You want a glass or do you drink from the bottle?"

"Don't tell my sister, but bottle." Her cheeks flame redder.

"Darn. How'd you know she was the first person I was going to text?" I snigger, handing her the bottle. "Why can't she know?"

Willa takes a swig, and my eyes latch onto her throat as she swallows. Though not a part of anyone's anatomy I usually give any attention, her neck is slender and long. Arched back to accommodate the bottle. It would look even better against a pillow . . .

Damn, I've got it bad.

Less than thirty-six hours, and I'm about to give my left nut for a roll in the sack.

It's been too long since I've been laid. That must be the issue.

"Too many germs." Her voice is tinnier as she mimics her sister.

"Are you two identical?"

"God, no." I nearly choke on my beer. "It's bad enough having someone share your birthday, your friends, your brain sometimes. I couldn't imagine sharing the same DNA."

"Tell me how you really feel, Willa."

"I don't know what it's like not to be a twin, so I can't say how I'd feel if I didn't have her. I'd be lonely, that's for sure. She keeps me entertained."

"Does she write, too?"

"No. She's creative in other ways. Painting, drawing, clay, jewelry. If you can make it with your hands, Clem can do it."

"Impressive."

"She's very talented. I'm not biased when I say that. She truly has a gift."

I love how there's not an iota of jealousy but only pride for her sister. Does she feel the same way about her gift? I hope I get the chance to find out.

As if that will happen. She's not here to get to know. She's only here until her car is fixed, a temporary pit stop on her road trip to other places.

Willa offers to clean up our dinner, and since I need a shower, I let go of the control to do it myself and agree. I can't complain too much about how her cleanup job after breakfast.

And when I've washed away the stress and stench of the day, I find a sparkling kitchen and Willa relaxing on the couch, her feet tucked under her, her beer on the ottoman. She changed into teal leggings and an oversized sweatshirt and swapped the glasses for the black ones. She doesn't look like a guest but someone who belongs in the space.

I *really* need to get laid.

9
willa

LAST NIGHT'S memories assault me.

Beckett chose a Hallmark movie that was unrelated to Christmas. It was unexpectedly entertaining, but what was more shocking was the way he was so into it. How he analyzed the character arcs, their goals and motivations. How he was spot-on.

He made homemade hot cocoa and used some sort of appliance to air-pop the popcorn. He drizzled it with butter and salt, and it was better than the movies.

I ate way too many of his mom's cookies, at least the ones with nuts and powdered sugar—I avoided the others like the plague. I appreciated how Beckett didn't call me out on it and almost saved the non-seasonal ones for me.

Our conversation was light and surface-level. Nothing was mentioned about the tree staying unlit nor about the exterior lights. There's some regret about how he's catering to my wishes when it's his house, but not enough to let him stop.

I felt a twinge of guilt when it was time for bed. He headed for his bedroom until he remembered his bed was the couch for the night. I didn't have a chance to offer to trade. He beat me to it when he insisted he was fine on the couch. While I don't think it's the truth, the idea of sleeping in his bed was too thrilling to pass up.

I went to bed blissed out on hot cocoa and snacks and again slept like the dead. I might have to ask him where his mattress is from because it's like sleeping on what I imagine a cloud would feel like.

Dragging myself from the comfort of the bed, after using the bathroom, I find the cabin empty. Beckett left a note on the counter. Even his handwriting is neat.

WILLAFRED,

I'M OFF TO FIX YOUR CAR. ENJOY THE LEFTOVER QUICHE, COOK SOME EGGS, OR EAT WHATEVER. YOU'RE AN ADULT. I TRUST YOU CAN FEND FOR YOURSELF AND YOU'RE COMFORTABLE ENOUGH TO MAKE YOURSELF AT HOME. I'M WORKING A HALF DAY, SO I'LL BE BACK BY TWO—ISH. HOPEFULLY WITH YOUR CAR FIXED. IF YOU NEED ME, I'M ONLY A TEXT AWAY.

BECKETT

I finish reading the note as my phone rings, the man of the hour's name displayed.

"Hey."

"So, bad news."

I slump into the chair I've claimed as mine for the past two days. "You can't fix my car."

"Unfortunately. The part I need is on back order. I have feelers out to see if I can find a used one, but with your car being newer, it's unlikely."

"So I'm stuck here longer?" I can't hide the disappointment in my voice.

"Your insurance might be able to get you a rental car, but pickings will be slim this time of year."

Slim most likely equates to nothing. But it's my only option.

Beckett's gone above and beyond being a gracious host, but I'm sure he's ready for me to be out of his hair. And I want to get to the rental if I can. It's already been two days of me paying for it without using it, and I'm looking forward to being in a space by myself and not surrounded by hideous decorations.

"Guess I know what I'll be doing this morning."

"If you need help, let me know. My office manager loves dealing with insurance and tracking down rental cars."

"Don't listen to him. I loathe it with a passion," booms a female voice.

There's a scuffle over the line, then I hear, "Willa, I'm Meredith. Listen, the boss has an extra SUV in his garage. He didn't offer it before now because of the snow and he truly thought he'd be able to fix your car today. Or so he's led me to believe. But there's an ulterior motive, too."

She pauses, and I wait for her to continue. When she's silent after a minute, I ask, "What's that?"

"It's not obvious?"

"No."

"He's—"

Whatever she was going to say gets cut off, and Beckett's gruff voice rumbles in my ear. "You don't want to come back to Winterberry to return my car."

He'd let me take his car? People in Winterberry sure are bred differently than where I grew up. Havenwood's similar, but I've yet to meet someone there as indulgent as Beckett.

"Not if I can help it." It didn't sound so grating in my head, but hearing it out loud makes me seem so ungrateful. Which I'm not in the slightest. He's been nothing but benevolent and all I've done is take. "But I'd still have to return for my car." My tone doesn't make up for my abrasiveness, but it's a little better.

An idea sparks.

"Wasn't your original plan to stay at the Airbnb you own?" I forgot about it until now, not even fazing me last night when he slept on the couch instead of heading to the rental.

"With the storm passed, I can do that."

"No. I didn't mean for you to leave. Let me go there. If I can't get a rental car, I'll stay there so I'm out of your space. You'll just have to drive me there. How bad can it be?"

"It's kinda bad. I checked it out this morning on the way to the shop. There's no working heat or running water. It's not an option."

The little elation I felt falters. "Oh. Guess it's kinda good you didn't go there the other night."

"I'm sorry, Willa. I didn't realize the undercarriage damage in the dark. I feel bad."

"You feel bad? Dude, I'm eating you out of house and home, sleeping in your bed, because I crashed my car. You have nothing to feel bad about."

"You could stay with me. If you can't find a rental," he presses. "I honestly don't mind. I kinda like having the company."

I'm not sure what to make of his suggestion.

Had you told me last week I'd be considering staying at this stranger's house, I would have told you you were crazy. But it hasn't been all that bad. Beyond the seizure-inducing lights and decorations. There's an odd sense of peace here. There's something about Beckett that sets me at ease, like someone had a hand in our paths crossing. As if we were meant to meet.

If Clem could hear me now . . .

"Let me call my insurance and see if they'll even pay for a rental car."

"Okay. Let me know what they say. Do you want steaks for dinner? I found a new recipe I want to try."

His sudden change of subject is jarring. So is his question. He asks like it's an everyday situation for the two of us. As if it's normal for him to be asking what I want for dinner.

"What if I can get a rental car?"

"You'll still need to eat, then you can be on your way, if that's your hesitation. Unless it's that you don't want steak or to help me try a new recipe. If that's the case, I can make something else."

"You're very accommodating." It's the first thing I think to say as I process his offer.

Do I want to stay for dinner?

Yes. I want to stay for more than just dinner.

The truth pummels me, but I don't have time to make sense of it because Beckett says, "It's purely selfish reasons. I have a plethora of recipes I want to try. You're bound to choose one of them."

"A plethora? No one uses that word except writers."

"Says you. I use it a lot."

"All the time," comes Meredith's voice.

I giggle, the sound freeing something inside me. "I want steak for dinner."

"Super." I can hear the smile in his voice. "Do you need anything else at the grocery store while I stop there? Or do you want to come?"

Why do I have a sudden urge to go grocery shopping?

Except for one thing . . .

"It'll be daylight, right?"

"Yes. No chance of any light-inducing medical conditions for you." It's like he can read my mind, knowing exactly why I asked.

"Cool. Text me when you're on the way and I'll be ready. I'm going to call my insurance company now."

"Good luck."

"Thanks. I'm going to need it."

After hanging up with Beckett, I called the insurance company, which approved a rental car. Except Beckett was onto something. Slim pickings amounted to nothing. Not anything in the close vicinity, at least. The nearest location that had a car with four-wheel drive is over fifty miles away and in the complete opposite direction from my final destination. I'd hate for Beckett to drive so far out of his way when he's already done so much for me. I don't doubt he'd do it in a heartbeat, but I don't want him to feel more obligated than he already does.

I reach out to the host of the rental cabin to let her know I wouldn't make it. Her understanding is evident, but when I mention I'm not worried about a refund, relief echoes across the line. It's not her fault I'm not coming. Besides, it's not like I'm paying to stay with Beckett. He's been more than generous allowing me to stay, not even considering taking me up on my offer to pay. I'll figure out a way to compensate him somehow.

By the time he texts he's on the way home, I've showered, checked in on my social media accounts—even posted on one of them—cleared my email inboxes, and opened my manuscript. I forced myself to stare at the blank page for thirty minutes, hoping it would spark something. Sadly, I'm still stuck, my brain still broken. Every day I don't write brings more frustration. It's why this week was supposed to be my week. Get my groove back, write for the fun of writing. It's like AJ Hart has gone silent or she's dealing with her own shit going on in her life.

I laugh at the absurdity, how if I said that aloud, the only people who would understand would be fellow writers.

A text from my sister interrupts my thoughts.

Checking that you're still alive

Still here. Car can't be fixed so I'm here for the foreseeable future

The phone rings in my hand.

"How do you feel about that?" is Clem's greeting.

I ponder how truthful to be. In the end, I go for brutal honesty. She'd see through anything less.

Exhaling, I begin, "I'm not sure I'm ready to leave. At least his house. I've settled in here, which is odd for me, but from the first moment I stepped in, a bigger power was at play, something bigger than myself. I can't explain it."

"Do your feelings have anything to do with one Beckett Nicholas?" she asks, her comment initiating a giggle.

"He doesn't seem like a stranger."

"And he's hot to look at. Damn, girl."

My lips pull into a frown. "How do you know?"

"A little thing called Google. He's Winterberry royalty. And he is f-i-n-e fine." She slips into a Southern drawl, and it's my turn to laugh. "You want to jump his bones. If you deny it, I will force Christmas upon you when you return."

I suck in a breath. "You wouldn't dare. The holiday will be over."

"Not in this house, it won't be. My boys will love another celebration. Might even have Santa bring more toys . . ."

"You're evil, Clementine."

"And yet, you're not denying it."

Because I can't.

While sleeping in his bed has been great rest, it's been hell for my neglected libido. Because my brain's worked overtime anytime I'm in it. And the thoughts are far from pure.

Closing my eyes and releasing a sigh, I admit, "I want to jump his bones."

"Who's the 'his' in this scenario?"

I jump out of my chair at Beckett's voice. Not only at the sound of it but the implication.

Shit.

Of course, he'd walk in at this exact moment.

He wears a playful smirk, an inkling of who I'm talking about. "Clem, gotta go."

"I want details" is all I hear before I jam my finger to end the call, my eyes never leaving Beckett's heated gaze.

"Time for the grocery store? Is the ground still snowy? Should I wear my boots? Is it freezing? Can I get away with this sweatshirt and no coat?" I rapid-fire questions at him, hoping to distract him from what I said.

His eyes narrow, and I don't know what he's thinking, but I wait him out. He crosses his arms against his chest and leans his hip against the counter. Damn, but he's sexy. I wonder what he's like in bed.

"Yes. Yes. Yes. Yes. No."

"Huh?"

"The answers. To your questions."

My eyes bug. "You followed those?"

He pushes from the counter, stalking to where I sit at the table. Resting his hands on the wood, he leans in. "Didn't miss any of yours nor the fact you've neglected to answer mine."

I swallow, stalling for time. His proximity is daunting, overwhelming. "Umm. Noticed that, did ya?"

"Yep." His head inclines closer until only a few inches separate us. My breath hitches, wondering what his next move is going to be. How much *closer* he's going to get. An inferno ignites inside me with the anticipation. "When you do it, be careful with my bones. I've broken several throughout the years." With a wink of his left eye, he withdraws from my personal space. "Be ready in five minutes. There's a fleece-lined hoodie in the hall closet."

I'm so flummoxed, I can't move nor make sense of what his latter comment means. Why would I need to know about his sweatshirt? I flash back to his answers, the only "no" the last one. What was the last question I asked? I take a few minutes to remember it was something about not needing a jacket.

There's a fleece-lined hoodie in the hall closet.

Is he suggesting I wear that instead?

It's only when his other comment sinks in do my cheeks blaze.

Be careful with my bones.

When I jump them.

Could this be more humiliating?

I rest my head in my hands, trying to wrap my thoughts around what's going on. How I redeem myself from this.

Except, he didn't seem bothered by it. And he was definitely encouraging me to do it with his warning of being careful. If he wasn't interested, he wouldn't have brought it up. He would have let the idea drop without acknowledging it. The fact he not only brought it to my attention but apprised me to be careful is a sign in my favor.

I haven't had thoughts of being with another man since Elias or barely looked at other men. Even if it's purely physical, a means to an end, to scratch an itch, I can't deny the chemistry between us. I can't deny the attraction.

"I see you're not good at following the one direction I gave you."

Again, his voice catches me by surprise. I peer up through spread fingers. "Has it been five minutes already? Oops." A nervous giggle escapes.

"Do you want the hoodie?"

He heads out of the kitchen to the closet ahead of me answering, and when he returns holding the sweatshirt, it's all I can do not to leap up and grab it from him. It looks warm, and it probably smells like him. Which is probably not my best move, but neither was agreeing to stay in a stranger's house two nights ago, and that's worked out in my favor.

Beckett holds the gray—not holiday-themed—hoodie out to me, and I snatch it out of his hands and shove my arms into the sleeves. It's about three sizes too big, but it's warm and cozy, exactly like the man who owns it.

"Not a straitjacket?" He quirks a brow.

"Not even a little. Thanks." I zip it up, shoving my hands in the pockets. The greatest urge to sniff it overcomes me, but he's watching my every move, so I refrain, using every ounce of willpower.

"Did you make a list?"

"I did."

"You have it?" he inquires when I make no move to produce it.

"It's in my phone."

"K."

He starts for the door, and without hesitating, I follow him.

At the rate I'm going, I'd follow him to the ends of the earth. Christmas decor and all.

10
beckett

I'M PLAYING WITH FIRE, but hell if I can stop.

Did I take it a little too far offering her my hoodie?

Maybe, but I don't regret it. It swims on her, but she's more adorable. And warm, which was my motivating factor.

Once in the SUV, I blast the heat. It's frigid out, and the snow on the ground doesn't help. Since I drove the truck to work, it's not warm, but it's a safer choice.

"What's the status of a rental car?" I look over at her, gauging her reaction. Her expression falters, and my mind works on ways to make it better.

"There's like one car the insurance will approve." My good mood sours because I don't want her to leave. "It's like over fifty miles away, so it won't work."

Best news ever. I can't let her sense my elation. Hearing her say she wanted to jump my bones solidified my decision of wanting her to stay. I've thrown the fact about her hating Christmas out the window. It's not like I'm marrying her. We can have a fling while she's in town without it impacting our opposing views of the holiday. If I get her going, it will probably make the sex even hotter.

"Ah, that's too bad. What are you going to do?"

"Not sure what I can do." She faces the window, her shoulders slumping. I take the time to drive down the driveway. "Can I, uh, stay a little longer? I'm happy to pay a rental fee for the room. I'll buy the groceries and treat you to meals."

"You should name a character after me." Because I can't control anything around this girl, the idea ejects from my mouth. Once it's out there, I kinda like it. A lot.

"Um, sure. I can do that, too."

Keeping my eyes trained on the road, I smile. The small victory somehow seems big. Maybe because she didn't even hesitate with her response and agreed immediately. Though I suppose if I never learn her pen name, she won't have to hold up her end of the bargain. How will I ever know whether she does it?

"That would be cool. I bet my niece would love it. I'd be famous."

"Famous? How would you ever prove it was you who inspired the name?"

She's got me there. "I'll find a way." Now that we've established she's staying, I give her a truth. "I won't be able to get the part for your car before the holiday."

"Yeah, I wasn't holding my breath you could, but I appreciate you letting me know. I hope I don't ruin your holiday. It's a me thing, and I try not to let it affect anyone else."

I bite my tongue to not ask, to not pry into her personal life. She's made it clear she doesn't want to talk about it, and it's not my business. But damn do I want to know.

Damn do I want to convince her otherwise.

Damn is it my luck she ended up here, that I didn't pass the call to Dax the night she crashed her car, to make her a believer.

I can't do anything until I know what I'm up against, and she won't give it up easily. I'm certain of that.

If she'll even give it up at all.

"I'm usually good about not taking on other people's bad moods, their bad juju, especially relating to Christmas. You can lock yourself in my room while I celebrate. No skin off my back."

The words are a lie. Despite knowing so little about her, I want to celebrate with her. However, I don't want my holiday ruined. It's a slippery slope, one I've found myself on several times before.

It's never quite worked out in my favor.

Perhaps this is the time it does.

Though it's not looking good.

Everyone and their mother are shopping at the local grocer. It takes triple the time to get the few things on our list because everyone stops to ask how the decorations are coming for the parade, if there are enough volunteers for the holiday breakfast, if there's enough food donated. You'd think I was in charge or something.

Oh, right. I kinda am.

August Myers, the man who owns the local stables, stops us in the bread aisle. "Beck, still need the horses for the parade?" A hopefulness hides in his voice.

He asks me every time I run into him in town, which is fairly often. I give him the same answer I've given him the last several occurrences. "We're good this year, August."

His expression falters, as if hearing the news for the first time. "Ah, okay. Maybe next year." Removing his cowboy hat, he runs a hand through his thinning, white hair. "See you around." He shuffles away from us, the frayed edges of his dirty overalls dragging along the floor.

Maybe he's going senile, but we haven't had live animals in the parade in several years.

In the produce section, we're accosted by Krystal Farnham. Decked out in holiday gear, including a light up sweater peeking from her unzipped jacket, she's all smiles. Owner of the candy shop, she graduated high school with Autumn.

"Hello, Beck." Her voice is jolly but not flirtatious. "Got a new recipe for the parade. Think you're going to love it." Her hand reaches out to touch my arm, but with a glimpse at Willa, she pulls it back.

"Hope it's something chocolate."

From beside me, Willa snickers. When I glance at her, her attention is on the tomatoes, holding one in each hand, weighing them for something to do.

"You know it," Krystal asserts. "Pop by early on Tuesday and I'll sneak you a taste."

"I'll do my best." I flash her a smile, sans dimple, and bring my focus to Willa, hoping she takes the hint and continues on her way. Thankfully, she does.

After our third invasion, Willa had enough. She texted me her list and stomped out of the produce aisle. I couldn't see where she went, but her feelings were adamant.

I do the best I can to hurry it along while also balancing my neighbors' desires to stall me. Everyone's excited about the festivities that begin in two days, their enthusiasm off the charts this year.

I'm trying not to let her bad mood pull me down, but my body's conflicted between making her happy and my happiness.

Never in my life has a woman wound me up so tightly, had so much sway over the decisions I make, even when she didn't ask for the control. It's unfamiliar, and I don't know what to do with it. The fact it's been two days and she's still a virtual stranger heightens the stakes.

After what seems like a full day on the job, I walk out of the store, shocked to find Willa huddled on a bench. Her thighs are pulled against her chest, my hoodie wrapped around her curled body.

I've never been so jealous of a hoodie.

I approach cautiously, not wanting to scare her. "Hey. Sorry about that." She picks up her head and wipes tears from her eyes. Gone is the anger, replaced by sorrow. "What's wrong?"

She unfolds her body, shakes her head, and laughs nervously, swiping the remaining tears off her cheeks. "Not here."

An anxious feeling sweeps through me, the kind I used to get before a big test at school. I want her to turn over her heavy burdens, let me carry them for a little while. Even if I don't know what those burdens are. But first, I ask, "Are you hurt?"

"No."

A wave of relief floods me that she's not in physical pain. Something made her cry. Something caused her to go from anger to sadness.

And I won't stop until I know why. I don't want to cause her tears, even if unintentional.

As the youngest of four, pushing and testing limits is my specialty. However, with women—more so, those I feel a connection with—I've learned the hard way to back off, that pushing them to the brink only results in hardship for me.

"Let's go."

She stands up, and I can't stop my arms from embracing her. There's a moment of hesitation on her part, but when she gives in, she completely melts against me. A jolt shoots to my core. Whatever she's feeling balls up tight in her, and strangely, I want her to give me whatever she's holding. I want to carry it for her, to take it off her plate and do the heavy lifting. It's a heady thought, something that should scare the shit out of me, but the feeling of terror never comes. What comes through is peace, rightness, clarity.

Perhaps the holiday spirit is getting to me this year.

I hug her until she pulls away. "If it's too much crazy, I'll understand."

"If what's too much crazy?" I ask, needing clarification.

Her left shoulder raises. "Me." Her fingers rub her earlobe, a quirk I find incredibly endearing.

"Two older sisters and a niece, remember? They cornered the market on crazy." A half-truth at best, but I can't let her know I'm not usually good with crazy, yet I can't get enough of her brand.

Maybe I've been drinking too much spiked eggnog and it's me who's crazy.

An air of a disheartening yule consumes our ride home. Willa seems less sad, but she's quiet, her usual spark diminished. When I try to engage, she shuts me down with one or two-word answers.

Back at the cabin, she's quick to grab the groceries, emptying the contents of the bags onto the table. "Tell me what you need for tonight, and I'll put away the rest."

"Do you have more work to do today?"

"No." Her response is immediate.

"Keep me company in the kitchen while I cook?" I sound needy. The mood's changed, but I wonder if there's still a part of her that's turned on. Or has that gone away, too?

"Sure. Just need to take out my contacts so gouging out my eyes isn't on today's agenda."

I can't help being intrigued by how she delivers these quips in such a monotone voice. I debate if it's intentional. Either way, it's the exact catharsis we need to break the tension, and my loud guffaw shakes the cabin.

"Let's keep the blood splatter to a minimum. At least until after we eat."

She cocks her head to the right, examining me. "Your brand of humor contrasts so much of what I know about you."

"According to my mother, I've been her biggest conundrum in life."

She allows the comment to sink in and permeate. Quick as her thinking is, she's also a ponderer when the situation calls for it. I admire that about her.

"Great word choice. I'd love to use it in my books, but my readers tend to not understand the big words. I'd have to use 'puzzle,' but your mom is spot-on about you. It's like she knows you well or something."

"Or something." She stands rooted in place, her arms crossed over her chest. "Go forth and remove your contacts. We've got work to do." I don't intend for it to sound so commanding, and I wouldn't be surprised if she fought me on it, telling me she doesn't have to listen to me or I'm not the boss of her. Except it's for *her* benefit. I'm merely encouraging her.

"Right. Be back in a jiff." She turns on her heel, and my eyes glue to her backside, watching her saunter to my bedroom. Only when she disappears do I shake out of the stupor she has me in and set to work on making dinner.

I prop the iPad on the stand and pull up the recipe for a pan-seared steak I've been wanting to try. Taking what I need from the table, I turn on some music, keeping it to non-seasonal tunes for her sake. I wouldn't want to be on the receiving end of a knife wound.

"I'm back, reporting for duty. What do you require me to do?"

So much innuendo in her question, so many ways I could respond.

Thankfully, I'm faced toward the counter and away from her so she can't see the way my cock takes notice. Although, if I move my hand to adjust myself, no way she'll miss that.

Over my shoulder, I call out, "You can put away the groceries in the fridge and pantry. Anywhere you can find room."

She calls me out with a humph. "Anywhere?"

"Anywhere your little heart desires, Bundy."

Could the nickname be any less appropriate? Yet, I'm not going to stop. It's extremely fitting for her. For us.

Man, I'm in trouble.

Forty-eight hours with her, and I'm creating new neural pathways in my brain to accommodate her and make exceptions for how I live.

It's because it's temporary.

Yeah, sure.

11
willa

WITH HIS PERMISSION TO put things anywhere, I do exactly that. It's not so much fun in the fridge with the limited options and space, but in the pantry, I go hog wild.

Not only are the shelves neatly organized by size and shape—ironically, not alphabetical—but there are multiples of each item all sorted neatly into plastic bins. For such a small area, it would have to be efficient to fit all this stuff.

I don't move anything that's already in a place, but I don't match the new stuff into his organizational pattern.

A can of black beans? Fit in with the boxes of pasta.

A box of cereal? Next to the flour.

Hot cocoa Oreos? Hidden behind the bags of chips.

Good luck finding those before the holiday, Beckett.

I'm surprised he purchased store-bought cookies. After his "it's cheating to bake brownies from a box," I would assume the same goes for cookies. Though I suppose Oreos aren't something people make from scratch. Still, a total conundrum.

I smile as I recall how his expression softened when he mentioned his mother. Same thing when we discussed his niece and sisters the other day. I'm a little downhearted I'll probably never meet them, to see how he fits in, where his personality comes from. From what he's said about them all, it would be entertaining.

"Groceries disseminated. What's next on my agenda?"

Music plays low from a speaker on the far counter. Should I feel guiltier he chose secular music for my sake?

"Rice or noodles?"

"Noodles."

"Are you capable of boiling water?"

I forgot we talked about my inability to cook. Based on his smirk, he's getting a lot of pleasure from rubbing my lack of skills in my face. Not sure I blame him. I am pretty pathetic.

"Yes, wiseass. I can even add the noodles to the pot and set a timer for when they're done." I grab a bag from the pantry. "And I can pour them into a strainer."

His expression serious, he sets the spatula down on the spoon rest and slow claps. "Color me amazed."

The thing is, two can play his game.

"Which pot do you want me to use? Going out on a limb here when I say you have a specific one." His mouth opens, but no words exit. "Not so condundrumy now, eh?"

"Oh, fancy author, making up fancy words. Is that how you get all your accolades? You take real words and make them into not-real words?"

I gasp, hand to heart to exaggerate it. "You've uncovered my secret. Whatever will I do now that you know?"

Beckett returns his attention to the stove, gives whatever he's got in the pan a stir before casting aside the spatula. His moves are practiced and full of ease, whereas I'd probably drop the utensil into the pan, panic while I figured out a way to get it out, and burn the ingredients in the meantime. I'm not jealous or anything, but damn this man.

"You ever have a one-night stand?"

I'm not expecting his question. While it processes through my mind, he moves my way.

"What?"

"A one-night stand," he repeats like I didn't hear what he said. Not the problem so much as the timing and implication of it.

"Didn't realize we were at this stage of getting to know each other." I stall, deciding how truthful to be.

"Yes or no, Willa." His heated gaze bores into me, friction palpitating between us. A sizzle scorching, hot enough to burn if I get too close to him. Good thing I'm keeping my distance. Even if it's a metaphorical burn.

"Ye-yes," I stutter.

He pinches his nose, suspecting a different answer maybe. "More than one?"

"Yes," I state with more certainty, still trying to decipher his angle. "You?"

"A plethora."

A chortle leaps out. "Not sure this is the time to prove your fixation with that word."

"Why?" He steps closer, crowding my personal space. He does this often, too. It should bother me more than it does.

"You've had a *plethora* of one-night stands?" He nods. "More than the average guy? An abundance of them? If your goal is to add me to your list, you're not selling yourself so well."

Honestly, I hadn't planned to say that so boldly.

Now it's his turn to be unsuspecting of my comment. He brushes his hand through his hair, causing a few of the front ends to stick up. Even with mussed hair, the guy is smoking hot.

He eliminates the tiny distance between us. "Is that so, Willafred?"

My eyes snap shut with his use of my full name, my lady bits calling for a ceasefire of surrender, campaigning for an end to the drought I've been in for two years.

His finger snakes under my chin, lifting gently. "Open those pretty eyes." Like earlier, it's a command. Unlike earlier, sexual undertones fill it. Like I'm not already hot and bothered.

My eyes flutter open, and an aroused Beckett fills my vision. I wish I weren't so easily attracted to him. It would be easier if he were some troll, someone I didn't visualize naked while sleeping in his bed. A hideous man who wouldn't dare do wicked things to me.

"Have you changed your mind about me?"

"No." The word breaches my mouth without thinking.

Because I haven't. His past doesn't change our magnetism. It doesn't change the depths of how much I want him. If there's no one else presently, I see no reason to keep myself off his list.

A timer dings, breaking the sexual hold he has over me.

"Shit. Dinner." He rushes to the stove, moving the pan from the hot burner to a cool one. "We'll pick this up after dinner, yeah?"

"We'd better. Now you have time to compose a well-thought-out response, a plan to get me into your bed."

"Unlike the last two nights?" he counters.

Ah, good point. That is where I've been sleeping and planned to be tonight, too. Guess he doesn't have to do much work.

I'm a blank slate about how to respond. Instead, I open the lower cabinet where he got the pan from and heave out a pot for boiling water. While the water fills, I sense Beckett watching me, waiting for a comeback. The longer I don't answer, the better my response has to be. Nothing like adding more pressure.

When a significant amount of time has passed and I've still said nothing, I sigh. "Accurate," I admit in defeat.

He shakes his head. "I expected more, Willa. A quip, a thesaurus word, something other than 'accurate.'" He changes his voice on the last word, but it sounds nothing like me.

"Sexual tension and coherent thoughts don't mingle."

"I see. And there's more of the former right now?" he astutely surmises.

"Lots. One might say a plethora." My brain kicks into gear, and it sets him in motion.

Beckett dashes to where I'm standing, and using one swoop

of his muscular arm, he crushes me against him. Our mouths crash together, and fireworks erupt. I feel the kiss everywhere, every nerve ending tingling. When his tongue invades—no other word could describe the action—my mouth, my knees weaken, and I crumble. Thank goodness for his arm under my ass holding me up. I steady myself by wrapping my arms around his waist, clasping my hands together, holding on for dear life.

All the while, he dominates the kiss. Lips slanted over mine, his plundering tongue, the most exquisite moans. Oh, that might be me.

My body vibrates with awareness, a sensation so strong, I could combust. I never want this to end, yet if it doesn't, I'm afraid it will be the end of me. I can barely breathe. If I don't get oxygen soon, I'll wither away to nothing. But what a way to go.

"God, Willa. You taste . . ." Beckett speaks with our lips still pressed together, somehow doing both and making some semblance of sense.

I smoosh my chest harder against his. "Don't stop, Beckett." But when I seek his mouth, he pulls away. "Not done yet," I whine.

His other arm meets the one holding me up, and with careful steps, he backs us to the table, taking a seat in the chair, pulling me onto his lap. Beckett situates me where he wants me, and my legs straddle his, his erect cock struggling to be set free. Our breathing's erratic, an unsteady pace of heaves and gulps.

With me steady on his lap, he loosens my messy topknot and twines his fingers in my hair. "Not done yet either, Bundy, but my lungs have a limited capacity. I'd imagine yours do, too." Words escaping me, I nod my agreement. Emotions swim through the swirling blues of his eyes, fine lines outlining the edges. "I wanted to do that to you the minute you asked if I was a serial killer."

His remark gives me pause. He's wanted to kiss me since we met?

"Did you now?"

"Until you revealed your disgust for Christmas. That shut the idea down real quick."

"Huh. What made you change your mind then?"

He taps the side of my head. "Your words. How you challenge me. The pain you carry." He delivers the words tenderly, each soaking into my brain and finding residence, the last one burrowing the hardest.

I don't let many people see my pain, the hidden scars of my past. Why I've let my walls down with him is a mystery, one not even AJ could solve. Despite knowing him for forty-eight hours, he's safe, a soft place to land among the planes of hardness on his exterior. His soul is kind, generous, a beacon of light in a storm.

"I don't want to talk about it," I murmur, hoping he doesn't force the issue. The connection between us severs the minute I drive away. Whatever we share during our time together will stay in Winterberry. It's the opposite of Vegas in every way, with the exception of lights this time of year, but the sentiment is the same. What happens here, stays here.

"Not even to let me help you carry it?"

"Why would you want to burden yourself with my problems?" I try to wiggle from his grasp, but he holds tighter. I don't have the strength to fight him.

Or maybe I don't want to.

"As I mentioned, I don't take on other people's emotions, but I'm a superb listener. You can ask anyone." His smile is shy but honest. So much truth embedded in his statement, I'm tempted to pour my heart out.

But I don't. It's not his business. I'm not his problem.

This time when I scooch away, he lets me go.

"You're not another name to add to my list, Willa. I don't know how I know, but I do. You're going to stand out. I'm sure of it."

He stands up and places the gentlest kiss on my head. A

storm of emotions kicks up inside me. Thank goodness it wasn't my forehead. I'm certain I couldn't handle that.

"Water's boiling," he announces, breaking me from the spell I'm under. The spell of Beckett and the *plethora* of emotions in me.

Maybe my best bet is to figure out a way to leave . . .

12

beckett

I WATCH HER EVERY MOVE. She wasn't lying about being less than handy in the kitchen. From the way she opens the bag—the noodles all but spilling out from how she rips it open—to how she awkwardly holds the pan by the handle to dump it into the strainer. Her elbows flail out at weird angles and her entire upper body twists with the movement. If I didn't think she'd get frustrated with me, I'd wrench it out of her hands. With the vicarious cliff we're dangling on, I keep my distance, preparing the veggies. But I don't let my sight stray from her.

She fixed her bun after I fluffed her hair. It leans adorably to the left, and it's all I can do not to take it out and fix it. Center it on her head.

Kiss her lips again.

The unrelated action stirs my cock. Damn, I can't wait to get her underneath me. Naked, willing, aroused. The kiss we shared awakened something inside me, a feral beast who won't be satisfied until he's fed.

Several times.

As many times as she'll agree.

Hell, they don't all have to be tonight.

We've got more days, and until she tells me no, I'm taking what I want.

"Do you stare at all the women in your kitchen?"

"If they look like you, I would."

She faces my way, one hip propped against the counter, her arms crossed over her chest. Today's hoodie depicts a bookshop logo, one I've never heard of. I wonder if it's local to where she lives. She's paired it with skinny jeans form-fitted to her legs.

"Should I take that as a compliment?"

"For sure. Especially because you're the only woman ever in my kitchen. Outside of my family."

Shock crowds her face. "No way."

"Way."

"This kitchen?" She points to the floor, in case I misinterpreted the question.

"Yes."

"And you've lived here for how long?"

"Four years."

She whistles. "None of your one-night stands?" A lack of judgment hides in her tone, which I appreciate.

"No."

"No girlfriends?"

I scratch my head, recalling whether they had ever been here. "Luna preferred to stay at her house. The cabin was 'sketch.' Her word, not mine."

Willa laughs at my impression, and the light chords unlock more emotion in my chest. She looks around. "Yeah, I can see it. Though it's very much growing on me. Minus anything related to Christmas. What do you usually have over there?" She motions toward the offending Christmas tree with a sneer.

"A bookshelf."

"I can get on board with that. What's your favorite book?"

"Grab the bottle of wine with the pink sticky note from the pantry and pour us each a glass while I plate dinner."

It warms my heart how she doesn't question my suggestion

nor call me out on not answering hers. I don't intend to ignore it. We'll continue the conversation over dinner.

Willa returns, her eyes analyzing the label of red wine. "Seriously? How long has this been labeled for this meal specifically?"

"Since you agreed to steaks. It's not like I'm anal."

Her nose scrunches. "Have you looked up the definition in the dictionary? There's most likely a picture of your pantry as a visual representation."

Removing the bottle from her hand and setting it on the counter, I can't fight the urge to grab her from behind and wrap my arms around her, trapping her in an embrace. She squeals, my dick further encouraged by the noise.

"You think I'm anal?" I peer down at her.

"Ridiculously so. I'm flabbergasted you don't have labels on the shelves in the pantry." I squeeze her tighter, eliciting a yelp. "Uncle," she wheezes. "Uncle."

I only let her go because if I don't, dinner will get cold with the things I want to do to her. I'm turned on by her making fun of me, and it's impossible to think straight, let alone do much of anything else.

"Pour the wine and set the table." My voice is raspy, lower than usual, spurred on by adrenaline and arousal. It will be a miracle to make it through dinner without ravaging her.

"K."

"Are you always so amenable to what's asked of you?"

She peers over her shoulder. "When the man asking treats me like you do? Guess so." Her attention transfers to choosing silverware.

"Noted for later activities."

The temptation to touch her too strong, I smack her ass as she passes me.

"Eep," she squeaks. "Watch it. I've got steak knives in my hand."

I fix the plates, piling on noodles, steak, and veggies. Her eyes grow into saucers when I put the plate down in front of her before taking my seat. "This I will miss when I leave here. This looks and smells delicious, Beckett."

"It'll taste delicious, too," I state, not ashamed to stroke my ego. "Oh, and to answer your earlier question, anything by James Patterson or John Grisham is my favorite book."

"By definition, 'favorite' implies one." She cuts her steak into bite-size pieces, stabs a piece with the fork, and puts it into her mouth. "Oh, damn." Her eyes sink closed, her expression sated. "This is so good. The flavors pop, and the steak's cooked to perfection. How am I ever supposed to leave this place?"

I'm sure she doesn't mean the last part literally, but damn if it doesn't inflate my already swollen ego.

"Stay" is on the tip of my tongue, but I swallow it back. It's not even a slight possibility. Not in any universe.

"Glad it lives up to the hype." I take a bite, curious to taste how it came out. One touch of the steak to my tongue, and I'm in heaven. I don't always get it right on the first try, but this one I nailed. It's a replica of the picture, and the flavors are exquisite, the garlic, rosemary, and butter creating the perfect sauce.

"Beyond the hype. I've been to five-star restaurants and never experienced a steak so delicious. Kudos to you."

My chest puffs with her exuded praise. "Thanks."

I savor the meal, the time spent with Willa high on my current priority list.

Eventually, she gets back to the book discussion. "If you could only read one book for the rest of your life—"

"Not a fair question. When am I ever going to be put in a situation to only read *one* book?"

"Everything in your house burns down except that book."

"Morbid." She shrugs, rolling noodles on her fork. "I'd go to the library or read on my e-reader."

"Your e-reader was lost in the fire. The library flooded, all the books ruined."

"The local bookstore."

"Bankrupt."

"Online bookstores. Goodwill. Thrift stores." The answers come fast, no deep thinking involved.

"All ran out of money and out of business."

"You're evil. But also, wouldn't that mean that you'd be out of a career?"

The comment perplexes her. "Hmm. Good point."

"What would you do if you weren't a writer?"

"A detective." She rattles it off without a pause, clearly having given it some thought.

"Solve all the crimes. I can see it."

"You? If you didn't fix cars?"

"A chef."

She holds up a forkful of steak. "Suits you. You ever work as a chef?"

"No. Culinary school and I weren't a match."

"What? Not enough order? Too much structure and routine?" She'd make an excellent detective. She's good at reading people and picking up on things even if they're not intentional clues.

"Couldn't handle the pressure. Everything had to be perfect—"

"You don't say," she mocks. Her tone is playful, but her expression is more serious.

"If I'm going to mess things up, I'd rather not be graded or judged. Mistakes in my kitchen are less stressful."

She listens attentively, absorbing my comments, contemplating her answer. "Are you sure you're the youngest kid? Seems to me you'd fit better as an eldest."

I point to my chest. "Conundrum at its finest."

"Right." She giggles. "Not all chefs go to culinary school. I'd say your method is working. If that was ever in the cards for you."

"Maybe once I figure out a way to grow a thicker skin. Any tips?"

"You can't take it personally. And don't read reviews."

"Simple as that, huh?"

Willa quiets, but the silence is refreshing. It's not awkward. All our conversations are constructive without being critical or a need to fill the silence.

"I'm not one to give advice. I gave up. After my first book was a wild success, hitting all the bestseller lists and bringing in more money than I could have imagined, I froze." She folds her hands together and leans her chin on them, staring at something behind me. "I didn't write for six months. I *couldn't* write. I was paralyzed with fear. No matter what I tried, nothing worked. I shut down, shut off from life, let the negative voices, the people telling me I wasn't good enough, win."

"What changed?" I ask when she gives me an opening.

"Met a guy. He wouldn't let me quit. Told me I had more stories to share with the world, that I was better than the haters. Even if the second book wasn't as amazing as the first, people were clamoring to read it."

"And it worked?"

"Drafted book two in ten days. When I handed it to my editor, she didn't even make many changes." Lost in the story, a wistful smile adorns her lips. "The second book did better than the first. And then subsequent books topped those numbers."

"How many books have you published?"

"Seven."

"Wow. That's amazing, Willa. Truly. How many more books are planned for the series?"

The color drains from her face. My heart squeezes. For her, for being the one to ask the question.

"Wait. What happened to the guy? The one who told you not to give up?"

"He, uh, he's gone."

"Oh, shit. I'm sorry. Was it a bad breakup? Is he the one who hurt you?"

Her complexion ashen, she stares straight ahead. "I ca-can't talk about it." Her fingers grip the table, her knuckles white.

Calmly, I slide my hand over one of hers, giving her a sense of comfort if she'll take it.

"You don't have to. I'm sorry you're upset."

"Thanks. Didn't mean to ruin dinner."

"You didn't. We're done." The plates are both scraped clean, the evidence of any morsels long gone.

She glances at her plate. "Because it was delicious."

"Are you still hungry? There are more noodles and veggies. We ate all the steak."

She waves my comment away. "No, plenty full. Until dessert, at least." She attempts a sad smile, and my heart wants to break in half with her pain. There's so much more she can't or won't talk about. I'm not sure she'll open up to me, but I'll let her know I'm here if she wants to. Whatever baggage she wants to unload on me, I'll take. When it's time for her to move on, she'll leave with a lighter load.

"My grandmother used to make a divine red velvet cake at the holidays. I'm not sure I've had it since she passed, but a sudden urge just hit me. You game?"

"That seems like a loaded question. Will it make you nostalgic for her?"

"Probably."

"Jealous I'm the only one feeling this way? Do you suddenly need to be depressed, too? "

It shouldn't be funny, but her monotone voice digs up buried emotions.

"Nailed it. I can't let you have all the fun." I think I've gone too far, but Willa cracks a smile.

She goes to speak, but the back door opens. "Uncle Beck, Gram says you've got her extra flour. So we're here to take it back 'cause me and mom have baking to do." Her comments precede my niece's arrival, and Willa sits up straight in her chair, a frozen expression molded on her face.

When Shania appears, my sister's on her heels. "Oh, didn't realize you had company. We'll get the flour and skedaddle."

Autumn looks over at Willa before disappearing into the pantry. Shania's taking in my guest, her eyes locked on her sweatshirt. Suddenly, she's on the move.

"Oh my gosh. Where did you get this from?"

Willa peeks down, like she forgot what she was wearing. "Oh, um. It's—"

"You read Hidden Clues Club? They're like my favorite ever. I love AJ Hart. She's my spirit animal. I want to be her. I can't wait for book eight, but it's taking for-ever. Which one's your favorite? I can't decide which one mine is. I love them all. And I love this sweatshirt. I need this sweatshirt. Mom!" she yells, louder than necessary. Autumn peeks her head from the pantry. "Add this to my birthday list, k?"

"Right away, my little dictator. Consider it added." Her deadpan is on point, and I stifle my laughter.

Shania smiles, too excited and missing her mother's sarcasm. She slaps her head. "Oh duh. I'm Shania. Are you and Uncle Beck dating?"

Willa's wild gaze finds mine. Shania's overwhelming on a good day, but when she's passionate about something? Watch out.

"Willa's just staying here until her car is fixed. What series did you say her sweatshirt was from?"

"Keep up, Uncle Beck. Hidden Clues Club."

My mind fits the pieces together, and Willa's horrified look makes sense.

"Who's the author?" I ask, my eyes not leaving Willa's. She gives a shake of her head.

"Evelyn Ravenhurst."

"Interesting." I commit the name to memory, planning to google it later.

"Yeah. She was supposed to do an author signing a few years ago in Burlington, but she was sick or something. I still want to meet her, even if I'm a little old for the books now. It would be so cool. She's like my favorite author, and I'm her biggest fan."

I can't betray Willa's trust, but I'd be solidified as favorite uncle forever if Shania only knew.

"I'm sure she'd love to meet her biggest fan."

Autumn reappears from the pantry with two bags of flour. Holding them up, she says, "Put these on my tab, k?"

I parrot her words from earlier. "Right away, my little dictator."

"What did you make for dinner?"

"Pan-seared steak with rosemary."

"Oh, damn. Was it as mouthwatering as the pictures?"

"It was better," Willa pipes in, finding her voice. To Shania, she says, "The first book in the series will always be my favorite. When AJ figures out it was the bus driver . . . even I didn't see that coming."

Shania lights up. "That's my favorite part of that book. I had no clue it was her!"

"Why's your tree dark?" my sister wonders.

"Yeah, and your outside lights are off, too," Shania adds, walking toward the switch. "Oh, the switch is off. Weird." She flicks it, bathing the room in the glow from outside. But does she stop there? Oh no. She walks to the tree and turns that on, too. "Ah, much better."

Before I can react, Willa pushes her chair out, rushing off to the bathroom with an "Excuse me."

Once the door's closed, Autumn jokes, "Hope it wasn't the meal."

If she only knew.

13
willa

PANIC INFILTRATES and a sick feeling eclipses me. Slamming the door shut a little harder than necessary, I lean against it, sliding to the floor. I kick my legs out in front of me, breathing heavy.

"Do not vomit. Do not vomit." I repeat the affirmation over and over out loud, willing the contents of the delicious dinner to stay inside where they belong.

I begin counting, controlling my breathing, clawing out from the wave of destruction attempting to wash me out to sea. Everything blurs for a moment, and when the dust settles, I determine it's embarrassment driving these emotions.

Not fear.

Not anxiety.

Pure humiliation.

I can't let Beckett's sister and niece see me like this. Oh my god, if she only knew my identity.

I about tossed my cookies when she recognized my sweatshirt. And then she professed her love for the books. *My* books. Now I'm glad I didn't tell her. And I respect Beckett for keeping the secret as well.

A knock comes on the door. "Willa? They're gone. I turned off the lights as soon as they left the driveway. It's safe to come out now."

What did I do in life to deserve this man? He's rescued me—literally, saved me from being stranded—he's fed me way more delicious meals than I'm used to eating in a month, and he doesn't demand to know my business. Oh, and he's super accommodating about my hatred of his favorite holiday. Who does that?

"Why are you so kind to me? I've done nothing to show you I deserve your kindness."

"It's who I am. You don't owe me anything, and I'll still be kind to you."

I believe that to be true. In the short time I've known him, he's proven it several times.

One might even say a plethora.

I laugh at my joke, the action cathartic.

"Can I come in?" he asks from the other side of the door.

"Wouldn't it be easier if I came out?"

"Are you ready?"

"Not really."

"Then I'm coming in. You might want to move away from the door."

How he knows this is beyond me. I didn't lock the door, so when he opens it, it pushes my back, my size no match for his strength.

His chuckle enters before him. "I see this time you ignored my suggestion."

Still on my butt, I scoot away from the door, swiveling around as he steps inside, shutting the door behind him. It's odd since we're alone in the house. The urge to get up and run floats through me, but I tamp it down, curious about what he's going to say.

"So that's your sister and your niece." I get the elephant out of the way. One of them, at least.

"Yep. Told you she was into books. Ironic, much?"

"Eerie," I murmur. What are the odds? My publicist would argue high because a lot of kids read the Hidden Clues Club books. Even without two years without a release, the books sell well. I shouldn't be so surprised to meet fans. Even when I'm incognito.

"Why didn't she recognize you?" His question is earnest and valid.

With the way social media and technology rule our lives, it should be more difficult to keep my identity a secret. To be fair, I've been out of the limelight for the last two years.

"My author photos are old and need to be updated, but it hasn't been a priority. My hair was a different color when I was younger, and I wear a pair of 'Evelyn' glasses in all the photos."

"What about social media? Author signings? Book tours? Or do you not do those?"

"It's, um, been a little while for either of those things. And Clem says when I'm Evelyn, even she doesn't recognize me sometimes." I lift a shoulder. Instead of continuing this discussion, I change subjects. "What did you tell them? To get them to leave?" I ask nervously, my fingers finding my earlobe. It's a nervous habit, yet it's self-soothing, too.

I doubt he'd tell them my distaste for decorations. He doesn't seem like the kind of guy to share someone else's secret.

He shrugs. "I played it off your eyes are sensitive to the lights, so while you're here, we're keeping them off. Not even Autumn questioned it."

"Uh, thanks. I appreciate it. Can't imagine what they'd say if they knew the truth."

"First, they wouldn't believe it. Second," he pauses, taking a seat on the floor near me. For only having one bathroom in the place, it's a decent size with plenty of room for us both to sit without being squished together. "Second, they'd interrogate you until the cows came home, wanting to know how it started and why. They'd be relentless, never taking 'I don't want to talk about it' as an answer." He glances at me, a burning desire encased in his features. He's asking without asking, like the gentleman he is.

I take Beckett's hand in mine, desperate to touch him, needing the odd sense of comfort he brings. Callouses dot his palm dwarfing mine, giving him character, telling his story. Even without words, he's a storyteller.

"If I weren't here, what would you be doing tonight?"

"Probably this."

"Sitting on the floor of your bathroom, pondering life?"

"Yep. It's my Saturday night routine," he deadpans. The raspy tone has my eyes closing. I could listen to him speak, no matter what he's saying, for hours and never get bored. He'd make a good audiobook narrator.

I shove my shoulder into his. "No, for real."

"I might be at my parents' house. I've got the next few days off to prepare for the town's festivities, so if anyone else needed my help, I'd lend a hand. Otherwise, I'd be home, boring as fuck, watching TV or reading a book, soaking up the last quiet night before chaos reigns. Probably have a fire going, with only the lights of the tree for lighting."

Guilt worms in at how much I'm ruining for him. I hate myself a little more for not confronting my own fears and demons, for not dealing with the effects of two years ago.

My ears perk up at the "festivities" and "chaos." As if my body knows something I don't, my breathing hitches.

"What kind of chaos?"

Beckett rubs his fingers along his chin, his five o'clock shadow more pronounced today than the past two days. Maybe he didn't shave this morning.

"It's probably better you don't know and plan to stay in the cabin after tomorrow. I'll be out of your hair. You can get some writing done."

I kinda love how he's so concerned with my work and making sure I get it done. I almost hate being so untruthful to him.

Our hands are still entwined, and he traces lines and patterns along my palm with his finger. I don't want him to let go.

From outside the bathroom, my phone rings. I peek at my watch to see my mom's name.

Beckett drops my hand and stands up. "I'll get out of your hair."

"Wait," I press, ignoring the phone. I'll call her back. His back to me, Beckett peers over his shoulder. "The thing we talked about earlier?"

A hint of recognition flares in his eyes. "Yeah?"

"Are we, uh, can it, um, still happen?" I hope he doesn't hear the desperation. Once he planted the seed, the need for him hasn't disappeared. It's dimmed, but not gone entirely.

"Sure thing."

A wave of relief washes over me. I wasn't sure where we stood after the grocery store and his family's visit. I'm glad I didn't have to beg.

"I'll clean up dinner and meet you in your room."

Beckett nods his agreement. "Feel free to have dessert, too."

"Are you not having any? Wasn't there mention of cake?"

His eyes rake down me, lingering longer on my groin. "Oh, I am. Can't wait to discover how you taste, Willa. The cake can wait." He exits the bathroom, leaving me aroused with one dirty comment.

I linger in the empty room, needing several moments to compose myself after the array of emotions assaulting me.

"Hope you know what you're getting yourself into," I address the woman in the mirror.

Beckett disappears outside, and before I start on the dishes, I rinse off in the shower, making sure I'm more presentable for sex. A quick shave of my legs, armpits, and the bikini area to eliminate the jungle they become over the winter.

I zip through the dishes, load the dishwasher, and let the others dry on the drying rack. The pot he cooked the steak in needs some elbow grease, so it takes a little longer.

Beckett returns soon after I finish the last of the dishes. "I'm going to lock up. Do you want anything to drink?" I lift the filled water glass. He nods and grabs a beer from the fridge. "Meet you in my room in a few."

"K."

While he locks up, I get comfortable in his room, slipping off my pants and hoodie, leaving me in only a bra and undies. I feel a little awkward, the tiny fluttering in my abdomen the only twinge of nerves.

I definitely thought I'd be more nervous when the time came to get naked with a man again. Somehow Beckett has extinguished my fears without even trying.

Probably because there's nothing at stake except sex. No strings, no expectations beyond my time here. No deep-seated feelings attached. No questioning what this means. Just two adults coming together to let off some steam. A way to enhance the physical connection between us, test out the chemistry.

A means to an end.

Beckett breaches the doorway with a plate and his beer.

"Oh, what did you bring us?" I inquire with a nod to the plate. He tips it down, revealing one cookie. Setting the dish and beer on his nightstand, he rips the cookie into two halves, extending one to me.

"A treat before. If I'm not too tired after, I'll make the cake."

I waste no time devouring the cookie, careful not to get crumbs in his sheets. If he was against food in his bed, *he* wouldn't have been the one to bring it in.

"Delicious. Wish I could ask for the recipe to replicate at home."

"Mom's probably got some in her freezer. Remind me to grab some before we part ways."

His use of "part ways" elicits a twinge in my chest, something I have to shut down before it grows out of control. Everything with Beckett is temporary.

The stay, the food, the feelings, the sex.

His cookie eaten, he shucks his T-shirt by grabbing it behind his neck. However, I'm more engrossed in what's hidden under the shirt.

A V dipping into his waistband.

Washboard abs.

A well-manscaped chest.

Muscular pecs.

It's evident he takes care of his body, works out to keep a fit shape, but not overly. He's trim and fit, not bulky like some guys who think more muscles are attractive.

My tongue sneaks out of my mouth, moistening my lips.

I've never been with a man who looks like Beckett. Like he stepped off a page in GQ, both with his clothes and without. I'm certain our attraction isn't based on physical attributes alone, but he is not an eyesore.

I try to walk a few times a week and meet a friend for different gym classes at least two or three times. Some days, those are the only reason I have to leave my house. I've never been more thankful she coerces me to join her than I am now. You can't bounce a quarter off my ass, but I've got some definition, and I don't cringe when looking at my naked body in the mirror.

He shucks his pants, leaving him standing in black boxers. He strides around the bed to the other nightstand, my eyes trained on him, my body contorting to watch his every move. Two dimples stand out on his back, but it's hard to delineate the shape of his ass. I don't *think* I'm drooling, but man, if I am, I'm not even an ounce ashamed.

Beckett Nicholas is one fine specimen.

I blame this complete obsession with his body on the situation I find myself in. I'm not usually into objectifying people's bodies, male or female, but that's exactly what I'm doing with

Beckett. I'm a proponent of what's on the inside matters more than the outside, but in Beckett's defense, I'd say they're equal.

"Got your fill?"

His words draw me out of my stupor, but the meaning doesn't process.

"Huh?"

"You're staring. Like I'm a piece of meat." His voice isn't its usual tone, and I can't tell if he's joking or not. His use of "meat" doesn't go unnoticed by my ears.

"With a body like yours, I can't imagine everyone doesn't stare."

"I'll take that as a compliment. I like your bra. You wear that for me?" Why does that thought light up my insides further?

Forgetting which one I'm wearing, I peek down at the floral embroidery mesh.

My lips tip into a smile. "Would you like it more if I say yes or no?"

He tips his head from side to side, his eyes never leaving my chest. "Honestly, either answer turns me on. Knowing you wore it so I'd see, like you had me in mind when you put it on, is powerful." He reaches into the drawer next to me, extracting a box of condoms. "But knowing it was hiding underneath your clothes?" The mattress depresses where he kneels next to my legs. "Damn. That's hot, Willa."

I give him my skewed truth. "I put it on this morning, before any of this was on the table." He climbs more on the bed, caging my legs with his knees. "But I kept it on for you. It's my favorite."

"Even when no one sees it?"

"Bras are my one indulgence, a treat to myself. Even at home, when I spend all day writing in sweats and don't leave my house, I wear a fancy bra. A best-kept secret, maybe? I've never had anyone ask before, and I've never tried to explain it." It's something I've done for a long time. Elias accepted it as who I was. If he thought it odd, he never said.

Beckett nods, his eyes glued to the bra. "While I admire it, love how it showcases your cleavage, mind if I take it off?"

I sit up, my arms reaching around behind me to unclasp it, but Beckett grunts, halting my movements.

"I asked, politely if you'll recall, to take it off. I didn't mention you doing the honors." There's a hint of hesitation in his voice, though he makes his motives clear.

"Okay."

He reaches around, unhooking the bra, allowing the straps to fall to my arms. Gentle fingers trace down my arms, eliciting goose bumps. He removes the lingerie, letting it drop to the floor on the side of the bed, his vision not once leaving my chest. Under his scrutiny, my chest heaves, my skin tingling.

"Beautiful. Gorgeous. Luxurious."

I can't contain my giggle. "Interesting list of synonyms."

He breaks the stare he has on my chest, bringing his gaze to mine. "Exquisite. Magnifique. Shall I keep going?"

His adoration for my breasts shouldn't be a turn-on, but damn if my pride doesn't swell. It's one thing for me to think they're nice boobs, but to hear him lavish this praise on them? It doesn't hurt to hear. With no expectations for this, he could have done the minimal foreplay, and I would have been satisfied. Yet the way he's taking his time, drawing it out, bestowing me with compliments? I could easily fall for him if I let myself get too carried away.

Good thing that's not happening.

Temporary, I remind myself.

"My pussy's feeling neglected." The statement shoots from my mouth like a cannon, no thought into it at all.

He glances down, scooting the blanket out of the way. "Patience," he croons before planting a kiss on the bow of my undies. "Your turn is coming."

I didn't expect him to be so . . . endearing in the bedroom. I expected demands, like the ones he's been giving all day.

Even in the bedroom, this man is a conundrum.

14
beckett

I DON'T WANT to rush this with Willa.

The connection we share is too strong, but I don't want it to be over too fast. Much to the chagrin of my cock, how hard it is, how it aches to get inside her, I'm taking my time. Going slow. Worshipping the heck out of her lithe body. Enjoying every minute I get with her.

Not that I intend for this to be a "one and done" deal. No way.

But no matter how many times we come together, I'm not sure I'll ever get enough before she leaves and I never see her again.

Since when do I think like this? Who am I?

Will the real Beckett Nicholas please stand up?

My cock twitches, letting me know its stance on things.

With my mouth near her belly button, I trail my tongue up the center of her abdomen, dragging it along the outer edge of her left breast. Willa rewards me with the softest moans, the most adorable mewls. It spurs me on to continue.

First the left breast, then the right.

I take her pert nipple in my mouth, swirling my tongue around it.

Willa's fingers meet my back, the tips digging in, encouraging me.

I want to do so much to her, have her in all the ways, fill up all her holes until she's fully sated.

And then I want to do it again.

And again.

Again, until she tells me it's too much.

Never have I wanted so much from a woman. Never have I wanted to give so much to a woman.

I only pop off when I need a breather. Can't have me wasting all my energy on her breasts. Not with so many other areas to explore.

And explore I will.

I already know what her mouth tastes like, but I can't help dipping my head, swallowing her noises, if only for a quick taste.

And because there are better things to do with my mouth, I rip my lips away from hers before I'm ready.

"I don't know what you're doing to me, but please don't ever stop." With hooded eyes, Willa blinks up at me, a sated smile on her puffy lips.

"Not likely, Bundy. I'm just getting started." I want to taste her other lips, to prove to myself she's sweet.

I lie next to her, my head resting on the pillow. Her scent engulfs me, and I realize it's not because she's right next to me. It's because her head has slept on this pillow the last two nights. Damn. I don't make it obvious, but I inhale, the decadent aroma crowding my senses.

Settling in against the bed, I propose, "Sit on my face." It's not quite a demand, merely a suggestion, one I'm highly motivated to carry out.

I turn my head to face her, to observe her reaction. A glimmer of an inexplicable emotion flickers over her face, but then she's on the move. Kicking off the covers, sliding her panties off her legs, dropping them with her discarded bra.

She pushes to her knees, her naked body on full display, including the area of neatly trimmed hair. A few shades darker than the hair on her head. Wonder if it's as soft. My fingers reach out and touch it, confirming it. And when they're fully indulged, they slide below, flitting across her clit and down her opening, which glistens with moisture.

"Let me take care of that for you. Climb on."

Her widened orbs seek mine. "I-I've never done it before."

"Let me be your first. I'll be easy and gentle."

She gives a tiny nod, but before she moves, a shiver wracks her. From the cold or the anticipation, I don't dare ask.

I reach out my hand, tugging her slightly when she lays her palm in mine. She comes easily, and I love how she's willing and open, not hiding herself away, not shy. With her help, I plant her where I want her: her pussy hovering above my mouth.

"Lower to your knees. Grab hold of the headboard." I initiate, she obeys.

This isn't all for my pleasure, but damn if I'm not getting harder at her cooperation. Means I have to up my game, make it worth her while, make sure she's pleasured.

My hands find her hips, and I bring her lower, her scent teasing, her pussy taunting.

"If it gets to be too much, take a break. Don't worry about hurting me. You won't. If I need a break or can't breathe, I'll take it. Tell me how you like it. You're in the driver's seat."

"K."

She widens her knees, sinking lower. The second I can reach her, my tongue licks up her seam. Willa moans, short and punchy. I do it again, wanting more.

Longer.

Deeper.

More guttural.

I swirl my tongue around her most sensitive spot. She tries to move, but I hold her in place. I told her she was in control, but having her exactly where I want her, I'm selfish. I want to give her pleasure the way I want, control be damned.

"Beckett. You dirty man. Making me feel all kinds of things. Don't stop that thing you're doing with your tongue." Willa's words are hardly audible, the only thing I truly understand is the "don't stop," which I don't plan to. Not for at least one orgasm.

Not until I'm fulfilled.

With her pussy in my face, I lap and lick, nip and nibble her clit and along her seam. Her breathing grows heavier, more pronounced, and her moans, too. Her sounds are music to my ears, the cadence pitching higher the closer I drive her to the brink.

And drive her, I do.

Up to the pinnacle of the cliff, sending her toppling over with a long lick of my flattened tongue.

"Beckett!" she screams, loud and unleashed. I love the way she prattles my name, how much I'm affecting her.

It's not supposed to be like this, to feel this . . . emotional. But damn does it.

And as I mentioned, I'm taking all she gives me and then some. We stop when I say we're done.

Way to be a selfish bastard.

She grinds against my face, her legs quaking next to my ears, riding out the power of the orgasm. My fingers didn't even get a chance in the action, something I'll have to remedy when she comes down from the high and I can breathe a little better.

The temporary interruption was worth it.

Perhaps not to my cock. It's an angry motherfucker, not patiently waiting its turn for pleasure.

With her in this position, I can't see her face, but I have a good idea what she might look like.

Red cheeks.

Glassy eyes.

Beautiful.

Willa's the one to break our connection, falling into a heap on the bed beside me. She angles her head my way, her eyes closed, face flushed, back heaving. "I'll take an order of that again, at your leisure. Ecstatic. Well done. Need more." The last phrase is murmured, almost as if she's afraid to ask for more, even though she made it clear moments ago what she wanted.

And she calls me a conundrum.

I flip to my side, working my boxers off to prepare for whatever comes next. 'Cause whatever it is, my cock needs to be free.

"There's plenty more. All night. Tomorrow. The next day." I stop short of going too far out. She's not here indefinitely. This won't be a regular occurrence.

Damn, do I wish it could be.

The thought wriggles deep within me, from a spot unearthed only by Willa. No one before her. Too bad we're not on the same page about so many things.

"Going to need recovery time. It's never been so . . . vigorous. So bewitching. So gratifying."

There's been only general talk about our past hookups and relationships. She's made it clear she had someone special, though where he went and why they're not still together remains a mystery.

Stupid fool to give someone like her up. Dude doesn't know what he's missing.

"Take the time you need. If you thought that was powerful, wait until I get my cock in you."

One eye cracks open. "*Cock*-y, much?" She emphasizes the first part of the word.

I thrust my hips. "I can back it up. You'll see."

She opens the other eye, rearranging to lie on her side. It offers a magnificent view of her boobs squished together. Despite being satiated, I want another taste.

My cock has other plans.

Because it wants to get inside her. To feel her sweet heat

around it. To know what it's like to be squeezed while she's coming undone.

Or, maybe that's more my thinking. Considering it doesn't have a brain and I'm the one who does.

I definitely need to see her face when she comes. To watch her reach the pinnacle and detonate all because of me.

These thoughts pummel me from out of the blue. I've never been so drawn to a woman, never felt so connected. Willa is making me feel all the things, things way beyond temporary.

I lie on my side, propped on my left forearm. Lust swims in the midnight orbs, the color intensified by our sensual act. "Your eyes are so pretty."

"Thanks." She accepts the compliment graciously. I appreciate that about her. She admits her flaws and faults but isn't afraid to accept praise for her strengths.

With my free hand, I trail a finger down her cheek, and her head curls toward it, a soft mewl spilling from her mouth. This isn't quite the recovery time she asked for, but hell if I can stop where it's going. I can maybe stretch the foreplay a little longer, but my dick's hard as steel. There's only so much pain a man in my circumstances can take.

Before I take this any further, I sink onto my back and sheathe myself, rolling the condom on quickly and securely. To protect us both. With wide eyes and bated breath, Willa watches my every movement. Every little move I make, she nods along, giving her permission for what I'm doing. Well, I assume that's what she's doing. I won't ask her, though her action incites me.

As if I need any added encouragement.

I situate myself above her body, resting on my forearms, caging her in. Another time I'll change up our perspective. Right now, the ability to memorize how she looks when she comes takes precedence. As long as I can get my dick inside her, the position is a formality.

"Enough of a reprieve for you?" My eyes leave her gaze, trailing down, scrutinizing her luscious breasts and admiring the sneak peek of definition on her abdomen, evidence of her working out.

Back on her face, her tongue darts out of her mouth, licking her bottom lip. "I'm amending my earlier statement. Take me, Beckett. Use me for your pleasure." I'm momentarily stunned by her words, which she quickly follows up with, "I meant, give us both pleasure. You and me. A pair of matching orgasms. Two—"

My mouth descends hers, swallowing whatever else she was going to ramble. There's time for rambling later. We've got more pressing matters.

In a dance I'm familiarizing with Willa, our mouths perform. Her head lifts off the bed to meet mine, and her arms circle my neck, tugging me closer.

"Need you," she murmurs against my mouth. The words are whispered, I barely make them out. But once they've penetrated and processed, I don't waste a single second giving her what she wants.

There will be time to sort out my reasoning later.

Pulling my mouth away, her breath whooshes out, like she'd been devoid of oxygen for days instead of minutes. When the kiss is that passionate, it's a good thing our bodies keep breathing on their own.

Widening her thighs, I settle between the crux of her legs, nudging her opening with the crown of my dick. Wetness seeps out, and it's all I can do not to thrust inside. To claim her body as mine.

"More, Beckett. Give me more than just the tip."

I stare down at her, a smirk alighting on my lips. "Impatient, much?"

"Yep." She pops the p, no trace of shame. The tips of her fingers knead my back. "Do I need to make it more clear?"

"Noted. On it. More than just the tip." I push in one inch more, drawing out a tiny moan. "Better hold on. I'll make it up to you later if I don't last."

It's the only warning I give her before I shove inside, moving her body with the action.

"Yassss," she draws out, tipping her head back, exposing her neck. Like she's serving it at a buffet, I run my tongue up and down, tasting the salt of her sweat. "More. Don't stop."

I literally haven't stopped moving, but Willa has other notions.

My tongue pauses long enough for me to mumble, "Highly unlikely," before it's back on her neck. Below, I drive inside her, pulling out, pushing back in, loving the way her pussy clamps on. Not willing to stop even when I come.

Which doesn't take long to get there, the need for release imminent.

Her pussy grips tighter, specifying she's close. I lift my head to feast on the beauty that's Willa. The rosy cheeks. The head writhing against the bed. The incoherent noises tumbling from her lips.

I can't say for certain she falls first. Because I'm so there. Right at the precipice. My balls draw up. And I don't hold back, knowing we're climaxing together.

Through grunts and growls, I ride out my release, using her body for my pleasure. Huh. Guess she knew what she was talking about.

But she's there, too. Using me for her pleasure.

The two of us, using each other. Coming together, each finding a beautiful release.

No matter how much baggage there'll be to unpack later, it will all be worth it for this piece of her.

A piece I didn't know was missing.

15
willa

THIS MAN IS INSATIABLE.

After the third orgasm, I lost track of how many he coerced.

Yes, coerced.

I swear, he looked at me with those hooded eyes, and my body gave him what he wanted.

He played my body like he was a conductor and I was his instruments. All different ones. Woodwinds, strings, brass, percussion. All of them.

And when I thought I was tired, he convinced me I had one more orgasm in me. And damn it, he was right.

If it weren't so pleasureful, I'd hate him on principle for being so pliable, so yielding to his every command.

My mind's a little hazy on all the details, but I don't think he slept on the couch last night. I remember drifting to sleep in his arms, waking once when he pried my eye open.

Did I tell him to fuck off and let me sleep?

Of course not. Hopped up on my knees and let him take me from behind.

He's unleashed this side of me I never knew existed.

It's not like my past sex life was bad, either. Elias and I had our share of playing with different positions, spicing it up. But last night's sex was on an entirely other level. A level I didn't realize was a possibility. For me, at least.

Now, it's half past dawn, or some crazy-ass time, and the man's disappeared from the bed. When the outside door slams, he's leaving or returning. Either way, I decide to investigate.

Pit stopping into the bathroom, all I can do is cackle at my flushed face and ratty hair. Attempting to corral it into even a messy bun proves fruitless, so I leave it down, running my fingers through it to tame some of the wildness.

Beckett's in the kitchen, his back to me while he stands at the counter. He wears a hoodie and gray sweatpants, and I can't resist the urge to wrap my arms around his front, laying my head against his back. If he's bothered by it, he doesn't show it.

It's strange how comforting it is, how familiar he feels after such a short time. I'm done questioning it, instead letting everything ride out until it's time for me to pack up and leave.

Which is something I'm not thinking about.

Elias would be so proud of me for living in the moment.

"Morning. I got donuts. Wasn't sure which were your favorites, but hopefully there's something you'll enjoy."

"Any combination of flour, sugar, and yeast will do. Add in some chocolate, even better."

He stops whatever he's doing and shimmies in my arms so we're face-to-face. His lips meet the top of my head, lingering before dropping a kiss. At least I showered yesterday, so the smell shouldn't match the mussed appearance.

"Should you leave the house today, it's cold out. Definitely can't skip a jacket."

Warmth infuses my body and soul. It's only been so long, and this man reads me like a book, offering advice before I even ask for it.

"Good thing I don't plan on leaving. What did you say you had to do today?" His expression sours, but I've let him beat around the bush for too long. I'm a big girl. I can pull up my panties. "Don't filter on my account."

"Gotta set up for the Christmas Eve parade. It's kinda an all-day project. I hate to leave you all alone again . . ." he trails off, his words somber.

"Don't feel bad. This week was for me to be alone. Granted, I'm not complaining about the orgasms, the food, the company, and if there's time later to get back to any of it, spending the day on my own will be well worth it." I smile, but it's half-hearted. I have an inkling why, but I'm not currently prepared to tackle it.

Beckett pushes a wayward strand off my face, his touch so gentle in contrast to him. I'm coming to appreciate all his sides, not being able to choose which one I enjoy most.

The one who gives you orgasms, an inner voice shouts. Can't say I disagree.

"What would it take for you to join me?"

I don't even think. "Nothing. Not happening." No way in hell am I that compliant.

He shrugs, not bothered by my response. "Had to try."

"When do you have to leave?"

"An hour or so. Why, did you have something in mind?" A twinkle gleams in his eye.

Fuck me.

And aloud I confirm, "Fuck me."

Had you asked me last week if I would agree to sex when my vagina already took a pounding, my answer would have been hell no.

However, despite already feeling sore, I let Beckett have his wicked way with me before he departs for the day.

But hey, nothing a long soak in his tub won't help ease.

While I'm in here, Clem calls.

"Any word on your car?"

"Still not ready. Won't be fixed until after the holiday."

"And you're okay with that?" Disbelief shrouds her tone.

"What other choice do I have?"

"I could fly to get you, drop you to the cabin, and bring you back after the holiday."

"Sweet of you, but I won't be the one to take away your kids' joy so close to the holiday. You know how I felt last year. That was the purpose of this trip. To not ruin the holidays for others."

And yet, here I am. Squashing Beckett's joy and fun.

Some houseguest I am.

"You can't let this get to you every year. It's not healthy."

I don't justify her response with one of my own.

I'm not saying she's wrong. It's just that I'm not prepared to deal with it, to face the emotions head-on.

My sigh echoes around the silent bathroom. "This isn't my year to do that." I close my eyes, deflecting the memories of my nephews' past celebrations. Their smiles, their excitement.

Am I prepared to give that all up forever?

"I can't talk about this, Clem." It's my go-to answer for when I don't want to deal with something I can't face. I shut down, run away, take the scaredy-cat route.

"Willafred. You can't forever run away from your problems." She sounds exactly like our mother. She gets a pass because she's my twin. Coming from her, it's not as derisive.

"I don't run away from all my problems."

A half-lie because running away from this one impacts so many aspects of my life.

"Can we talk about this next week when I'm home? You're stealing all the joy from my bath." I slink down lower in the water and rest my head against the back of the tub, fluttering my eyes shut.

"How's the book coming?"

"Fuck off, Clementine."

"Love you, too, Willa. Enjoy your bath. Talk soon."

The line goes dead. I'm grateful for the technology of the iPhone to hang my side up once the call disconnects. I'm too relaxed to move.

I soak for a good thirty minutes, my mind vacillating between replaying my conversation with Clem and my night with Beckett. Those memories are more fun, and because I'm apparently a woman possessed, my fingers make their way under the water. At home, I'd use the handheld shower for situations like this, but Beckett's bathroom only has the one on the wall.

It's Beckett's name on my lips when I work myself over, crashing down hard after the fall. So hard, a well opens up, a dam unleashed, spilling devastation everywhere.

A slew of memories pummel me.

The last time Elias and I were intimate.

The text messages.

The phone calls.

The realization he was gone and never coming back.

The seal broken, I can't control the tears. Ugly, snot-inducing tears cascade down my cheeks. A cry so hard, I can't catch my breath. My lungs seize, my chest constricting and heaving with the sobs wracking my body. I don't know how I'll stop, how to let go of this crippling emotion trying to drag me under.

I push to sit up, trying to stop the intense feelings, to catch my breath, but nothing works.

Not telling myself to breathe.

Not demanding I stop crying.

Not pushing away the onslaught of memories.

Until someone calls my name.

"Willafred."

It's Elias's voice, yet it sounds so real. So earthly. So in the room.

"Open your eyes." So close, so demanding. "Willa, honey. Let me see those pretty blues." A hand on my arm rattles me, and I gulp for fresh air, dragging it into my lungs.

My eyes fly open, but it's not Elias staring back at me. It's Beckett, his eyes wild, terrified, a storm brewing in the wild blue.

Without another word, he lifts me from the bath like I weigh nothing. Not caring about how wet I am, the mess we're making on the way to his bedroom, he holds me close. The tears fall faster, but they're silent now.

When he sits on the bed, he doesn't let me go. He wraps me in the blanket, whispering, "It's gonna be okay. Shh. Don't cry. Try and relax," and other calming words into my ears. With one hand, I search for purpose on his hoodie, holding on tighter, afraid to let go. With the other, I rub my earlobe, searching for any small sliver of comfort.

I can't speak, can't explain what's happening, can't pull away so he doesn't get more soaked.

And I can't stop crying. The tears won't dry up.

My body's fraught with sentiment that has been holed up inside for the better part of two years. It's all coming to a head. Here, of all places.

If I were thinking clearly, I'd blame Beckett for doing this to me. For unlocking the key to a chest I've kept locked since that fateful day.

But it's not really his fault. It's mine.

It's mine for not confronting my issues two years ago.

It's mine for shoving down every ounce of feeling.

It's mine for running away from life, for shutting down, for blaming Elias for dying.

My body quakes, but Beckett squeezes me tighter.

I can't contemplate what he must be thinking, the thoughts consuming his head at what's going on. It's too much to focus on regulating my breathing and stopping the tears.

I rest my head against his chest, not caring how wet he's going to be when this passes.

If this passes. At this rate, it feels like it won't end.

I'm not sure how long we sit in his bed, me crying in his arms, him offering nothing but comfort and soothing. His hand trails up and down my back, tracing the same pattern.

Up and down.

Up and down.

Up and down.

Centering on his movements helps relieve some of the ache, some of the angst tormenting my body. But my body's stubborn, not ready to give up the fight. I'm too weak to mount a defense.

After what feels like hours, the tears dry up, but the emotions don't stop their assault. Beckett's comfort seeps into me, fighting my battles I'm too worn out to tackle on my own.

Though I'm still naked, the blanket's dried and warmed me up. Or maybe that's the warmth wafting off Beckett.

From my position in his lap, I peer up at him. Worry lines outline his face, his expression a mask of concern. His fingers trail along the edges of my jaw, big hands cupping my face.

"We're talking about it," he growls. "All of it. The only choice you get is here or the living room. Nothing else is up for negotiation."

His demands are so impossible to combat. As much as I don't want to talk about it, arguing isn't an option. But I can't help but refute, "I need to get dressed. Dry my hair."

He blows out a long-winded captured breath. "I'll allow you ten minutes. Bed or the couch? Coffee or tea?"

"Coffee. In the living room. Will you start a fire?"

"Absolutely, Bundy." He slips his mouth over mine. The kiss is chaste, a way of showing he cares.

As if I needed more evidence.

"If you're not on the couch in ten minutes, I'm coming for you."

"Right. I understand." When he stands up, I notice his entire outfit is soaked. I point to his front and sheepishly add, "Sorry." Except I'm not the one who pulled me from the bath soaking wet.

He glances down to assess it. Instead of addressing it, he stammers, "Ten minutes." He stalks to his dresser, ripping open the drawer and wrenching clothes out. He disappears from sight, holing up in the bathroom.

I don't dare think he won't follow through on his "ten-minute" order, so I follow his lead and get dressed.

16
beckett

HER LOUD CRIES tore through me. The harrowing sobs, the hallowed wails, the pain.

At first, I thought she was hurt. That someone was hurting her. It took me a minute or two of panic to find her in the bathroom, to realize what was happening. By that time, my heart was a mess, my pulse skyrocketed to the worst-case scenario.

But what truly wrecked me was her expression. The pain and sorrow etched on her face. The shame she wore like a mask, branded into every pore.

I didn't think. I reacted.

When I couldn't get her immediate attention—she was too lost in a different time—panic gripped me like a vise, a hold so strong, I didn't think I could fight for her. It didn't occur to me I'd be soaked when I reached out and lifted her from the water. I had one goal: to make her stop crying. Not because I couldn't handle the tears and the noise, but because she couldn't. She needed comfort, and I was the one to give it to her.

Even now, dressed in dry clothes, trying to process what the hell happened, making coffee and sugary snacks, I wouldn't have reacted differently if I had stopped to think about my actions. The woman is going through something, and despite her propensity to not want to talk about it, that stops now. I can't let her be alone with this. No matter how hard it is to talk about, she needs to get it out, to confront it.

Whatever *it* is.

I'm not sure how well I'll do to help, but I'm here to listen, to lend all the support I can give her, to hear her out, to make things better.

Except that's not always the case. I can't "fix" everything. Not for myself, and not for the people around me. Especially if they don't want help. What I know about Willa, she's going to refuse the help as much as she can. But when she lets her guard down even one bit, that's when I'll pounce.

The bathroom door opens, and Willa emerges. Her eyes red and swollen hidden behind her glasses, her cheeks puffy. Exactly how long had she been crying? How much emotion was she trying to purge?

What the hell has this girl been through?

A shiver races up my spine. What if it's something I can't handle? What will I do then?

I tamp those thoughts down, needing to get a better grasp on what we're dealing with.

"Hey." Her voice is strained, weak, the usual soft cadence now rough.

"Are you hungry? Did you eat today?"

A coping mechanism I learned long ago—food makes everything seem less bleak. The more sugar and fat, the better.

She wraps her arms around her abdomen, giving herself a hug. I itch to pull her into my arms, but I don't want to upset her more. "I had a late lunch. What time is it?"

"Almost seven. I'll heat some soup my mom sent. Are you okay with mushrooms?"

"Sure." The one-word agreement is lackluster, but at least she's willing to eat. "About before—"

I cut her off. "Food first, then we'll talk." I shake my head.

"You'll talk, I'll listen," I amend, in case she thinks she can get out of it.

Her hand is balled in the sleeve of her hoodie, and she won't meet my gaze, but she gives a tiny bob of her head. She can have this time now to figure out how to share her story because once I get her on the couch, she's not leaving until I have it all. No matter how raw and horrible, she's not omitting any details.

While the coffee percolates, I warm up the soup Mom sent home with me, making a bowl for Willa and me. When I set it in front of her, she accepts it graciously. Her expression is blank, devoid of emotion. It's eerie but understandable. I blame her heightened state for what I do next.

"Stand up." It sounds less harsh in my head, so I'm not offended when Willa stares blankly at me rather than doing as I demand. "Please."

With guarded emotions, she slowly pushes the chair back and stands. As evidenced by her "oof," she's not expecting me to crush her to me.

And that's exactly what I do.

Hold on to her tightly, like if I let go, she'd float away, never to be seen again.

Her body's stiff at first, but within moments of my arms encasing her, she melts against me, wrapping her arms around my back, clutching on tight.

No words are exchanged. No words are needed. Our actions say it all.

I allow her the space she needs, except this isn't all for her.

I don't do this, take on other people's emotions. I'm not heartless and have loads of sympathy for people I love. But I'm not usually such an empath. So why the need to take on Willa's stress and tension? Hell if I can understand it. However, the only thing going to stop the ache in my heart is helping her.

If only she'd let me be her hero.

I balk at the suggestion. Never in a million years would she agree to that. As if she needs a hero who's her total opposite.

We stand wrapped in each other for what feels like forever. A solid five minutes if I had to guess. When she moves to pull away, I don't stop her. Moisture pools in the corner of her eyes, but she doesn't let it escape. Strong in the face of adversity.

"Bet you're wishing you were a serial killer now, huh?"

With everything going on, I don't understand her comment immediately, but when it sinks in, I cackle. "So I could do away with you?"

"Well, yeah. I'm a lot more unbalanced than you bargained for."

"Isn't that the truth," I confirm with a laugh. "Turns out, I like unhinged women. Who knew?"

Though I'm uncertain that's true.

I like an unhinged woman. Singular. One.

Willafred . . . whatever her last name is.

I keep the chatter light over soup, but once we're finished and move to the living room, the fire I started earlier—at her request—roars, illuminating the room with its embers. What I wouldn't give to have the tree on as well.

At this point, I'm not even questioning why I'm bending over backward for her.

With a mug of hot cocoa in her hands, Willa sits in the corner of the couch, her legs scrunched up, her torso folded over them. I can't imagine this will be easy for her, and even before I know what she's going to say, I'm proud she's not backing down.

She totally could. I didn't give her much of a choice in the matter, but if she was extremely opposed to talking about it, all she'd have to do was say the word and I'd shut it down.

Cue the pussy-whipped jokes. And she's not even someone I'm dating or in a relationship with.

"Remember when I told you there was a guy?"

"Yep." Asshole for leaving her. Though it gave me a chance

to spend time with her, and these past few days have been great. I wasn't kidding when I said she'd move to the top of my list of one-night stands. And that was before we had sex. Now that I've had her? No other on the list holds a candle to her.

She sucks in a breath, releasing it slowly, deliberately, stalling for time. I scooch closer to her but leave the decision of where she wants me up to her. She reaches one hand out, and I entwine our fingers.

"He didn't leave me because our relationship didn't work out." She pauses, and I allow her words to sink in, processing them without reacting.

"I'm not sure I'm following. You're not with him still?"

"No."

"But it's not because your relationship ended. What else is there?" My black-and-white brain is having trouble making sense of her statement.

"He died. On Christmas."

"Oh, shit."

I'm not sure which part is worse, but man does it explain her behavior and her hatred of the holiday. I can see how something like that would put a huge damper on the joy of the season.

Right about now, I'm super delighted I didn't push the issue past that first night. I also understand why she didn't tell me. Why she never would have told me except for her breakdown.

"I'm so sorry, Willa. Can I ask how?"

She stares into the fire, almost as if she didn't hear my question. My brain whirls with what could have happened.

Was he sick?

Was he killed?

Was he murdered?

Okay, the last one is highly unlikely, but I won't eliminate the possibility. I also won't prod until she's ready to explain.

I work her onto my lap, her body still tucked into a ball. She doesn't fight me, and I'm glad I give her whatever comfort she needs. My hand rubs circles on her back, letting her know to take her time, but I'm here. For whatever she needs, I'm here.

"It was early Christmas morning. He was a runner and training for a marathon in January. We lived in North Carolina then, and the weather was mild, 'perfect running weather' according to him. He hated missing a day of training. While I supported his training, I urged him to go out early, before breakfast, so it wouldn't interfere with our celebration. He agreed, but on the condition I could only write while he was gone. If he had to be present for the entire day, so did I." She laughs, but it's devoid of humor. "When I wrote, I could get lost for hours. Forget to eat. Forget the outside world existed. If there was one bone of contention in our relationship, that was it. That's not to say he didn't champion my writing and my career. Elias was my biggest cheerleader, advocate, and fan. But not on Christmas. If I wanted to get lost in my world on Christmas, it was while he was gone."

"Seems like a suitable compromise to me, a win-win for both of you."

"Totally." She pauses, moving her head to a different spot on my chest, directly above my heart. I'm eager to hear the rest of her story, but I don't want to rush her. "Except I got so caught up in my story, I lost track of time. Before I realized, three hours had passed, and he wasn't back yet. He'd told me when he left it wouldn't be a long run. An hour at most." She pauses again, sighing deeply before she delves back in. "When I discovered I hadn't checked my phone in all that time, a bad feeling niggled in. I didn't know then, but it was the time he took his last breath. He was saying goodbye."

My heart about cracks in my chest, and my arms squeeze her tighter on their own. It's like I'm experiencing it with her for the first time. Her realization is heart-wrenching and guttural, even years after the fact.

"How long has he been gone?" I venture to ask.

"It'll be two years this Christmas." Even saying the word is painful. Now I understand why.

Jeez. No wonder the girl needed an escape.

She peeks at me. "My phone was blowing up with calls from the hospital, but I missed them all. Too stuck in my own damn head. I didn't even get to say go-goodbye." She chokes the last word out, the memory still raw.

Tucked against me, her shoulders quake, another crying fit ensuing. All I can do is hold her, let her get it out, be there for her, give her a semblance of comfort.

My mind reels with the information, so many questions swirling around about what happened next. How long they were together. Their relationship status.

I want to know everything she'll tell me. I want her to give me her pain.

A twinge pangs in my chest, a feeling so unfamiliar, it catches me off guard. I can't deduce what it is, so I don't try.

I hold Willa until her silent cries subside, rubbing her back, offering compassion. A part of me wishes I could have met the girl she was before.

Was she as quirky?

Was she as quick-witted?

Was she as strong and resilient?

"The driver who hit him was drunk. At eight o'clock in the morning. From the night before." Her voice is raspy, like her throat's raw and scratchy.

Bastard.

"Was it a hit and run?"

"No. Guy was so wasted, after driving over Elias, he hit a brick wall. Bastard didn't die. Had he not hit Elias, he would have been killed on impact. He wasn't going as fast when he hit the wall. I lost the love of my life, and he walked away with a broken leg and some jail time. Hardly seems fair."

"It never is in these situations. I'm so sorry, Willa. I can't imagine what something like this does to a person."

"Christmas is forever ruined. I haven't been able to write even a chapter—"

I cut her off. "What do you mean? I thought that's what this week was about. A writing retreat." How it's so much more, I now understand.

She sits up, positioning herself next to me instead of on my lap. "I've had writer's block since that day. Haven't written a damn word. How can I? Had I not gotten lost in my book, I could have maybe made it to the hospital. Said goodbye. Told him I loved him one last time."

I want to tell her not to think that way, it wasn't her fault, and who knows if things would have ended otherwise. My mouth opens, but no words come out. Who am I to tell her how to feel?

I try a different tactic. "I can see how this tragedy would destroy your mojo. So you weren't planning on writing this week?"

"I truly hoped by escaping my normal life, being somewhere secluded, I'd find inspiration. Or maybe it's more like finding peace with writing. Forgiveness of sorts. Elias would be the first in line to be pissed at me for giving up, for running away. If he knew, if he were here, he'd force my fingers to the keys to type. It wouldn't matter what the words were, I just had to type something. Anything. It could be gibberish, and he'd be happy." A sardonic laugh bubbles from her, a minute levity in the current situation.

"Well, have you tried that?"

She faces me. "Uh, no."

"Why not?"

Her expression turns serious. "I don't speak gibberish. What if I spell words wrong?"

I ponder my response to her earnest question. "Does it matter if they aren't real words?"

"In reality, no. But in my current situation? It's one more excuse so I don't have to actually write."

A wacky idea strikes me, lighting me up with its brilliance.

Sure, it's odd, but what with Willa hasn't been?
I hope she sees it for what I mean it to be: encouragement.

17

willa

"GET UP." Beckett stands up in a flash, like there's a fire outside of the fireplace he needs to put out. When I don't immediately follow his issued demand, he holds his arms out. "Please, Willa. Come with me." His tone softens, a layer of sadness and some other emotion clinging to it.

"Where are we going?"

"Kitchen table. Get your laptop. You trust me?"

There's so much hope in his question and his matching expression. I can't say no.

Besides, if I did, it would be a lie.

Bizarre as it may be, I trust this man with my life.

"Yes."

He pulls me to standing, ushering me on my way to grab my laptop while he disappears into a closet I haven't yet explored. We both meet at the kitchen table, each with our computers.

"It's been a long while—longer than you—since I've had to write anything but an estimate or an email. Forgive my rustiness."

His statements make no sense, but he's giddy. I'm curious to see what he has planned.

I feel lighter after unloading on him, telling the story few people know. Between the crying spell and spilling my guts, it's a catharsis I needed. Something I've needed for over a year.

The irony isn't lost on me who helped me find it.

We sit across the table from each other. He plugs his computer in mentioning how he doesn't use it often. Still in the dark about what we're doing, I don't question it.

Once his laptop is up and running, he studies the screen. "Microsoft Word. Is that still the thing to use for word processing?" His inquisitive glare makes him so appealing. His curiosity is high on the list of what I enjoy most about him.

"I suppose. Some people use Google Docs."

"What do you write in?"

"A program called Scrivener."

He stares a beat too long, then chuckles. The sound is a balm to my soul. Not quite like one of Beckett's hugs, but close. "Word it is. You use scrive—that program you said."

It's my turn to laugh. "I have Word for exchanging manuscripts with my editor. If whatever we're doing is being shared."

He points a finger in my direction. "Yes. Good idea. Word all around."

How this man elicits so much excitement from me is a mystery.

"What are we doing exactly?"

"Writing."

"Wr-writing?" I stutter. My pulse quickens, fear clutching me in its grip. "Writing what?"

"Gibberish." He doesn't offer me a chance to interrogate what he means and continues, "Spelling and grammar don't count. And of course, it doesn't have to make sense. It just has to be letters and words on a page."

It dawns on me what he's doing—persuading me to write. Doesn't matter what. Like I told him Elias would do.

I gasp, staring at this man who's been more than a gentleman since I first spoke with him on the phone. This man who's taken care of me the past three days, who's cooked meals for me, who's given me more orgasms in a twenty-four hour period than I've had the last two years. My heart clenches, a swell of sentiment coursing through me at his compassion.

"Beckett. I don't know what to say."

"Good. Don't *say* anything. Write it. Gibberish, English, Greek, Parseltongue, just get words on the page."

A smile creeps on my lips. "Parseltongue, huh?"

He shrugs. "Did you not meet my niece, your biggest fan? She's also into Harry Potter. I read them all, but I'm not sure I remember how to spell any of the words. Luckily for me, it doesn't matter."

"How long?"

His right brow raises. "How long what?"

"How long are we writing for?"

"You pick."

I think for a moment. No matter how long it is, it's going to feel like an eternity. Might as well start small.

"Five minutes."

"K." He peers down at his screen. "Whoever gets the most words wins."

"Wins what?" I ask. My brain needs to know why it has to be a competition, yet my mouth has other ideas.

"The movie choice for tonight."

I groan, already knowing I'm going to lose. I have no capability to write anymore. Even gibberish.

"Would you rather the prize be something else?"

Another night with you, my brain fills in, but I don't express it aloud. After today's emotional roller coaster, I'm not in any headspace for sex.

Cuddles? Absolutely.

Sex? Negative.

"No, it's fine. Start thinking of what you're going to pick because you'll be winning."

"We'll see."

I used to hate when my parents would use that phrase. It was always no. But the way Beckett uses it has a different connotation, even if it's not a yes or no answer.

"Ready?" He stretches his hands in the air, palms linked, bending back his fingers in a warm-up.

"Not even a little," I mumble.

To make him happy, I open up a new Word document, the blinking cursor taunting me.

Write words.

Write words.

Write words, it seems to blink.

Beckett messes with his phone and declares, "Go."

I stare at the blank screen.

Words. I can do this. They don't even need to be actual words. Letters strung together in any order. That's what Beckett said, right?

From the other side of the table, I hear the hunt and peck of Beckett's fingers pressing one key at a time. I crack a smile. Elias hated typing on the laptop, too. He was more of an iPad guy, using the laptop only when forced.

My fingers type *Elias.* Then the words *I miss you. I miss you so much. I wish you were here. But if you were here, I wouldn't be here, and that makes me kinda sad. Because Beckett is the best kind of host, even when he doesn't have to be.*

The words pour out of me. A love letter to Elias, filling him in on the last two years and all he's missed. The good parts and the bad, the highs and lows, even the lowest of lows. The words leap from my fingers. Words locked up in a box with a missing key. Until Beckett found it and set them free.

"Time."

So involved with the words, Beckett's voice makes me jump.

I scan the screen. It's at least a page of words, sentences, and paragraphs. My eyes find the time.

"That was not five minutes," I grumble. A smirk rests on Beckett's mouth.

"No joke about you getting in the zone. I didn't want to stop you. How much gibberish did you write?"

I survey the page. Some random typos, but it's filled with real words.

"None, actually. All English."

His brows rise. "Really? Excellent. Anything worth sharing?" He wears anticipation like a badge. But I'm not ready to share what I wrote.

"No. Just some ideas for a new story," I lie easily.

"Secretive. Fair."

"How did you do?"

Beckett pushes his laptop toward me. On his screen is a grocery list of ingredients and a Costco list.

"This took you thirty minutes?"

He shakes his head. "Five. Spent the rest of the time watching you. You squint a lot when you're looking at the screen. It's adorable."

I roll my eyes. "It's a bad habit. The glasses are supposed to help, but most of the time, I'm not even reading the words. I wasn't this time. I suppose it could be gibberish."

Except I know it's not. Elias's name is written too many times to be gibberish. And let's not forget Beckett's, too.

"I'm going out on a limb to say you won."

"I did," I confirm. Not the movie choice, but a victory over writer's block. Even if only for today and a topic that has nothing to do with Hidden Clues Club, it's a win.

A huge win.

"Thanks, Beckett. Your idea was brilliant."

He sits up taller, his chest physically puffing out with pride. I'd knock it, but it's well-deserved. He closes his computer, laying his folded hands on top. "Can I ask a follow-up question to your confession?"

"Sure."

His eyes meet mine, the sky blue of his holding mine steady. "Did you always hate Christmas?"

My guffaw is loud, tearing out of me like a wild animal released from a cage. "I did not. Used to be my favorite. But losing the love of my life sucked all the happiness from it. The lights, the decorations, the joy. It doesn't seem right to celebrate without him."

Beckett nods, his understanding acknowledged. "How long were you together?"

"Almost four years, though some days it felt like I'd never not known him. In a good way." I sigh, a rush of memories flooding in. "The best way."

"You lost a lot that day."

"Everything." It sounds cliché, but it's true. Every plan I'd had went up in smoke when he died.

The future we were building.

My writing career.

Christmas.

I lost it all.

"I'm sorry, Willa. I'm so sorry."

"Thank you. It means a lot."

There have been a lot of "I'm sorrys" over the last two years, enough to last a lifetime. Beckett's feels different, more important. The most important. Heck if I can explain it.

"Hey, any chance you're up for making that cake you teased me with last night?"

"Yeah, sure."

Damn do I love how agreeable he is.

"With your help."

I take it back.

I hate how agreeable he is.

The cake in the oven, I inspect the kitchen. Beckett's workspace neat and tidy, like the man himself. Mine, a disaster. I'd say it mirrors me, but I hate to put myself down. It's more of a mess because I haven't a clue what I'm doing in the kitchen.

"What do you eat for meals at home?" he asked as he attempted to "teach" me to bake. Wasted breath on his part. His smile never faded, the man didn't get frustrated, and I kinda loved it.

"I order takeout or use a meal delivery service. Someone else does the shopping and prepping, and all I have to do is heat them up. My microwave sees more action than my stove."

"Your stove must get jealous." I thought he was kidding, but his expression remained stoic. I wasn't sure what to make of the comment, so I shrugged it off.

Though something poked at me the rest of the time we prepared the cake.

The most pleasurable part of the night is now, licking the beaters, something I missed from living with my mom. She didn't bake often, but Clem's and my job was to lick the beaters, utensils, and the bowl. I'm *really* good at those jobs.

Fantastic, even.

"I promised myself sex was off the table tonight."

Mid-lick, I stare at Beckett watching me, his eyes hooded and oozing sexiness.

"O-kay." I draw out the word, my comprehension of his words nonexistent.

His eyes float shut, a rough exhale expelling. "It's *hard* to do that with your tongue . . . doing what it's doing."

"Sorry?" Not sorry. Not for him and not for me enjoying this batter entirely too much. I can't wait to taste the cake.

Beckett swears under his breath and stands. "I'm showering. You, clean the kitchen so it's not so much a disaster zone." He retreats from the table, stopping directly in front of me. "Thank you for trusting me with your story." Tucking a loose strand behind my ear, his lips brush my cheek. "You're the strongest person I know." One more kiss to the top of my head before he disappears into the bathroom.

Like forehead kisses are to Elias, top of the head kisses will always belong to Beckett.

The notion pummels me. Hard. As if someone smacked me.

What am I even thinking?

Nothing "belongs" to Beckett, least of all something related to a relationship. The idea is laughable at best.

So why am I not laughing?

And why do I want them to belong to him? Give that spot over to him. To have no one after him reclaim it.

Perhaps I'm still on a roller coaster, this one being my life. There sure have been a lot of peaks and valleys, ups and downs, some spirals and twists thrown in for good measure. Life has been a lot, especially these last two years. Being here with Beckett is giving me some semblance of reality back, even if this week doesn't resemble real life in the slightest. Not even a little.

While he showers, I clean the kitchen. Like it's my job.

Wiping down the table and counters.

Washing the dishes and loading the dishwasher.

Mopping the floor.

I make it shine. Because if I can do one nice thing in exchange for all the things Beckett's done for me, I'm doing it.

Beckett emerges from his room with wet hair, sweats, and bare feet. His eyes scan the kitchen, his teeth whistling in appreciation.

"Damn, Bundy. How long was I in the shower?"

"Long enough for me to do this." I hold my arm out, twirling around to show off my progress.

The timer buzzes, signaling the cake is ready. It smells delicious, and my mouth waters. Beckett made it clear it would have to cool, but he confirmed it's worth the wait. He hasn't led me astray yet, especially with food, so I'm trusting him.

Damn, how much I trust this man.

A puzzled look breaches his face. "What?"

"I'll be sad when I have to leave." *Oops.* So not the words I meant to say. I slap my hand over my mouth. "Goodness, I don't mean that."

"So you won't be sad to leave?" A smirk claims his mouth, the action jarring to my libido and every other part of me that wants more of him.

"I will be. I wasn't supposed to say those words out loud. Internal thoughts should stay inside." Now I'm babbling.

"I disagree. Tell me more of these internal thoughts." Bending down, his sweatpants showcase the ass hidden beneath. With oven mitts on each hand, he carefully removes the cake from the oven, setting it on top of the stove. "Did you decide on a movie?"

"I want your thoughts on another Hallmark one. I don't care which one. Non-seasonal, of course." Something makes me add the qualifier, even though I don't think he'd do that to me.

"Got it. I have just the one."

"Why am I not surprised?"

"Hot cocoa or spiked coffee?"

As if that's even a question. "Spiked coffee, duh." I don't let my eyes roll.

"Pull up the Hallmark app. I'll make the drinks. Once the cake cools a bit, I'll cut pieces."

His proposition is so natural, so Beckett. How he's such a great host when he doesn't entertain people is beyond me. I'm not knocking it. It's been one of the best parts of this unexpected detour.

The other is the sex.

I tamp down those thoughts immediately. I'm not opposed to more sex, but not tonight. After last night's marathon and today's breakdown, my body needs a rest.

However, I sure wish it didn't. No matter how sad I'll be, my time here will end. Everything with Beckett will be boxed up and become a memory.

Surely one of the best.

18
beckett

AS THE CREDITS ROLL, my eyes train to the beauty beside me. She put up a good fight, but sleep claimed her about twenty minutes ago, which is a lot later than I thought it would. I figured she'd conk out as soon as it started.

Exhaustion layers her face, but it's no wonder. We got little—if any—sleep last night, and no doubt her meltdown took an emotional toll on her body.

I hate to wake her, but she needs to sleep in a bed. *My* bed.

I nudge her shoulder. "Willa, let's get you in bed."

She rouses slowly, her eyes blinking, zeroing in on me. "Sorry. Was more tired than I realized."

"Not a problem. You can watch the ending tomorrow."

She nods, her eyes catching on something in the corner of the room.

The lighted tree.

I couldn't help flicking the switch after she fell asleep. I needed the fix, like an addict with drugs. Even if only a bit of a high. My body relaxed immediately. Tension rolled off in waves, and I felt like I could fully take a breath. It's not all from the tree. The heaviness of Willa's story took its toll on me, too.

"Shit, sorry. Let me turn it off."

Willa grabs my wrist. "It's okay." She winces as she says the words, though the statement is genuine.

"They have to go off anyway at bedtime." Soon as I clean up the cake and mugs and lock the doors, I'm turning in, too. Another big day of prepping and working tomorrow.

She sits on the couch, her eyes still adjusting to the light from the TV, her legs tucked into her chest. "Will you, um, lay with me, until I fall asleep? I don't want to be alone tonight."

Should I be giving in to her every request? No.

Will it stop me? Also no.

My decision isn't only for her, but I don't have the brainpower to unpack all of what it means. Perhaps I don't want to.

"You got it. I'll lock up and meet you in there."

Her smile is small but grateful.

What I wouldn't give to see more of her smiles. More expressive ones. I sense I haven't seen Willa experiencing pure joy.

After sending her on the way to my bedroom, I load the dessert dishes in the dishwasher, turn off the lights on the tree, and make sure all the doors are locked. I plug in my phone next to the couch, confirming the alarm's set.

Joining Willa in the bedroom, I find her tucked into my bed— on my side—her tired eyes tracking my movements. She holds up the comforter, inviting me under. I can't refuse.

Just until she falls asleep, then I'll move to the couch.

A shrill noise wakes me from a peaceful slumber.

"Make it stop," the woman in my arms grumbles.

I take a minute to realize what the noise is and why Willa's in my bed.

Or rather, why I'm in bed with her. Not that I'm complaining. Best night's sleep I've had in a while. Having her in my arms isn't a hardship.

Except I have to take care of the deafening noise first.

Reluctantly, I climb out from the warmth of the bed, leaving her there. I shuffle to the living room, turning off the phone's alarm.

I left it out here thinking I'd be sleeping on the couch. Instead, I fell asleep with her.

I don't regret it even a little.

It's earlier than I need to get up, but if I climb back into bed, I won't want to leave it.

Won't want to leave her.

However, I don't have that luxury today, and I hardly doubt she'll want to come with me. She won't start enjoying Christmas because she told me her story. Though now that I know the real reason, a part of me wants to give her some joy back, even if it's minuscule and temporary.

Temporary. There's that word again.

"What time is it?" Willa's groggy question interrupts my thoughts. She's starfished on the bed. If only I could join her. Instead, I keep my feet rooted in the doorway.

"Early. I have an errand to run, then I'm off to work on the holiday breakfast with Dax. Coffee? Breakfast? Cake?"

Even in the dim light of the hallway, I can make out her smile at the last suggestion.

"Cake is an acceptable breakfast, don't you think? And coffee. Must have coffee. Your choice since you're making it and all."

"Who makes it every morning for you?"

"Me, myself, and I. But yours is super better. A whole lot. A plethora times better than mine."

"You're super adorable." The comment blasts from my mouth with abandon. I swear she lights up more. Rather than dwell on my awkwardness, I change the subject. "What are your plans for the day?"

She sits up as I get dressed. "My only goal is to avoid a breakdown of any kind. If nothing else gets done, I'll consider today a success. How long will you be gone?"

It doesn't escape my notice how domestic this conversation is.

Or how right it feels.

"Most likely all day. The busy season is upon us. If you want to leave, you can use the SUV in the garage. Keys are hanging on the key hook by the back door. I'll take the truck just in case. It's not as great with all the snow still hanging around."

"Where would I go?"

"Wherever you want. No lights during the day, but most stores blast Christmas music. We could meet for lunch." Meeting her for lunch will push my arrival home later, but the way the idea perks her up, I'm glad I suggested it.

She sits up straighter, her eyes dazzling with interest. "Yes. At your favorite place."

"K. I'll write down the name. You can put it in your GPS, but it's just off Main Street." I debate whether to add the next thing, but figure what the heck. If she turns me down, it won't be the end of the world. "Mom's making a pot of chili and wanted to extend the invite to you. No pressure, but Mom's chili is out of this world. But my siblings will all be there, and there will definitely be a discussion about the holiday. You don't have to let me know right now. There's always room at the table, even at the last minute. Think about it."

Why am I so nervous for her to say yes?

Because I want her there.

I want her to meet my family.

I want . . .

I shut down these paths of thinking. What I want and what's reality are two different things. No use even thinking about her in any capacity other than temporary.

"Will do." Her fingers rub her ear. The more she does it, the more endearing it is. So much of it is subconscious, which makes it more beguiling. "Thanks for indulging my request last night."

I'm momentarily confused by which request she's referring to, but I say, "You're welcome."

"It was kinda nice to have you in the bed with me."

"Only 'kinda' nice?" I tease.

"I'm so used to sleeping on my own, I missed a warm body. And yours was warm."

I'm not sure if she insinuates about it being *my* warm body or if I hear that because it's what I want to hear. Either way, I'm taking it as a compliment. Not only about my body being warm.

"It's a first for me."

Her lips turn into a frown. "Sleeping next to someone else?" she surmises.

I shrug. "In my bed."

"Hmm," she hums. "That's . . . interesting."

My eyes spy the time. "Shit. I have to get going. I'll make the coffee, but then I'm running out the door. You'll find something for breakfast?"

"There was mention of cake. I'm fine." Her lazy smile twists my heart. The urge to climb back into bed with her is so strong, but I resist.

"Cool."

If I don't walk away now, I won't. However, I can't resist the pull to her, so I drop a kiss on the top of her head.

I don't misinterpret the hitch in her breath.

Or was that mine?

My mind wanders to Willa as I drive through town to the elementary school where this year's holiday breakfast is being held. Specifically, what she's doing while I'm gone for the morning. It doesn't take much to think about her. She's the star of my waking fantasies and the nighttime ones. A stupid grin springs to my mouth.

Stupid only because it's ridiculous how much she's embedded herself in me. Without my permission. Probably without even trying. Despite her crazy tendencies, the woman inserted herself into my life in such a way I'm accommodating her every whim.

And I don't hate it.

Dax's truck idles in a spot near the cafeteria door, his concentration engrossed in his phone. He doesn't notice when I pull up, park, or get out, and only does when I knock on the passenger window. He jumps in his seat, his phone flying from his fingers. I chuckle as his lips mutter curse words I'm not privy to until he lowers the window.

"You scared me, dipshit."

"I gave you ample time to figure out I was here. What's so riveting on your phone? I thought you gave up porn."

His eyes narrow. His middle finger closest to me scratches his head.

It's been this way all our lives. I'd do anything for him, but riling each other and giving the other a hard time is what we do best. Just ask anyone at the garage. He's the mechanic while I do the auto body work and only clash on the occasional wreck we need to work together. I'm astonished he agreed to co-chair breakfast with me this year. He clearly forgot all the bitching and moaning he did three years ago when I put him to work serving the food.

This year, he's been extremely helpful throughout the planning process, something that begins in the summer. We've only had one small argument about the theme, but after we finally agreed on Reindeer Games, it was smooth sailing. It helps that he let me be in charge of the food and he took lead on the activities, and we agreed outsourcing the decorations was the best plan. As good as I am with creative endeavors, transforming the cafeteria into a place that incorporates the theme is outside my wheelhouse. Thankfully, there are plenty of people in town willing to create decorations. I can't wait to see how it all comes together.

The Winterberry Junction holiday breakfast has been a staple in town for as long as I can remember. The chairperson from the previous year appoints his or her successor when necessary. Nominated five years ago, I'm not ready to give it up yet.

A gust of wind picks up, reminding me I'm standing in the cold, with snow still on the ground from the other day's storm. "Let's go inside and make sure it's all coming together."

Blowing into my hands, I wait at the front of the truck while Dax turns off his engine and fishes his phone from the floor. Still mumbling to himself, when he joins me, his first question is, "When do I get to meet Willa? Shania hasn't stopped talking about her."

I love how much my niece is so captivated by Willa, even though she doesn't know her secret identity. When she finds out, it's going to blow her mind.

"I invited her to dinner tonight."

"Why didn't you bring her along to help with breakfast?"

"She's working." It's not a complete lie. She's supposed to be working. I can't tell him the real reason she wouldn't come to breakfast. She wouldn't get one foot in the door before she'd freak out. After what she shared about her loss, I can't completely blame her. Sharing her secret relieved her of some of the stress and tension she's been carrying around the last two years.

It may have even grown her grinchy heart a centimeter or two.

Wishful thinking.

I shouldn't care so much about her like or dislike of Christmas, but I can't help myself. Once she leaves, her abhorrence of the greatest holiday will be a blip on my radar, a person I knew for a short time.

My heart twists with the thought of her leaving, of never seeing her again.

"Becks?" Dax's voice penetrates my brain, diverting the runaway train my thoughts are on.

"Yep."

He raises an eyebrow. "You have no idea what I said, do you?"

I don't even lie. He'd see right through it. He may be the biggest pain in my ass, but he's my best friend. "Nope."

He smirks. "You definitely have to bring Willa to dinner."

"Why?"

"Because I gotta meet the woman who finally flustered you enough to knock you down a peg." He strides away, sneaking inside the open door before I can refute his claim.

Except I'd be lying if I said it wasn't true.

Damn him for being so observant.

Or am I to blame for being so transparent?

19
willa

I SPEND my morning lazing around the cabin, eating cake, and drinking the pot of coffee. I can't understand how it's so good, but it is. Since Beckett won't be home for a while, I savor it, making it last for most of the morning.

Beckett texts around eleven.

> Meet you at the Wildflower Cafe around noon.

> Great. I'm going to head out soon to scope out your town

> I'll give you a tour after lunch

> if you want

> Sure

> See you in an hour

I put my phone to the side, but he texts again.

> Hope you're having a good morning

My smile is automatic.

I just finished the pot of coffee. Now I'm going
to explore the parts of the cabin I haven't yet to
find your skeletons

Have at it. I've got nothing to hide

I love how you think I'm serious. I'm going to
shower and then head out. My sleuthing will
have to wait until after lunch

That's too bad for you

Get back to work

I'm finished but wasn't sure if you'd be ready
for lunch yet

I could eat earlier and explore after

Want me to pick you up? I'll drop you back off
after our tour and then finish what I have to do

Because you don't trust me to drive your car?

I wouldn't have suggested it if I didn't trust you

Oh, good point.

So what then?

He doesn't respond right away, so I put on socks and
shoes.

What's the weather?

Hoodie weather

My hoodie

Territorial much?

A week ago, I would have said no . . .

The dots jump, but no message appears. I'm forced to confront his unanswered question.

So are we meeting at the cafe?

be at the cabin in seven

Guess that answers my question. Why am I not surprised? Why am I not upset?

eep. Better get ready

I finish the last sip of coffee and dart to the bedroom to change out of my pajamas and into clothes. Since my trip involved lounging around the cabin, I don't have much in terms of "leaving the house and looking like a presentable human for a cafe" clothes, but I pair a clean pair of black leggings with a crewneck sweatshirt and hope for the best. Doing my hair would take away some of the sting, but the sound of the back door opening has me rushing to run a brush through it. I'll tie it back out of my face so it's not so wavy. Even though I dried it yesterday, it's taken on a life of its own this morning.

"Leave it down," Beckett barks from the bathroom doorway as I'm struggling to tame it into a less messy version of a lazy bun.

Yes, *barks.*

"It's crazy," I note, pointing to the out-of-control strands.

"It's beautiful."

His words cause me to stumble, needing to steady myself on the sink. Our gazes meet in the mirror. He breaks it to rake his down my body, eating me up like I'm his next meal.

"I can't wait to see what color and style your undergarments are later today. Meet you in the driveway."

His comment whirls around my brain. The man makes me so unhinged with one comment. It's maddening. Yet, I love it at the same time.

Glad to know I'm not completely broken.

You're welcome. Elias's voice echoes around me on an exhale.

Wildflower Cafe is packed. Half a dozen booths line the back wall with low and high tables scattered throughout the rest of the floor. The usual casual decor is embellished with holiday decorations. They're not so "in your face" as the outdoor spectacle of Main Street, and I can—possibly—admit they're tasteful.

Like the grocery store the other day, people bombard Beckett with greetings, smiles, and questions.

A man in his fifties approaches first. His skin is like tanned leather, like he works outside a lot of the year.

Reaching his hand out to Beckett, his gaze slides my way before returning to Beckett's. "Didn't have a chance to congratulate a job well done. Or, jobs I should say. The lights, the breakfast, the parade. Is there any part of the town festivities you didn't have your hand in?" A deep laugh rumbles from him, and his cheeks blush a rosy red.

Beckett shakes his hand. "Thanks, Mert. It was a busy year."

"What will you do now that you've won this year's contest?"

Beckett smirks like the Grinch. "Oh, don't you worry. I've got lots of ideas up my sleeves." Again, Mert's attention draws my way, but Beckett dismisses him with a, "See you around."

Mert seems perplexed at Beckett's cursory tone but eventually takes the hint. "Oh, right. I'll be seeing you." He strolls back to his table.

We get a small reprieve until an older woman, probably my grandmother's age, ambles to the table, leaning heavily on her cane.

"Beckett Nicholas. Just the man I wanted to see." In a move I'm not expecting, she twists her body, angling her ass toward the booth seat, using the back of the booth and the table as leverage to sit down next to Beckett.

"Hey, Birdie," he mumbles courteously but without the enthusiasm I've seen from him. Can't blame him, though. She's interrupting our chat, taking up residence in the booth like we invited her to join us. He smiles at her, but his dimple doesn't make an appearance.

"We must chat about next year's holiday breakfast."

Beckett sighs, mouthing, "Sorry" to me.

I excuse myself to the bathroom. An inkling of guilt tries to worm in, but I shove it away. He suggested lunch, knowing full well how his town works. Mostly keeping to myself at home, I don't spend too much time out and about in Havenwood, so I'm not sure how it compares to Winterberry Junction. Here, it seems like everyone knows everyone else, and a few of Beckett's comments corroborate the notion.

I don't stall in the bathroom, but I don't *not* either. Hoping I've given Birdie enough time to chat about next year's breakfast —like if they don't get started immediately, they'll run out of time for something happening in twelve months—I make my way toward the table in time to catch Beckett's eye roll and his "save me." I stifle my laughter, but he looks like he needs saving.

Sliding into the seat across from them, I don't waste time interrupting Birdie's speech. Something about red versus green decorations. "Um, Birdie, was it?" I raise my voice to be heard over hers.

Her glare swings my way, almost offended I'm impeding her conversation. Ironic since she's the one who first muscled into my and Beckett's discussion. "And you are?" Her tone isn't quite rude, but it's more abrasive than other Winterberry residents, something I file away to inquire about later.

"Willa." Do I tell her I'm staying with Beckett? That we're fuck buddies for the week? She's not innocent, but that doesn't mean she won't take offense to it.

"Willa," she repeats. "But who are you? You're not from Winterberry. I'd know." She crosses her pudgy arms over her chest, tilting her head down to peer over her glasses. Like a light bulb goes off, she snaps her fingers, surmising, "Oh, you're the woman staying with Beckett. I heard about you."

"Looks like the Winterberry gossip mill is at it again," Beckett chimes in with a shake of his head. "Actually, she's only here for a few more days. I'll catch up with you next week about your ideas for next year's breakfast." Beckett stresses *next* and *year*. Hopefully, Birdie comprehends.

She's slow but eventually she harrumphs, and with a struggle, awkwardly pushes out of the booth. Once she's standing, leaning heavily on her cane with one hand and the table with the other, she stares at Beckett. "I expect to see you next week. I'll have Marlene block out some time on my calendar. Plan for an hour." One last scowl in my direction, she hobbles off.

Beckett lets out his breath and slumps against the booth, his fingers running through his hair. Before I can get him to explain, a cute teenager arrives to take our order, her eyes akin to googly ones, her smile ear to ear, her focus solely on Beckett.

"Hey, Beckett. How's it going?"

"Great, Justine."

If possible, her smile widens at the use of her name. She's got it bad for him, but he doesn't indicate the attraction is mutual. Only because she's too young for him. Or I'd assume that's what he'd say. He's a handsome, single guy. How he doesn't have women falling all over him is beyond me.

Or maybe he does. He's spent a lot of time out of the cabin. Sure, he says he's at work, but he could be with someone else and using me as a backup. With this being so sudden and also temporary, it's not like we set rules or boundaries. And if he is getting it from someone else, good for him. Maybe she'll be more permanent.

Even considering him with another woman sours my stomach. Which is the stupidest ever because he's a fun time for the time being. Nothing more.

"Willa?" Beckett's voice breaks me out of the trance. He regards me with an unusual expression, almost as if I'm a stranger. Oh, right. I am. "Have you decided what you wanted?"

"No. Can we get a few more minutes?"

Justine smiles at me, but it's not as bright as the one for Beckett. "Sure thing. I'll come back in a bit. Something to drink while you wait?"

"Water, please."

"I'll have a Coke."

"Be right back." Justine flitters away, leaving us to get back to the menu.

"What's good here? What's your favorite?"

"For breakfast, their avocado toast. For lunch, the grilled cheese and tomato soup combo is my go-to."

"Is that what you're getting?"

"Was waiting to see what you want. If you want to share something, we could do that. If you want to each order our own, we can do that, too."

I scan the menu again, getting stuck on the sandwiches section. "I'm a sucker for buffalo chicken sandwiches."

Beckett nods. "Good choice."

"But the tomato soup and grilled cheese combo sounds good, too. Want to go halfsies on the meals?"

"Sure."

I stare into his blue eyes, the color deepened by the dark green sweatshirt he sports, his auto body shop logo front and center. "Are you agreeing with me for me or are you agreeing because that's what you want?"

He ponders my question before shrugging. "Honestly, a little of both. I'm not too picky when the food's good, but I get a rise out of making you smile. If sharing sandwiches will do that for you, I'm here for it."

"You know how to sweet-talk the ladies, make them swoon. The ladies of Winterberry Junction are a lucky bunch." Like earlier, something yanks at my heart at the suggestion of him with another woman. Even when Elias and I first started dating,

I wasn't this territorial, and that relationship had the potential to turn into more.

I don't know what to make of this realization. It's probably a good idea not to delve into it.

Beckett laughs. "Not when you've known them all since before elementary school. Or rather, they've known me for that long. Hard to find a solid relationship with someone you've known your entire life."

"Valid point. Guess it's the tourists who have an advantage."

"Like you."

"For sure. Women like me." My cheeks heat under his watchful examination. Thankfully, Justine reappears with our drinks.

"All set?" Her pen hovers above her notepad.

"Yep. Two bowls of the tomato soup, grilled cheese on sour-dough, and the buffalo chicken wrap, substitute ranch instead of bleu cheese."

"What kind of cheese for the grilled cheese?"

He defaults to me. "Swiss or American?" I propose.

"Swiss," he confirms to Justine, handing our menus to her.

"Super. I'll go put this in." With a last glance in Beckett's direction, she skirts away from the table.

"Not a fan of bleu cheese?" I infer.

"I'll eat it if there's nothing else available, but Bonnie's ranch —she's the chef and owner here—is out of this world fantastic."

I admire him for not asking if I'd mind the substitution and instead making the change. Not that I'll let him know it.

"What if I want bleu cheese?"

"I'll get you some on the side."

Damn, didn't account for him to have a reasonable answer ready. It's not flippant, but genuine, like the man himself.

I forgo asking more about Marlene and Birdie. I don't care enough to know. They'll be a distant memory as soon as I hit the town limits. Instead, I ask, "How was the holiday breakfast?" I'm proud of myself for speaking without a stutter.

"Fun and rowdy. Participants enjoyed themselves." A full-on smile broaches his lips, his enthusiasm infectious until I remember why he's excited. He takes a sip of his Coke. "What did you do? Get any words?"

I shake my head. "I didn't feel like dealing with a blank screen, so I didn't attempt to write. I'll try after lunch, but I'm not hopeful."

He raises a brow. "Even after unlocking all those words yesterday?"

"A fluke, I'm sure."

"Ah. We could do it again tonight. I have something I can't get out of, but after dinner at my parents, my top agenda item is discovering what's under your clothing and completely free for anything else."

My cheeks flame hotter. "Beckett," I hiss, lowering my voice. "This is not appropriate lunch chatter. In a public place."

He leans in closer, motioning for me to do the same. "It would be inappropriate for me to ask to see them at lunch. Talking about it is on the table."

"It's all inappropriate at lunch." He's got me all hot and bothered, feelings that have laid dormant until a few days ago. I want nothing more than to act on them, but this isn't the place. "Save the foreplay for the cabin."

"Ever done it in public?" Straight-faced and even toned, he poses the question. Like he was asking if he needed an umbrella if it was raining.

I survey the cafe. The tables aren't close enough together for other patrons to hear us in our hushed tones. But still, I make sure only Beckett can hear me. "How public is considered public?"

"Outside the house. In a parking lot. Where people might see."

"Yes to a parking lot. No to the last one."

Beckett rests back against the booth, his arms crossing over his chest. "Interesting. Was the parking lot crowded? Any chance for people to look in?"

I swallow. "No."

"Did you feel scandalous?"

"So much," I deadpan.

Beckett rolls his eyes. "How about at a make-out spot? Where people go to have sex."

"No. Too much of a chance to get caught there, of it getting back to my parents. My mother would have a conniption."

"Nice word choice. So, you were always the good girl?"

It's my turn to roll my eyes. "Hardly. But with things that might tarnish my mother's reputation, I was."

"Gotcha. And this parking lot sex. Was that Elias?"

"Nope. He was more of an 'in the house' kind of guy." It's a bit awkward talking about my past sex life with Beckett, but it's less awkward in public than if he were to bring this up in the bedroom. Don't ask me why because I won't have an answer.

"Adding it to my agenda for later."

"Um, should I be afraid to ask what 'it' is?"

"Afraid? No. Intrigued? Definitely."

Justine delivers our meals, prompting a brief pause in our conversation. "Can I get you anything else at the moment?"

"Drink refills, please." The smile she sends Beckett's way has more wattage than before, yet he's oblivious to it.

"You got it." She's back in two minutes, long enough for me to sample the soup.

"This is delicious," I compliment.

Justine beams, her attention on me for the briefest moment. "I'll let the chef know. Enjoy." She flitters away again, and Beckett splits the sandwiches so we get one half of each.

"Dip the grilled cheese in the soup. You won't regret it. And eat those first. The other sandwich isn't hot."

If his command wasn't rational, I'd fight it, but it makes sense.

"Good plan." I submerge a corner of the grilled cheese in the tomato soup and put it in my mouth. It's the ideal temperature and the perfect combination of savory flavors. Beckett watches my every move, waiting for my reaction. "Wow. Delicious."

"There's something special about Bonnie's soup. I've tried recreating it, yet it's never as good."

"That shocks me. The meals coming out of your kitchen are delicious, too."

He nods, not quite accepting the praise. I'm no food critic, but when flavors and ingredients appeal to me, I'm the first one to let the cook know.

We fill the rest of the meal with idle chitchat, not getting back to his earlier proposition. Once our tummies are full and fed, Beckett doesn't allow me to pay the bill. We walk out of the cafe, his hand on the small of my back. It's not possessive or anything but a quiet gesture, a comfort. His touch alone sends warmth through my body. It's both a good and bad problem to have.

"What time do your duties require your attention?" He switched the truck for the SUV and opens the passenger door for me.

"I'm trying to get out of them, but I don't think my sister will let me."

My lips draw into a frown. "Why would you want to get out of them?"

"More time with you." He doesn't allow me to get a response to his statement. He also doesn't take his eyes off me as he rounds the hood of the car, his expression stoic. Does he do these things on purpose to rile me up?

I'm guessing yes. He likes the rise he gets and enjoys throwing me off-kilter.

Well, he hasn't seen anything yet.

20

beckett

I EXPECTED A RESPONSE. Any answer to my statement. Instead, I'm met with silence as I climb behind the wheel.

Maybe I finally pushed her too far out of her comfort zone and I need to back down. The combination of the conversation about having sex in public and wanting to shirk my duties to spend more time with her is her breaking point.

Damn, if I fucked this up for myself, I'm gonna be pissed. Guess I should have let what was transpiring between us happen naturally. I always have to be the nudge, the one to take it just beyond the line of uncomfortableness.

"Shit, I can't do this."

Her words filter in slowly through the hazy fog of uncertainty in my mind.

I've yet to start the car, so I twist to face her. "Can't do what?" I hesitate, not sure I want the answer but asking it anyway, needing to be on the same page as her. Even if it's not where I want to be, I'm not the guy to take what she isn't offering.

"Feign indifference of wanting to spend more time with you. Pretend I don't want to find out what else is on your agenda for today. Fake that our earlier conversation didn't dredge up feelings to turn me on." Her sentences come out in a long whoosh, and Willa gulps air to refill her lungs.

Instead of responding with words, I pick up my wallet from the console, checking I have at least one condom, praying for two. They're not expired because it hasn't been long since I put them in there. Holding them out to her, I inquire, "You trust me?"

"Yes." No hesitation. Which I admire and love about her.

Errr, not love. Greatly like. I greatly like the way she doesn't hesitate.

For fuck's sake. It's way too soon for the "L" word in any capacity with Willa.

I abolish these wayward thoughts. "Great. Let's do it."

I start the car and work out where this can happen. When I suggested it, I didn't think it all through. Where we would go if she said yes. I hadn't planned for her agreement. I had hope, but I couldn't gauge how she'd react. If she'd accept it. Now that she has, I have to reassess the plan.

It's too cold for much. If it was spring or fall, I'd take her to the park, set up a blanket, and go to town.

I don't really want to do it in the car, but it's a last resort.

Willa rearranges the strap of her bra that's fallen and the best idea hits me. And it hits on three different pleasure points: sex in public, getting to see what's underneath her clothes sooner rather than later, and letting her pick out something new. A souvenir to remember me—and this escapade.

I direct the car to the mall in the next city over. She'll have her choice of Victoria's Secret or Soma. From what I can gather, hers come from less commercialized stores, but this will do in a pinch.

The only hitch is how busy the mall is. Because of course, the fact it's the holiday week escaped me when this brilliant plan came to fruition. Also, no way we can avoid all the holiday decorations. Thinking fast, I try to preemptively strike down her dissent.

"I have an idea. It's not the best I've ever had, but it's an idea which I put some thought into."

"O-kay." She draws out the last syllable.

"My plan is threefold."

She giggles, and my cock takes notice. "Threefold. Interesting. Let's hear it."

I find a spot about halfway from the door and put the car in park, leaving the engine to idle in the chance she disagrees. "One. Public sex."

She gasps, darts her eyes to the building and back to me. "At the mall? At the busiest time of the year?" Her voice pitches higher, anxiety creeping in.

"In the dressing room. Of Victoria's Secret or Soma."

Her shoulders fall from her ears, but she's not convinced. "It might be busy in there. We could get caught."

I wiggle my eyebrows. "Half the fun of public sex."

"You speak from experience?" she wonders.

I neither confirm nor deny but continue. "Two. I get to see what undergarments you're wearing today."

"We could do that at home."

My ears catch on her use of "home," but I can't dwell on it presently. I'll come back to it later.

"We'd have to wait until later. I've been imagining what they look like since this morning. The wait is killing me."

She calls my bluff with a raised brow but instead of refuting, speculates, "And the third?"

"Three. You pick out stuff to try on, hence why we need a dressing room, and then when we're done, I'll slip my card into the machine to pay for your purchase of a new matching set." Her eyes ignite, and I don't question whether she'll agree.

She's in.

She doesn't answer immediately, her gaze staring out the windshield. "We'll have to be quiet. And quick. We'll need napkins, something to clean up the mess."

Before she can change her mind, I reach into the console,

producing a wad of napkins. "Stuff these in your purse. Oh, and these, too." I dig the condoms from my wallet and hand them over.

Her aghast look halts my movements. "We won't have enough time for both." She tries to push one back to me, but I grab her purse from the ground and shove them inside.

"Maybe you'll need a bra from both Victoria's Secret *and* Soma."

She wants to be shocked, to not want that, but her eyes give her away. Like lights on a Christmas tree, they twinkle with exuberance.

And just like that, I'm introducing Willa to public sex.

If I thought the parking lot was packed, it's nothing compared to the inside. Hordes of people congregate everywhere. Last-minute shopping at its finest. Normally, crowds don't bother me, but the ache in my pants since Willa agreed to my plan begs to differ.

"Where to first?"

"Soma."

I stop at the map to find exactly where it's located, then I drag her by the hand to our destination, doing my best to avoid the most decorated areas, shielding her from the visual aspects. Her body is tense, but I'm guessing it's more from the anticipation of what we're about to do than the decor.

Fighting through throngs of people—from crying kids to senior citizens mall walking—we make it to Soma in one piece. The closer we get, the harder it is to conceal the erection in my pants.

"What's your size?"

Willa doesn't answer, and when I face her, narrowed eyes greet me. "I think this is all a ploy for you to learn my clothing size."

I shrug. "And?"

"And . . . 36C."

"Panties preference?"

"Cheeky, boy shorts, thongs. Medium." A flash of red coats her cheeks, but it doesn't make residence there. She's into this, which only makes getting to the dressing room more imperative.

"I'll pick some out, you pick some out, too. Meet by the dressing room in the back left." I point out the sign in case she's confused. "Three minutes. Go."

"Eep." She drops my hand and rushes away to a table on the right. For about thirty seconds, I watch her, drinking her in, puffing my chest about being the lucky bastard who's going to make her mine in five minutes.

Shaking out of my stupor, I flick through a rack of bras I think she'll like based on the two I've seen her wear. I also pick out one I like. Black mesh with a red heart pattern. I don't bother with the underwear. There will be time for her to choose more once the deed is done.

Adding one more to my stack, I walk to the back of the store. Willa's already there, a stack of apparel in her hands. "Are you ready for this?"

She nods sheepishly, her fingers kneading her left ear. "I'm nervously excited. I love that we could get caught, but no one knows me here, so who cares, right?"

"Exactly. It's a great temptation."

We step up to the attendant, who opens up a room for her. If she's appalled I follow her in, she doesn't show it. Inside, I flip the lock. The space isn't big, but it's enough for what we need. Stacking the clothes on the bench, I unbutton my pants, pushing them to my knees.

"Not wasting any time," Willa notes.

"You said we had to be quick."

While she removes her undies and leggings, I fish a condom out of her purse and sheath myself.

"No foreplay?" she muses softly, a teasing lilt in her tone.

"Come here." I motion to my lap. With her legs free from restraints, she kneels with widened legs on the bench, straddling my thighs, her ass hovering above my knees. I swipe one finger through her slit, my finger covered in wetness. "Foreplay, my ass." With gentle fingers, I grip her hips, lifting her up and positioning her above my hardened cock. "Stroke me once." My words are a growl, a whispered demand.

"I don't think I can be quiet," she admits, her voice barely audible.

"If you want me to buy you a gift, we can't be kicked out. Do your best."

Hormones surge through me. With her poised above my dick, coupled with the clandestine location, the need for release is palpable.

"Sink down. I won't last long. I'll make it up to you later."

Our gazes lock, hunger and devotion swimming in the kaleidoscope of colors. How did I get so lucky with this girl? Even temporarily, I'm the luckiest guy on the planet.

"It's not like we have unlimited time right now, but this is already super hot. I'm so keyed up, I don't care if you come with one thrust."

"That's about what it will be."

She plants her hands on my shoulder as she sinks onto my dick. "Fuckkkkk," she stretches out, an inaudible moan accompanying it. "Move, Beckett. Please."

"You gotta move, babe. Have you never been a cowgirl?"

"No."

There's so much to unpack in the one word and her expression, but now's not the time. We'll come back to that after, but we're definitely coming back to it.

"Up and down. Ride me. I'll hold your hips." I widen my legs, making sure my feet are grounded. "Keep your hands on my shoulders, eyes on me." I encourage her to lift two inches. Before I can instruct otherwise, she lowers back down, squeezing my dick. "That's it. Use me to get yourself off. I'll follow."

Soon, she finds a rhythm, bouncing up and down, her finger-tips digging into my flesh, creating a good kind of pain and pleasure. Each time she's down, her walls clamp tighter around my cock.

"You close?"

"Yep." The word not out of her mouth, her head falls back, and she detonates. Her mouth opens, but her orgasm is silent. While she rides out hers, my own hits, and I pump into her, thrusting my hips once, twice, three times, emptying everything inside the condom. Willa slumps against me, her arms falling and looping around my waist. "That was . . . invigorating. Reckless. Seductive." She glances at me. "I think you were right."

"About which part?" I move her, cautious to keep the condom in place. Once she's off, I remove it carefully, tying it off, dropping it in the plastic bag Willa holds out. She hands over napkins, and we clean up. I didn't account for the lack of wipes or a wet paper towel. Thank goodness one of us had the where-withal to think about the cleanup.

She shimmies into her undies, sorting the new ones into two piles. "Once wasn't enough." She holds up a bra. "Victoria's Secret has bigger dressing rooms. What are your thoughts about up against the wall?" There's a twinkle in her eye, and I love knowing I'm the one who put it there.

"It's brilliant." With a huge smile, she takes off her sweatshirt and cami, leaving her naked breasts on display. I can't resist not touching them. With her left breast cupped in my hand, I reach around for the black and red hearts bra. "Try this one?"

"Sure."

New kink unlocked: seeing how far I can push Willa to the edge without toppling over by massaging her breasts as she tries on different bras.

Man, this is going to be fun.

21
willa

TWO HOURS LATER, we leave the mall. I'm sated and hyped up on the three orgasms Beckett doled out between the two dressing rooms. I'm also the proud new owner of three new bras and a weekly set of underwear.

There was something so thrilling about what we did. Knowing people were on the other side of the door as his dick was inside me was an experience I won't ever forget. Though they were both fast and furious, I've never participated in anything as sensual, sexy, or hot. Had he tried to convince me to go for a third time, I could have been persuaded. There's got to be a store in the mall selling condoms.

On the way back to Winterberry, I interrogate, "What else is on your agenda for tonight? Were you able to get out of whatever it was you needed to?"

While I tried on different bras, when he wasn't driving me insane bringing the third orgasm by massaging my breasts, he was on his phone.

"I have to make one quick stop at the bed-and-breakfast to help my brother-in-law, and I promised you a tour. Have you decided on dinner yet? Chili at my parents," he reminds.

Which I had forgotten he'd mentioned it this morning.

Between lunch and covert sexual acts, his invitation got buried in my mind. As much as I'm not sure I'm ready for his parents to meet me, I have little to lose. Also, I heard the hope in his voice this morning. He's optimistic I'll join him. I can do this for him. Not in exchange for everything he's done for me, but as a bonus.

"I accept. Though perhaps a change of clothes is in order." I didn't bother putting my underwear back on. Not with how soaked they were. My hair's more of a disheveled mess, courtesy of Beckett's fingers. I tried my best to tame it, but it was no use. Wearing the evidence of our tryst like a badge of honor out of the mall is one thing. In front of his parents is another level.

"Dinner is at six-thirty. My errand at the B and B shouldn't take more than an hour, less if I'm lucky, but we should probably hold off on round three until after dinner. I want to take my time with you, not have to rush to shower and get dressed."

I thought sex with Elias was good, the best I'd ever had, for sure. The best I'd ever have, I assumed. While he won't ever be truly replaced, sex with Beckett is showing me what I was missing out on. It's addicting, and as much as I want to get my fill, the more we do it, the harder it will be to give it up. To accept it's over.

"I think hot cocoa should be added for tonight. And cake. Definitely cake."

"Sure. However, Mom will have some kind of dessert, too. Probably not cake, but something festive."

"Clem made sure I knew vacation calories don't count."

"And think how many you're working off. Tonight, too. Anticipate little sleep."

"But isn't tomorrow a busy day? Don't you need sleep?"

"The festivities don't start until later in the day. After tonight's stop, everything will be in place. We'll sleep in."

"We will, will we?"

Beckett peeks over at me. "After what I have planned, you'll be too exhausted not to sleep in." He smirks, and damn if it doesn't send shivers down my spine at the mere suggestion of sex with him. Of being up all night. Of being so thoroughly fucked, I'm exhausted.

I rub my thighs together. Apparently, three orgasms at the mall aren't quite enough of a fill.

"Willa, meet Lenny and Heidi. This is Willa," Beckett introduces once we're inside the front door of the B and B. He towers over his sister by a foot, but only a few inches taller than her husband.

Lenny holds out his hand for me to shake, but his sister pulls me into a hug.

"Shania hasn't stopped talking about meeting another fan of the Hidden Clues Club. The way she's carried on and on, I almost want to read it myself." She chuckles, her cheeks blooming red.

"You should. You can still enjoy it as an adult."

"Right. In my spare time, I'll get right on it."

"Which will be never," Beckett explains. "The woman doesn't know the meaning of 'free time' or rest, nor can she read."

Heidi swats his arm. "I *can* read. I choose not to."

"It's iffy at best." Beckett makes a so-so motion with his hand. The playful sibling banter is adorable.

I only have Clem, and being a twin has its unique circumstances, but I never wanted a brother. Not for any other reason than Mom and Dad's attention was hard enough to come by. Having to share with another sibling—brother or sister—would have been tough.

"Shut it, Elfie, or I'll spill all your embarrassing stories to Willa while you and Lenny bring down the boxes from the attic."

"Actually," Lenny butts in, "you've got to check on dinner so it's set for the guests if you want to be on time for your parents' tonight." An unspoken conversation happens between the two of them, and she huffs.

"Fine. Only because of the thing." She winks at her husband

and brushes a kiss on his cheek. It's easy to see the love shared between the two of them. "Come with me, Willa. I want to know all the things."

"Uh . . ."

Before she can lead me away, Beckett leans next to my ear. "If you get uncomfortable, bring up Taylor Swift. She won't be able to shut up." He pauses, scratching his head, almost stalling. I try to conjure what he might be thinking. "She's going to ask if there's something going on between us. So we're on the same page, what are you going to tell her?"

My heart flutters. I hate being put on the spot. More so about something of this magnitude, something I should have expected to come up.

In the long run, does it matter if his family knows we're intimate? For Beckett's sake, it might. He's the one who has to deal with them once I leave.

I toss it to him. "What do you want me to say?"

"It'll be hard to lie to my family, to keep my hands to myself, to pretend I haven't licked every inch of your skin from head to toe."

The mouth on this man. Goose bumps pepper my skin.

"I'm not the one who will have the questions to answer after I leave. So it's up to you."

In pure Beckett fashion, instead of responding with words, he leaves a kiss on the top of my head.

"Okay, let's get to moving boxes."

Once the guys are out of earshot, it takes Heidi less than three seconds to say, "So, you and my brother." There's little emotion attached to her statement, and I can't decide if that's good or bad.

"I blame the snowstorm for making me stir-crazy and falling into bed with him."

She nods, accepting the half-truth. "I'd be willing to bet the same's not true for him. Especially after what Meredith told me."

She doesn't elaborate, forcing me to follow her to the kitchen at the back of the house.

Though I spend zero time in kitchens, I'm wowed the moment I step into it. It's large, modern, and welcoming. There's a lot of white—cabinets, counters, drawers, the backsplash tile—with accents of gray on the lower half of the island where four stools offer seats. A huge Viking stove takes up most of one wall with one of those faucets mounted off to the side. Clem would know what they're called. The white farmhouse sink is kitty-cornered across from the island.

My eyes travel around the room, taking in the expansive picture windows with a window seat along it presenting a view of the backyard. It's covered in a layer of snow from the storm, but it seems to go for a bit before butting up against woods. There's a door to what I assume is a pantry—probably much bigger than Beckett's if I had to guess—and a doorway on the far wall leads to a communal dining area. Completing the look are high ceilings with wood-exposed beams and a rustic wooden floor. It's every chef's dream.

"This is a beautiful kitchen."

Heidi beams. "Thank you. We renovated it about three years ago. Next year, we'll start on the one at our other B and B to match. Though if not done before the baby comes, it'll be stupid to start so late in the year with not enough time before the holidays. So maybe it's a project for the year after that."

"Congrats."

Her forehead furrows. "On a kitchen?"

"On the baby?" I swear she mentioned baby. Did I hear her incorrectly?

"Oh. Right. The baby. Pregnancy brain." She smacks her forehead lightly. "Shit. Do not tell Beckett or Lenny. And can you feign shock when we announce it tonight at dinner? You're coming to dinner tonight, right? Beckett invited you? If not, here's your invite."

"My lips are sealed. Yes, he invited me to dinner. I'd offer to bring something, but I'm a disaster in the kitchen. Though we can stop and pick up some alcohol or something. Would that be good? What does everyone like?" Once I start rambling, it's hard to stop.

She dismisses my offer with a wave. "Nonsense. You're a guest. And Dax is always on alcohol duty. If there's something you want, I'll text him now before he goes to the store." She pulls her phone out, poised at the ready for my order.

"I'm not too picky. I'm sure there'll be something I can drink."

She sets the phone down on the counter and sets to work making dinner for the guests. As she prepares the meal—roast beef, mashed potatoes, green beans, and a salad—she tells me about how she got into the bed-and-breakfast business, how she met her husband, too much history about Winterberry I'll never remember, and as promised, embarrassing stories about Beckett. Those are my favorite. I don't think he'll be pleased to learn she spilled the beans, but he's not the angry type either. Beyond the first night when he found out I'm not into Christmas.

"Do you provide meals every night?"

"No. We try to do our best during the busier seasons, but it's not included in the room's price nor is it advertised. Depends on how busy my week or days are or if I feel like cooking. I try to plan out when I'll do it, but it doesn't always work out. Some weeks, I'll cook every night, especially if I'm mad or upset. Other weeks, I don't cook at all for the guests."

"Did you learn to cook from your grandmother, too?"

She smiles and places her hand over her heart, nostalgia washing over her features. "He told you about Nana. He can be such a pain in my rear, but he's got this soft, sweet side that makes it hard to stay mad at him. Ever since he was little, I often forgot he was the younger brother the way he'd taken care of me. Too bad he hasn't found the right woman yet. With his sympathy for everyone in spades, he's going to make a great husband."

"You're right. He will."

My heart pangs. *Lucky bitch.*

She starts to say something else, but the guys entering interrupt it.

"The men have moved the boxes," Lenny boasts, his chest puffed with pride. No one mentioned what kind of boxes needed moving, so maybe his pride is warranted.

Heidi rolls her eyes at her husband. "Knew you could do it."

"Willa and I are off to change and head to Mom and Dad's," Beckett exclaims. To me, he says, "Did you hear all the embarrassing stories?"

"I did. Sounds like you were a bit of a troublemaker back in the day."

Beckett glares at his sister. "Whatever she told you, I can top with stupid shit she did."

Heidi goes to protest, but her husband wraps her up in his arms, planting a kiss on her lips.

Their love is evident. Blessed woman.

"Willa, we must escape before they make out. It'll scar you for life."

"Love you too, little bro. See you soon, Willa." I catch the tail end of Heidi's comment as Beckett tugs me out of the kitchen, down the hall, and out the front door.

"Do you need to shower or just change your clothes?"

"I'm kinda thinking I need to wash off the sex smell before meeting your parents."

Beckett halts his retreat to the car. "You smell perfect to me."

"You'd think that since it's your fault I smell like this."

"If I let you shower now—"

I cut him off. "I'm sorry. If you *let* me?" Though I'm half joking, I'm reminded of my mission to rile him up. "How about I tell you I'm showering when we get home?"

"Great, fine. Then tonight, after coitus, sleep next to me still smelling like sex."

"Nice use of coitus."

He bends in half, taking a bow. "Thank you. Do we have a deal?"

"Thought there wasn't much sleeping going on tonight."

"Wiseass. For that quip, I'm choosing your undergarments."

"Not any you bought today. Those have to be washed before wearing." I shudder at the grossness of wearing them without washing.

He scratches his head. "Damn. Really wanted to see you in the black and red one. Will it be dry for tomorrow if I wash it when we get home?"

"You're going to do my laundry?" I squeal at the thought. Elias would barely fold his own clothes, let alone wash and dry them.

"Yes. Give me anything else you want washed." My mouth opens, but the man anticipates my question. "I'll do them on delicate. I think I even have one of those mesh bags leftover from . . . never mind. That's not important."

I cross over to where he stands, looking up at him. "You spoil me."

He pushes a lock of hair behind my ear. "You deserve it." He leans in, his lips meeting the top of my head. I'm going to miss those the most.

If this thing between us wasn't temporary, would it have a chance of going the distance?

22
willa

DESPITE HAVING to hide my distaste for the Nicholas's Christmas decorations—and there are a *plethora*—I love Beckett's family. His mom, Bethany, welcomed me into the fold the minute I walked into the house, wrapping her arms around me in the tightest hug ever. In all my twenty-eight years, my mother hasn't once hugged me so tight and for so long. No wonder Beckett is the way he is.

If he met my mom, would he think the same of me? I dismissed the thought as quickly as it came, not needing anything to bring me down tonight.

Bethany introduced me to the rest of the family as "Beck's Willa."

Heck if I didn't mind belonging to him for the night.

Except to me, he's Beckett, not Beck. And no amount of spending time with his family is going to change that.

"Family, we have an announcement," Heidi proclaims once everyone's arrived.

"You're knocked up," Shania guesses, much to her aunt's chagrin. Heidi schools her expression quickly, but if I noticed, no doubt others did, too.

"Yes. Best Christmas present ever." Lenny wraps her up in his arms, his hands splayed over her tiny belly.

"Congrats!"

"So exciting!"

"Well done, Lenny." That's their dad, Merritt. Beckett's a younger version of him, without the beard. I'm kinda partial to the scruff and stubble Beckett's had these past few days. My thighs especially.

Heat flames my cheeks. I shouldn't be thinking about Beckett going down on me while there are other people around.

When we're at his parents' house.

When his sister just announced she's pregnant.

But hell if I can help it. Because the man is striking to ogle. And of course, he doesn't miss my staring. Caught in the act, he winks at me, once from each eye, like he knows exactly what I'm thinking.

Based on the color of my face, he probably does.

Hugs, high-fives, and congrats are shared among the family members, and Merritt proposes a toast.

With spiked eggnog.

Gag me.

I raise my glass handed to me by Dax in solidarity, but I can't force myself to drink it. In a move only Beckett could orchestrate, he turns us around, swaps our glasses, and chugs my full one, spinning us back around in a matter of thirty seconds.

"Whiplash, much?" I mutter, but I'm grateful he's here to protect me from having to explain why I'm not drinking the toast.

"Are you okay? The Nicholas clan can be a little overwhelming." He drapes his arms over my shoulder, inching me closer to him.

"Compared to the Gibson clan, 'a little' is an understatement." I chuckle, the sound dying shortly after. "I'm good, thanks. There's a lot of love in this room, and if my family had half of it, life growing up would have been better."

It's not that my parents were horrible, but affection and love didn't come easily. They aren't the touchy-feely type, which was harder on Clem than me. She craved it, and who better to give it to her than her twin sister? Ironically, she's the one who still lives by our parents, but after Elias died, I needed a change of pace. When I announced I was moving to Vermont where Elias had grown up and went to college, no one but Clem tried to stop me. For her sake, I hate that we're so far, but for my sanity, it's better this way.

"I'm not sorry you're here, Willa."

It's the only thing he says before he's pulled away by his father for some before-dinner tradition.

His words play on repeat in my mind, my brain trying to make sense of his statement.

Does he mean *here* as in tonight?

Does he mean *here* as in Winterberry?

Does he mean *here* as in with him?

Is it a combination of the three?

"You seem lost." Autumn appears next to me, studying my appearance.

I blow out a breath. "Not lost. Overwhelmed. Your family dynamic differs from mine."

"Ah. I don't get it, but it's understandable. Shania's dad couldn't handle our brand of nutty. Took off before her first birthday. For a hot minute, I thought about packing up and following him, but I couldn't do it. I want her to grow up like I did. Sometimes I feel guilty she's growing up without him, but it's his loss."

"She's an incredible kid. You've done an amazing job with her."

"Eh." She does that so-so motion with her hand I've seen from Beckett. "She has her moments, but I couldn't ask for a better kid. And even though she's got a lot of her dad's personality, it's the parts I loved most about him." Wistfulness clings to every word, the emotion palpable around us. "Don't mind me.

Much as I love Christmas, it doesn't mean it isn't hard. The life I thought I'd have, so different from this one."

"Preach it, girl." I mumble the words, not sure I want her to hear me but relating to the sentiment. It occurs to me I never apologized for my erratic behavior the other night at Beckett's. "I'm sorry I was so skittish the other night. I'm not quite myself lately."

She waves away my apology. "No worries. Beck explained you weren't feeling well. How long are you in town for?"

"Until Beckett gets the part for my car."

"Huh."

I can't decipher the one word, but a commotion at the door saves me from having to. The guys have returned dressed in the ugliest Christmas sweaters I've ever laid eyes on. To hide my discomfort, I join in the others' laughter.

Greens and reds of all shades adorn the guys' chests. I home in on Beckett's. An ugly green and red argyle pattern covers his chest with the words "Don't stare at my package" stretched across. The alternating silver and black letters seem hand-sewn onto the material. The best part is a crocheted green present, complete with a red bow, attached to the bottom hem of the sweater inches above Beckett's package. It's hideous. The colors and patterns don't match in the slightest, but a huge grin plasters Beckett's face. I can't *not* match it with one of my own.

Merritt hands out a pencil and a scrap of green paper to the girls. When he hands me mine, he explains, "It's a contest. Best sweater wins."

"By best, you mean . . ."

His grin lights up the already bright room. "The most hideous, of course."

"Right. Got it." I take the pencil and paper with nimble fingers, hopefully hiding the shakiness.

The women gathered at the far end of the living room, the other guys stand in a line at the front. When Merritt joins them, he speaks. "Reminder of the rules: ignore who's wearing the sweater and vote on the ugliest one. Not about who wears it best or your affiliation with that person." He slides his eyes my way before resuming. "May the best man win."

From a speaker on the fireplace comes the sound of *America's Next Top Model* theme song, and then, I couldn't make this up, but one by one, each guy struts his stuff down the "runway"—aka, the middle of the living room floor. Each is more stoic than the last, getting into character, their chests showing off their sweater proudly. It goes in age order, so Beckett is last. With his gaze fixated on the wall in front of him, he strides across the carpet, one foot crossing in front of the other, like the models do. Why it amazes me he knows exactly what to do is beyond me.

About the middle of the room, he pauses, doing a slow and complete three hundred sixty-degree turn, the sweater covering his chest on full display. I wish I could rate his pose, his walk, his presence. Hands down, he'd win. Though his sweater is ugly, too. But I need a critical eye to assess them all fairly and unbiased.

For a moment, I forget they're Christmas-themed and lose myself in the fun of the game.

Each man takes one final step away from the line, our last look at each sweater. I jot the winner down on the paper and fold it up. Beckett collects them, a wink for me when our hands meet.

"We're talking later about your runway walk."

One brow rises. "You should see me on the stage. The *stripper* stage." He enunciates stripper, but his voice gives nothing away. I can't tell if he's serious.

My imagination fills in the gaps. Instead of Channing Tatum, I picture him as Magic Mike. Losing his clothes, thrusting his hips in tune with the music, giving lap dances. It's a vivid picture. Another thing to add to the list to discuss tonight.

Beckett hands over the papers to his father to tally the scores.

"Well, looks like we have a new champion. Drum roll, please." I watch in awe as every family member pounds on a solid surface until Merritt closes his fingers into a fist in the air to silence them. "The winner of this year's Nicholas sweater contest is . . . " He pauses, making eyes with his sons and son-in-law. "None other than . . . Beck." A raucous chorus of "hooray" and "congrats" erupts in the room. Even the "losers" chime in.

From behind the couch, a trophy is produced. With a spray-painted gold Christmas tree on top, it appears to be years old. Vintage, almost. Bethany also produces a notebook, handing it over to her husband. He flips through the pages, scanning whatever's written on each one until he comes to a blank page. A sharpie in his hand, he scribbles something on the page, holding it up once he's done.

"After a few years' hiatus, he's back in the winner's circle. Well done, Beck. Nice choice of sweater. Tell us, where did you find this monstrosity?"

Holding the trophy, Beckett radiates joy and excitement. Elation oozes off him, his dimple front and center, and I can't help but bask in his glow. It's less about the holiday sweater and more about the victory. What I wouldn't do to feel his warmth on a more permanent basis.

Beckett waits until everyone's quiet. "I couldn't find what I wanted, so I embellished it. I bought a plain red sweater at Target and created the argyle pattern, then sewed on the letters. If you don't believe me, I have pictures to prove it."

Is there anything this guy can't do? So far, I've yet to find it.

"Impressive." His mom comes closer to inspect his handiwork. "Very impressive. Nice use of crochet. Nana would be proud."

"That part was simple. It was the embroidery that was a bitch. Poked my fingers a few too many times over the months I worked on it."

As his family interrogates him more, I watch their interactions. All the decorations are making me kind of twitchy, but for Beckett, I'm trying not to let it show. With the way this family goes all out in their celebrating, it's almost hard not to want to join in on the joy.

Telling Beckett about Elias unlocked something inside me, a box I'd kept secured tightly with a padlock. With it opened, some tension of holding onto the anger lessened, paving the way for more acceptance. More celebrating the joy.

Perhaps this year's holiday won't be the sob fest I've been dreading.

Dinner is interesting, to say the least. Bethany made a feast, more so than chili, salad, and cornbread. I get the sense not every family dinner night is like this, but holiday dinner night definitely is.

Covered by a holiday tablecloth, the dining table seats us comfortably. I'm seated next to Beckett and across from Heidi, with his parents each at one end. The discussion centers on the festivities over the next few days. Bethany made it clear the next two days were appetizers and finger foods, though there was mention of a brunch Christmas morning. My ears perked up on brunch, and damn if I don't want to come for this mouthwatering feast. I'd have to put aside a lot—more than a plethora—of feelings to allow myself to appreciate the work going into something like that and not freaking out or hyperventilating at anything Christmas-related.

I'm honestly not sure I'm up to the task. Could I break the pattern from last year, knock down the walls I built to guard my heart against allowing myself to feel . . . happy?

Time will tell.

I won't come if I don't think I can handle it. I won't do that to Beckett or his family. If I'm not completely on board with whatever the Nicholas holiday traditions are, I'll stay away.

Beckett knocks his shoulder into my arm. "You're quiet."

"Ruminating things."

"I like that one. Ruminating." He nods, trying it out on his tongue. "In place of pondering or wondering."

"Exactly that."

"What are you ruminating about?" Under the table, he laces our fingers, my palm fitting perfectly in his larger one.

I give him a half-truth. "Life. Your mom's chili is delicious. Much better than my mom's. I was almost scared. She scarred me for life with hers." A shudder passes through me. She'd make it at least every other week, forcing Clem and me to eat at least one bowl of the congealed crap.

"Nana's recipe. It's been so long since I've had hers, I can't remember whose was better."

I pat my stomach. "I'd be so fat if I ate this regularly. That, or I'd have to participate in the classes a friend drags me to."

Beckett waggles his brows. "You could work it off in the bedroom. Did you know sex burns three point two calories per minute?"

Warmth creeps into my cheeks. "Beckett! You did not just say that at your family's dinner table."

"I did, and I'll say it again. Se—"

I twist in my seat and slap my free hand over his mouth. "Hush. Not dinner table conversation."

His tongue sneaks out of his mouth, licking my palm. I should move my hand . . . but what I should do and what I do are different things.

That is, until he snakes his free hand along my inner thigh.

"You are so bad," I whisper-hiss, looking around to make sure no one is paying us any attention. "Your mom is *right* there." However, after today's escapades in the dressing room, I'm having a harder time convincing him to stop.

But no. This isn't the time or the place.

"So, Willa. What is it you do?"

The question comes from Autumn, and I freeze on the spot. How do I tell them what I do? Not after the other night with Shania. But how do I lie to these kind people? What even will I tell them?

As I'm internally panicking, Beckett rescues me. "She works

with authors helping to market their books on social media." The lie slides smoothly off his tongue, like it was practiced. It's so fluid and plausible, I stop to consider if anything else he's told me could be a fabrication of the truth.

Shania pipes up first. "That's so cool. Do you know authors in real life?" I nod, not trusting what will spill out without my permission. "I've always wanted to meet an author, ask them questions. Like Evelyn Ravenhurst. Man, I've got so many questions for her."

"Eep," I squeak, and it's Beckett's turn to cover my mouth.

"If Willa ever meets her, she'll tell her she knows her biggest fan."

Shania smiles broadly at her uncle. "I really hope *Santa* got the memo about the collection I put on my list. I have the perfect spot on my shelf for them." The way she says Santa leads me to suspect she's not a true believer.

Beckett leans in close, his mouth right behind my ear. "I have it on good authority her shelves will be sporting new books. Maybe before you leave, you'll sign them for her?"

"Yes, of course," I breathe out, letting go of the pent-up breath zinging through me.

Beckett's smile matches Shania's.

One word plays on repeat in my mind.

Leave.

As much as I know it's inevitable, why does the thought have me squirming in my seat worse than the thought of celebrating Christmas?

23

beckett

WILLA'S quiet on the drive to the cabin, her gaze trained outside her window. I avoided Main Street, not wanting to upset her, knowing she must be over her limit after spending hours listening to plans for the holiday and surrounded by decorations all night.

It's not until I've parked in the garage and we're inside the cabin does she regard me. "I had fun. Your family is truly great. Overbearing, overwhelming, and all. Thanks."

"Glad you had a good time. Was it too much?"

She chortles. "At times? For sure. But I lived to tell about it. Clem's going to be so proud of me." At the mention of her sister, her voice changes. "I can't wait to tell her tomorrow."

"Speaking of tomorrow, are your plans to stay in the cabin all day?"

In the dim light of the entryway, her swallow is hard to miss. "It's probably best. I don't want to ruin anything for you."

The bit of hope I had she'd join me deflates. "K." After sharing why she detests the holiday—man, I'm not sure even I can blame her after something like that—I hoped she was making progress, albeit small. I won't force her out of her comfort zone. I have too many obligations to the town tomorrow to worry about Willa, too.

"What time do you have to leave for the parade?"

"It starts at two, so I have to be in place around one-thirty. Probably leave here around one. I can throw something together for breakfast and lunch, though I'm not sure what we have. Or you can order something. Most places stop delivering around noon, so it'll have to be early."

Her gaze casts down, but I can't tell why. I itch to tip her chin back up, read her expression, know what she's thinking.

Ah, fuck it.

Gently, I reach my fingers under her chin, lifting it. Her expression is unreadable, a mix of emotions.

"I wasn't asking to guarantee you'd provide the food. I didn't want to be in your way when you're getting ready."

I share a small smile. "Ironically, I like cooking for you, Willa. Gives me purpose. It's more fun to cook for two than one."

"You have so much purpose in your life, Beckett. Why you feel the need to find more in feeding me is a mystery."

The words to answer her get stuck in my throat.

This is temporary. *She's* temporary.

She'll be gone in a few days, never to return. And I'll go back to living my life, forever changed by this stranger who crashed into my life unannounced and stole a piece of my heart, altering the fabric of my entire being.

Heidi's right. I watch too many Hallmark movies.

I wouldn't change a thing about this week, even if it means never again experiencing the feelings she brings out in me. Never finding my true love.

She is not your true love, the rational part of my brain argues.

I shake out of my stupor, this trance she has me in.

"I owe you orgasms. Let me lock up, and I'll meet you in bed."

A shy smile crests her lips. She steps closer to me, the traces of whatever seemed to bother her moments ago diminished. Her finger rakes over my chest, trailing a soft, zigzag line along the hard planes. "Let's start with your blow job. You've been waiting longer than this afternoon."

It isn't what I expected her to say, but I'm not at all disappointed. Who am I to deprive her of what she wants?

I didn't bother setting an alarm last night. I'm always up before the sun. Creature of habit and my internal clock. However, I made good on my promise to Willa and kept her up most of the night worshipping her body. She reciprocated, starting with an out-of-this-world blow job, helping me feel more manly after questioning if I was too soft, too delicate.

After the way she let me fuck her mouth, I decided I can be both—hard and soft as needed.

A conundrum through and through.

Lazily, I move my head to watch her sleep. Even at rest, she's beautiful. The fine lines around her eyes are smoothed out. She's got one arm tucked under the pillow, her hair messy and framing her head. Needing to feel the silky strands in my fingers, I broke her hair tie when I ripped it out of her hair.

"Don't be a creeper," her groggy voice instructs. Her eyes remain closed, but her mouth parts.

"You don't know I'm watching you."

One eye peeks open. "You confirmed what I believed. Your thoughts are loud. Shut them off."

I chuckle at her use of imagery, as if she can hear my thoughts. Better yet, as if I could *shut them off*. Not a chance. Not with her.

"No can do, beautiful. Not with you in my bed." I stop myself from adding any more. That's enough of a reason I can't shut them off.

Because she's the freaking star of my thoughts, and I don't want to shut them off.

"What time is it? And don't say early. The actual time, Beckett."

I suppress my chortle. "Hardass. Almost seven. I slept late today."

She flips from her stomach to her side, keeping that same arm tucked under her pillow.

My pillow.

"Maybe if you had the decency to let us get some sleep overnight, you'd have been up at your normal time. But no. It was 'one more, Willa. You can give me one more,' and 'that's it. Another one just like that. Come for me.'"

"Didn't hear any complaints last night."

So maybe that's a lie. She wasn't complaining, but I pushed her beyond where she was comfortable. Or at least, where her previous comfort zone was. The last round was hard and fast, yet she took it like a champ. I would think if she was truly uncomfortable, she would have said so. I hope.

"That was delirious Willa. Whatever she said and did, you can't use against me today."

"Okay, sure. Got it. Which Willa am I having this conversation with?"

"Hungry Willa. Also, needs coffee Willa." She bats her eyes, her expression what my sister calls Shania's "puppy dog face." Do I have to mention I'm a sucker for it?

"Keep me company in the kitchen. Regale me with more tales about young Willa and growing up in North Carolina."

"If I must."

Not able to resist her lips any longer, I lean in and plant a kiss on them. A quick one, so she doesn't yell at me for proper hygiene or anything.

"You must."

She flops to her back, the blanket falling from where she had it tucked under her. She was adamant about sleeping in a T-shirt, but I convinced her one of mine was the best choice. Thank goodness it's too cold for her to leave the bedroom wearing only that. I'd probably lay her out on the table and let her be breakfast.

Hmm. Even with clothes, it's not a bad idea, though she'd still be hungry.

"What are your thoughts on cinnamon rolls?"

She moans, and my dick takes notice. Guess it's not too tired from last night's action. A few hours of sleep has it raring to go again. Not that we have much time today.

Unless we're quick or take advantage of the buffer of time the dough needs to rise.

"Love them. Even know how to cook them myself." She beams at her compliment.

"From scratch?" I tease, knowing her answer before she speaks.

Her expression sours. "Um, that would be no. You're going to make cinnamon rolls from scratch? How long does that take?"

"The longest part is waiting for the dough to rise. Any ideas what we could do while we wait?"

She shakes her head. "I'm too sore already. I can't take anymore. My vagina wasn't built for all-night sexathons. Nope. No."

"Get your head out of the gutter. I was going to suggest a movie. Lying on the couch, maybe cuddling. But I see where your mind's at." I climb out of bed, not able to face her and keep a serious face.

"Uh, sorry. A movie would be great, actually. A fire would be better."

As much as sex is always on my mind—she wasn't wrong—cuddling on the couch with her, under blankets, a fire roaring in the fireplace, has merit. I turn back around. "Are you in the 'Die Hard is a Christmas movie' camp?"

"Hardly."

"Awesome. *Die Hard* it is. The dough's going to take some time to prepare, then I'll get the fire started. Want some fruit to hold you over?"

"Did we eat all the berries? Man, those were good."

"Why don't you check while I make the dough? Put together a plate of fruit. You're up for that task, right?"

She nods, though I'm not convinced she has faith in herself. If I had more time with her, I'd make sure she gained more confidence in the kitchen. Though it definitely wouldn't be at the top of the priority list.

"Oh, Beckett. I can wash fruit and make the plate look so fancy, you're going to think you bought it at the store."

I raise a brow, calling her bluff. But hey, if she's cocky about it, this I gotta see. "Prove it."

She wants to back down, I can read it in her eyes, but she doesn't. She's a proud one, and I'm here for it. Even if it's not up to par, it's fruit on a plate. Not much to mess up.

A kiss to the top of her head elicits a moan and has her swooning. Does she realize she gives up her tells so easily? Much as she's guarded, she's let down some of her walls, letting me in one tell at a time.

I exit the bedroom, make a stop in the bathroom, then move to the kitchen, seeking the recipe for the rolls and the ingredients.

Some traditions never die. Cinnamon rolls were Mom's specialty on Christmas Eve morning. The first year I moved out, I showed up early, anxious about the recipe she made once a year. Turns out, it was a kids' tradition, and once we were gone, she stopped. I argued Shania was still a kid who'd need the tradition to continue, but Mom stood her ground. The only time in my life she was stubborn. I griped about it way too long, but no one played into it. Not even playing the youngest card convinced her to make them.

The next year, I made them myself, but it wasn't the same. The appeal was gone.

Yet, the year after that, it was like I couldn't *not* make them. I ended up delivering them to a homeless shelter a few towns over, and as much as I wanted that tradition to continue, the place closed down the next summer.

Last year, I made them for the B and B, but Heidi told me, in no uncertain terms, "This tradition isn't welcome here." It was harsh and a definite blow to my ego, but I understood when she whipped out plates of baked French toast. And okay, she wasn't wrong.

Resignedly, my plan this year was to forgo my tradition and have breakfast with her and Lenny. Until Willa came crashing—no pun intended—into my life.

The memories assault me as I whip up the dough, watching it transform from a bunch of ingredients into a ball on the dough hook of the mixer. I'm so lost in the motion, I don't realize Willa has appeared.

"I didn't know dough could be so entertaining."

I'm startled by her voice, but I don't let it show. "Gobs better than watching paint dry."

A hearty chuckle is her response. I assume she's laughing at my metaphor, but she says, "I used gobs in a book once. My readers weren't too keen on it. Will never make that mistake again."

I tear my attention away from the mixer, seeking her ensemble. As predicted, she's wearing a pair of flannel pants she's yet to wear and an Aspenridge sweatshirt. She tied her hair up in a knot, her glasses perched on her nose. She's a vision of beauty. I won't even try telling her that. She wouldn't hear it and would start an argument for argument's sake.

I've never been drawn to women who need a full face of makeup to feel beautiful. A woman's natural beauty is more my speed. Willa has it in spades, even first thing in the morning, dressed in PJs. She bears some effects of exhaustion, but it enhances her charm.

"Beckett." My name at a decibel louder than inside appropriate breaks the trance.

"What?"

"You're zoning out and staring. Creepy." She pinches the bridge of her nose. "I'll need a large platter or a cutting board will do." Confusion settles in, so she continues, "For my fancy fruit plate."

"Right. Bottom shelf in the pantry. On the left."

"Of course he knows exactly where they are," she mocks.

"I do live here," I defend. Not very well. It's not my best comeback.

She retreats to the pantry, returning with a serving platter. It's red, but that's the most "festive" part. If memory serves, it was on the bottom of the pile.

Baby steps. Getting her to leap won't help anyone.

24
willa

THE MORNING FLIES BY.

We consume the most mouthwatering cinnamon rolls I've ever tasted, view *Die Hard,* and after Beckett compliments my fruit platter, we devour it.

When Beckett mentions napping, I wonder if he'll stay on the couch. When he follows me to the bedroom, I'm ecstatic. I can't get enough cuddles with this man. The thought is heady, sobering, because this isn't permanent.

I shouldn't be this preoccupied with him.

I shouldn't be this comfortable, this giddy, with wanting to spend time with him.

I certainly shouldn't be falling for him.

But I am. Undoubtedly.

Perhaps it's my body's way of finding some closure, especially after my meltdown a couple of days ago. Or it's my version of casual, and when I leave in a few days, the feelings will stay here. As if casual feelings are only synonymous with Winterberry.

I laugh at the absurdity of that being true.

The fun side of my brain convinces me to stop thinking about it as a negative, to embrace the time I've been given with him, and let it happen. It's not like I'm going to leave here with another broken heart for a future guy to mend.

Thoughts for another day and time.

"I'm gonna go work out in the garage before I have to report for duties. You, write some words."

Beckett leans against the doorjamb, his feet crossed at the ankles, dressed in workout pants and a T-shirt with the sleeves cut off. Leave it to Beckett to prove that's a look I enjoy. From my vantage point in the bed, I wish I wasn't so freaking sore. Because if we had time, I'd jump his bones.

Gingerly, of course, to not break any.

Except, no. Good thing we don't have time because my vagina needs a rest.

That's something I never thought I'd think.

"I'll see what I can do. My editor will thank you if I manage any."

He scratches his head, the movement causing the shirt to rise and showcase a band of skin. I soak it up, as if I wasn't intimately acquainted with every inch twelve hours ago.

"Does incentivizing help you?"

"Depends on the incentive."

He stares a moment, his eyes blinking slowly. "Sex, Willa."

My vagina weeps with the thought.

"Sex won't do it today. Before last night's pounding, I probably would have said yes."

"Dessert?"

My mouth waters. I want to tell him no, but damn if whatever he's thinking isn't appealing. Even if I don't know what it is.

"Maybe."

He snaps a finger. "New lingerie."

Damn. I was hoping he wouldn't go there . . .

My eyes shut, a moan escaping. "Don't tease me. I'm weak regarding that, but I'll just fail. And then be mad at myself for not earning new bras and underwear and having no words. It's a trap I can't fall into."

As much as I want what he's offering.

Incentives used to work. Even small rewards. A small piece of chocolate for every one thousand words written. A new notebook for every ten chapters written. A massage when my book was finished.

That was before. Before Elias died.

Now, nothing works. Not even the "open the manuscript" as the one task. Some days, that was too much. This week was supposed to be a jump-start to writing again, but look where that's gotten me.

Being spoiled rotten by this hottie.

Which isn't at all conducive to writing books.

"Got it. No lingerie. Fancy candy? The candy shop in town sells imported chocolates. I'll pick some up and see what you get done. If you earn any. Otherwise, I'll have to eat them myself."

I open my eyes. "Bet you'd enjoy that," I mumble, crossing my arms over my chest.

He mimics my position, though his biceps are more attractive to look at. A smirk catches on his lips. "Yep. Though I'd rather share it with you." Sincerity laces each word.

How is he so perfect? So single? Granted, our current living situation is unconventional and temporary, but what could be so particular that other women might fault him for?

"I'll do my best," I promise. It's a loose promise, but one I can attempt. For his sake. Heck, for my sake. For the sake of my readers and everyone waiting for the next installment of the Hidden Clues Club.

"I'll be back." He turns around, and I ogle his ass as he walks away. "Words, Willa," comes his stern directive.

"Too bad I don't write romance," I lament. "I'd have lots of fodder and inspiration."

With nothing else to do, I untuck myself from under the

covers and push out of bed. I look up at the ceiling. "Any help is much appreciated."

The back door opening startles me. My fingers freeze on the keyboard, the "mys" of mystery interrupted. Beckett materializes, beads of sweat on his brow and under his nose. His hair is tousled and damp spots dot his shirt.

My time shouldn't be wasted on writing when this hot specimen is available for the taking. If I only get several days with him, why am I wasting it writing a book? I can do that when I get home. I should take advantage of this well-abled man and get my fill of orgasms.

If only that were a real possibility.

"How was your workout?"

"Demanding. Quiet, yet loud. I had to blast music to drown out my thoughts."

It's a nod to our conversation earlier. Wonder if he'll tell me what the thoughts were.

Before I can ask, he interrogates, "Get some words?"

I can't keep the smile off my face. Because I did. Not a love letter to my dead boyfriend, but a rough outline of the next AJ Hart book.

I squint at the screen. "Just shy of one thousand. Holy shit." I look at Beckett. "Ho-ly shit. That's the most I've written in two years." I stare at the number, convinced it has to be wrong. Nope. 995. Wow.

His broad smile is not a reaction to my enthusiasm. His is genuine pride for my accomplishment. "That's amazing, Willa." In socked feet, he trudges to the fridge, removing two bottles of water. He places one in front of me. "Drink."

The one-word blasts me to the past, a vivid memory of Elias placing a cup of water in my hand, forcing me to take sips.

"Drink," he'd command, knowing I tended to go long periods without hydrating.

I blink back to the present, Beckett sitting across the table. He drains half the bottle, wiping his mouth with the back of his hand. "What?"

"No-nothing." But it's not nothing. It's so much *not* nothing. "How did you know?" I blurt.

Confusion furrows his brows. "Know what?"

"I needed water." I unscrew the top, taking a healthy sip, invigorating my body for the next round. Excitement rattles through me at the possibility of another round of words.

He shrugs, finishing his water. "You looked thirsty. I'm sorry?"

"No, don't be. It's just . . . it's what Elias would do. Put water in front of me and tell me to drink. It's like you knew but you didn't know. Eerie."

"Yeah," he agrees, blowing out a breath, his eyes darting around the room, not focusing on any one spot. "I'm gonna hit the shower. Almost time to head out for the parade." Sorrow fills his tone. I hate I'm the cause of it.

"Where would one go to watch the parade? If one had free time and wanted to check it out. For research," I tack on.

His brows quirk, but that's his only tell. His stoicism doesn't falter. "For research purposes, park in the lower lot of the high school and walk to the front lawn. For the best view, though? I'd suggest the driveway of the Fernwood Fables B and B. Fewer people. Better snacks."

I nod, soaking up his advice. "What time did you say the roads close?"

"On the back roads to the B and B, you're good until two-ish easy. Straight down Main and to the high school? By one-thirty." There's more excitement in his voice the more he speaks.

"And which vehicle do you drive?"

"The last one. You can't miss it." He stands up, stretching his arms above his head, giving me another delicious view of his abs. "I'm going to be late if I don't shower. If you want a ride, be ready in twenty." He doesn't give another option. Because his choice is for me to ride with him. Yet, I haven't even decided if I'm going.

Part of me feels like I owe it to him. He's done so much for me, the least I can do is sit and watch a parade, something he takes great pride in. He's been so invested in my stuff, I should do the same. The whole celebrating, being joyous and festive, has me hesitating.

What if it's too much?

What if I have another emotional breakdown?

What if I ruin a parade for a town that adores Christmas?

"Okay." It's a whisper, all I can manage. I don't want to give in and not be okay, but I also want to support him, not be the one to cause the smile on his face and the spark in his eyes to disappear. I can't be that person.

I *won't* be that person.

It's time to shit or get off the pot.

Kinda wish I knew which way to lean . . .

My heart in my chest, my nerves are running the show.

I follow Beckett's directions to the B and B, maneuvering his SUV down the long driveway. Holiday lights illuminate the old white Victorian house, but against the daytime sky, they aren't as luminous. A small crowd of people gathers to the right of the driveway, but he mentioned by the time the parade rolls down the street, the front lawn would be packed. I find a spot in the back lot, one of the last few.

I chose not to have Beckett drop me off because I wanted the freedom of the car in case an immediate escape was necessary. Not that I'll be able to get the car out if something happens, but it gave me a little more peace of mind. The way my brain's going crazy and keeping up with my erratic heart rate, I'm grabbing onto any slice of peace and clinging with both hands. It's giving me the grounding I need.

Because I'm not grounded in the slightest. I'm all out of sorts, wondering what the hell I'm doing here and why I made this decision.

Beckett.

A smile finds my lips at the mere thought of the man. I'm here for him. And maybe a little for myself, too. To prove I can do this. Not ruin other people's fun and take away their joy. To reclaim my own. Elias isn't coming back. It's not the holiday's fault he was killed. I've got to let go of these depressed feelings and let myself live again.

One event at a time, I'm going to regain the happiness, the delight, the Christmas holiday offers. I doubt it will be easy, but if not now, when?

Seems like Winterberry Junction is the perfect place to start. And if my emotions overwhelm me, it will be a distant memory in a few days. No one will remember the crazy girl who ruined the town's Christmas.

My phone rings, and I dig it out from my bag.

"How are you holding up?" is Clem's greeting.

We texted yesterday about dinner with the Nicholas family, but I didn't tell her what I was up to.

"I'm a little freaking out, to be honest." I whisper the words, so they don't get past the car. As if anyone's around and paying me any attention.

"Is he pressuring you to celebrate today?"

"No, the opposite." I suck in a big breath, exhaling it out slowly. "I'm choosing to celebrate. Rather, watch the town's parade."

"Willa, that's—"

I cut her off. "Crazy? Idiotic? Insane? The worst decision I've ever made in my life?" I'm more dramatic than I'm pretending to be.

"I was going to say amazing. I'm proud of you, kid."

Her words uncover something buried deep inside, first shaken loose by circumstances of the past few days. Tears spring to my eyes, but I will them not to fall. I can't get out of the car and take part in the festivities this emotional.

"Thank you. You don't know how much I needed to hear that. I'll even excuse the 'kid' part."

Her chuckle vibrates my ear. "I'll let you get to your parade. Got an inkling I needed to check in on you."

"Thanks for not ignoring this one."

"Sure thing. Have fun at the parade and what comes next. Call me tonight. No matter how late. I want to hear all about your day."

"It may be really late . . . or early." I cringe at my implication. "I don't want to interrupt any plans you've got with the boys and Keith."

"You won't be. I promise." Her voice is lower, and there's something she's not saying, but I let it go.

"Great. Talk later. And thanks again, Clem. Thanks for sharing half my brain and knowing what I need before I do."

"Always, kid. I've got your back. Love you. You've got this."

I can't let the guilt wiggle in. The guilt about ruining her Christmas last year. Her pride is genuine. And she's right. I can do this.

"Oh. I wrote almost one thousand words today. Useful words, some of which might even make it to the final draft." I laugh, letting go of more of the tension circulating through me. Clem's voice helped dislodge unneeded anxiety.

"Willafred! Go you. We've got so much to catch up on when you get home. You can come for a visit, and we'll do a day just the two of us. Keith can wrangle the misfits. But go. You've got a parade to watch."

"Love you, sis." I hang up, a renewed sense of pride from our conversation. Until my heart jumps into my throat at the knock on the passenger window. I lower it about halfway.

"Willa? Beckett told me you'd be coming. Parade's arriving

soon." Heidi holds up a plate of cookies. My mouth waters, even with the green and red colors, the sprinkles, and other festive decorations.

"Hey. Yes, sorry. Finishing up a call." I hold up my phone in case she thinks I'm lying. "I'm coming." I return the phone to my bag and grab the thermos of coffee Beckett poured for me. *"Spiked,"* he informed. *"Will help keep you warm. That and my hoodie."*

Not once in all the time we were together did Elias try to understand my aversion to coats. Not once did he suggest I wear something of his to keep warm. He'd often roll his eyes when I'd get super frustrated by having to wear it when the weather was extremely chilly when we'd go to Vermont for a visit.

Yet, one action and Beckett not only didn't question why I couldn't stand the coat but made sure I had something less constraining and more to my liking. His reasons aren't purely for me, but it's easy to pretend they are. Especially because I'm not the one fighting suffocation, and as a bonus, I get to smell like him. Win-win in my book, no matter the ulterior motive.

With a smile on my mouth and glee in my steps, I reach into the back seat and slide my arms into the sleeves of the hoodie. Making sure the car is locked, I join Heidi at the back of the car, stealing a cookie from her plate.

"Okay, let's do this."

25

willa

TWENTY MINUTES LATER, the parade rolls down Main Street. A marching band from the high school, floats from shops in town (I assume), a dance team decked out in elf costumes, and a full-on rendition of *A Christmas Carol*—complete with costumes and a set—round out my favorites.

I didn't ask Beckett or Heidi how long it lasted, but I figure it must be almost done. How much more can they fit into a Christmas Eve parade?

Beckett wasn't wrong about the crowd of people congregating here. Mostly families with kids, their grandparents, and a few groups of teenagers. Not once did the teenagers get rowdy, and the only time they were on their phones was to take pictures. I'm so used to zombie-like ones hanging around the coffee shop, it was refreshing to see them so excited about a parade. Some of their infectious joy leaked to me, and I'm not sad about it.

My therapist will have a field day when I see her in January. I can't wait to tell her.

"Ah, here comes Beck," Heidi calls out, enthusiasm dripping with it.

I take a step in front of the crowd, trying to get a glimpse of him and what kind of float he's driving. All I can see is an old red Chevy truck, like vintage old. From the sixties, maybe. I thought he said he'd be driving it, but upon closer look, he's not the driver. Another guy his age sits behind the wheel, and Dax is in the passenger seat. I'm so confused.

"I don't see him," I grumble, mostly to myself, but Lenny overhears it.

His smirk is sinister as he points to the back of the truck.

The only person in the back of the truck is . . . wait for it . . . Santa!

It takes several moments for what I'm seeing to sink in.

"Wait, what? *That's* Beckett?" I blink, attempting to clear my vision. Between my contacts and the cold weather, my eyes are bothering me more than usual. I stare at the man currently waving to the crowd, sporting a huge smile.

The white beard affixed to his face.

The overstuffed red coat with a black buckle holding it in place.

The *jolly* expression.

It's Santa, alright. Beckett as Santa.

Why am I so astounded he's dressed as Santa? The clues were all there this week. AJ Hart would sass me so hard right now that I didn't see this coming.

All I can do is laugh.

A hearty laugh, one sounding a lot like Santa's, pulled deep from the pit of my stomach. It's been so long since I've laughed like this. I can't remember the last time.

Joy radiates through me, the excitement making me giddy. It invigorates me, eclipsing every doubt I had that I'd ruin this for other people.

I'm glad he didn't tell me, and I'm also delighted I decided it was important to come. I wouldn't have wanted to miss this.

"Of course he's Santa," I state aloud, still reeling with laughter.

When I seek Beckett out again, his back is to me, waving to

the crowd on the opposite side of the street. He hasn't noticed me yet, but when he shifts toward the driveway, ecstasy pours off him in ripples. His smile widens, his eyes sparkle. That's the only way I can describe how bright they are. Our gazes lock, and my smile grows.

A week ago, the thought of being near Santa would have crippled me, sending me running for the hills. Instead, here I am, wishing I could jump into the back of the truck with him.

Sure, it's not "Santa" I'm interested in so much as Beckett. A guy who's turned my life topsy-turvy in a matter of days, including making me a believer again. I don't know when it happened, but he worked his charms, and here I am.

His arm swings wildly yet controlled. "Ho, ho, ho," he croons. "Merry Christmas." My arm raises to return his wave, my excitement not contained. He bangs on the top of the cab, calling out, "Hold up a minute." Slowly, the truck rolls to a stop, and Beckett jumps from the bed, strolling my way, not forgetting the part he's playing. His hands splay his round stomach, and he saunters more than strolls, his focus not leaving me.

My stomach leaps, wondering what he's up to, why he's stopped the parade to find me.

About two feet in front of me, he halts, his eyes never leaving mine. "Hey."

"Hey, yourself." I shake my head. "Santa!"

A tinge of red stains his cheeks. Not like the "rosy cheeks" in the song, but from self-consciousness. "Glad you made it. Worried for a second you'd miss all this." He reaches an arm out, motioning to the surrounding crowd.

"I wouldn't have missed it for the world." The truth gushes out, the words genuine and frank. The only reason I'm here is because of Beckett. I owe it all to him. I'm not sure I'll ever be able to show my complete gratitude for how much he's helped me this week.

"I have something for you. Hold on." He breaks our trance, returning to the truck, reaching into the window of the cab, not once breaking character. He doesn't ignore the cheers of "Santa" on his way back, giving his fans a wave. When he reaches me, his hands are behind his back, but his smirk tells me he's up to something.

"Whatcha got there, Santa?"

"Close your eyes, Willa." His demand is gentle, softer than his usual tone. I don't bother fighting it, fluttering my eyes shut. He removes the wool hat I'm wearing, replacing it with a different one. "Okay, open."

My eyes open, and I'm met with his phone's camera in selfie mode. A Santa hat has taken the place of the winter one, but I can't get a word out before he pulls me flush against him, instructing me to smile when I'm where he wants me. The screen reflects our bliss, and I only hope the picture accurately illustrates it.

"Do you trust me?"

"Wholeheartedly."

A devilish gleam in his eyes, he wraps his hand around my wrist and pulls me to the other side of the hedges. I don't have to wonder for long what he's up to when his arms clasp around my waist and lean me backward. A flurry of butterflies kicks up with the comprehension of what he's doing.

"Beckett," I squeal, as he crashes his lips to mine, my protest dying.

During the Hallmark movie the other night, we talked about how the hero sweeps the heroine off her feet—metaphorically—and dips her back for the grand finale of kisses.

And what a finale it is.

Fireworks explode in front of my eyes.

Tingles erupt, coursing through my body at warp speed.

My cheeks flush not only from the cold, but the heat exchanged between the two of us.

All too quickly, it's over.

Beckett rights me, making sure I'm not swaying, steadying me with his hands on my shoulders.

"Such a dirty Santa," I coo, my lips zinging with feeling.

Beckett chuckles, leaning in close. "If you're not too sore, maybe later I put the suit back on and you can help me take it off? I'll show you how dirty I can be."

His comment lands between my thighs, the parts of me still super achy from our fun yesterday. But damn if I don't want more, no matter how sore I'll be for the next couple of days.

"Yes, please."

His smile so broad, his dimple pops, and he leaves a kiss on my head. I will myself to stay upright and not embarrass myself by falling over as I swoon.

"I have a few things to get back to once the parade wraps up. Stay here and wait for me?"

"Where else would I go?"

He boops my nose. "Right answer, Bundy. Be back soon. Go warm up inside with Heidi." His lips sweep over mine, and then he's gone. A little more hastily this time, the role pushed aside as I catch the back side of him climbing into the truck to finish the parade. "Nothing to see here, folks. I must be getting back to rest up for my long night ahead of me. Merry Christmas Eve," Beckett shouts to the crowd. He taps the cab again, and the truck moves on past the B and B, the crowd clapping and cheering his departure.

The parade ends with a bang, and I'm still recovering from the hidden kiss.

"Wowza. That was hot. Much as I don't like to think of my brother like that, the way he looked at you . . ." Heidi fans herself, mouthing, "Hawt."

"Did he really just do that?"

"Believe it, Willa. He did," she confirms, tugging on the white pompom. "Shall we go inside? We've got hot cocoa."

"The kind Beckett makes?" I can't help but ask.

She winks. "Better."

What a day this is turning out to be. Elias would be so proud I didn't let my fear win.

26

beckett

JOVIAL LAUGHTER GREETS me as I enter through the back door of the bed-and-breakfast. I'm a little nervous about Willa's reaction after the stunt I pulled. She didn't seem upset during it, though she was shocked. Which is exactly what I was going for and why I didn't tell her who I played in the parade. She *never* would have come had she known. Once the cat was out of the bag, she embraced it.

Or seemed to anyway.

I'm second-guessing myself now. Is this the time I went too far and tossed her so far out of her comfort zone, she won't recognize it anymore?

Please don't let that be the case.

I find them in the private living room: Willa, my sister, and my brother-in-law, laughing as if they have no cares in the world. Like they have no better place to be than right here. In truth, it's exactly where I want Willa. For purely selfish reasons, which I will only admit to myself and others under pure duress.

Damn, I've got it bad for this woman. Never been in this situation before, it's making me feel all kinds of things I shouldn't be feeling for a woman who's breezing through town. A tourist. A fleeting moment in time. That's all she is.

My chest twinges. It's a horrible description of her, even if it is the truth.

"Hey." My voice cracks, so I try again. "How's it going?"

All three heads spin my way, Willa's smile the brightest.

"Santa. You're here." Willa stands, rushes over, and leaps into my arms. Her legs wrap around my waist, and she clings like a koala. My arms envelop her, bringing her impossibly closer. When she doesn't fight it, I hug tighter. My eyes close on their own accord. I try to hide my inhalation of her scent, my body wash mixed with her vanilla aroma making the sweetest combination. "I missed you," she breathes out.

Damn, but I fall.

I tumble into oblivion, into a place I won't recover from. A piece of my heart will forever belong to Willafred Gibson.

I'm in deep trouble.

"Everything okay, Beck? You're looking a little woozy." Of course, Heidi picks up on my mood change. She's always been keen on my emotions.

"Fi-fine," I stammer, opening my eyes. Willa's concerned expression nearly guts me. "All good," I reiterate. I can't be the one to hurt her, to make her feel any more sadness in her life. "Missed you, too." I peck her cheek and lower her to the ground, feeling the loss of our connection immediately.

"Your sister was telling me all about growing up in Winterberry and how you got the job of playing Santa in the parade."

"Awesome," I deadpan. "Is there more hot chocolate?" I point to their mugs.

"I'll make more." Heidi looks from me to Willa to Lenny. "Stay for dinner. We're making beef Wellington and have plenty. Mom and Dad are staying home, eating their appetizers and finger foods."

I address Willa. "What do you say, Bundy?"

My sister's face contorts to confusion and Lenny snickers. *Oops.*

"I'm game for any food I don't have to cook." She snorts, the sound one I haven't heard but ridiculously cute. Ashamed, she covers her mouth with her hand.

"What time is dinner?"

"Suppertime. Around five?" Heidi checks in with us.

A glance at my phone informs me it's nearing four. In case she got her words done, I stopped at the candy store earlier and grabbed a bunch of different rewards. As much as I want her to experience it for herself, we didn't have time today. Perhaps the day after Christmas.

Before she leaves.

Nope, not thinking about that now. I've still got her for the next forty-eight hours give or take. I'm going to soak them up. Every minute.

"Do you need help with anything for dinner?"

Heidi shakes her head. "It just needs to be cooked. Lenny can put it in the oven now. It takes about an hour to cook and rest."

"Great, then Willa and I are going to drop one car off at the cabin and be back in time for dinner."

Heidi raises a brow. "'Drop off a car?' That's what you're going with, bro?"

"Because that's what we're doing. Besides, an hour isn't enough time for what I have planned for Willa."

Okay, maybe I went too far with that comment.

Willa's cheeks flush the color of my Santa suit. "Beckett!" she hisses, slapping her arm across my chest.

"I can't lie to my sister. She knows all my secrets."

"Not those," Heidi protests loudly. "I'm not thinking about that." She shudders. Serves her right. "Be back before five. And bring a bottle of wine. Something red that goes with beef. You know best."

"Got it. We'll be back." I fit my fingers into Willa's hand, her mood a little more disillusioned than when I first walked in. Once outside, she zips up the hoodie, pulling it closer around her in the colder air. "Sorry. Didn't mean to put you on the spot and make you feel uncomfortable."

"Yes, you did," she challenges. "But I get it. An hour's not long enough for dirty Santa's appearance." The little minx sashays to the SUV, her hip sway exaggerated. "I'll follow you to the cabin."

As much as I'm enjoying her company, the aftermath of when she leaves won't be pretty.

"Guess what?" Willa asks the minute we breach the threshold of the cabin's back door.

"What?"

"I wrote almost one thousand words today." Pride oozes off her. And the woman should be proud. Damn proud.

"That's huge." I can't help but take a small amount of pride knowing it has something to do with me.

"I know. And I have unlocked more ideas than I've had in the past two years. I almost can't wait to get back to it. But I'm not. I'm taking the holiday to enjoy." Her eyes roam up and down me. "And you. I'm taking you to enjoy while I have you, too. The words can wait. I'll be home soon enough."

I can't read her opinion of her statements. Except the part about her being proud of her accomplishment. As for the rest of it, I'm lost. I have my feelings on the matter, but I can't put them on her. Not even a little.

If today and tomorrow are all we have left, we'll make the best of them. We won't let the future taint them.

"Awesome." I remember the candy I bought her, which I left in the truck. "I have another surprise for you."

She eyes me warily. "Another one? I'm not surprised out by you today?" She's still wearing the Santa hat and she looks adorable. Almost enough to say fuck it to joining my sister for dinner . . .

No. We'll get our fill tonight, after dinner. We can do both.

I race out to the truck, grabbing the bag of candy. Back inside,

I hold it behind my back, drawing out the suspense. "What's 'almost one thousand words' worth in terms of a reward?"

"On a good day, two pieces of chocolate. Today? After not writing for two years? I'd say any and all rewards are appropriate."

Her words cause emotion to swell my chest, a wish of not having to let her go.

What's gotten into me lately? Why can't I accept this for what it is? A casual hookup between two people who just met. I don't want to call her a stranger because getting to know her the past several days, I've uncovered more than my share of information about her. More than a stranger would know. But that doesn't change the fact this isn't anything more than casual. Less than that. A fling.

"Beckett?"

Willa's voice brings me out from a path not leading anywhere good. I hand over the bag. "Hopefully we can hit the candy store before you leave, to stock up on your favorites. For now, these will do."

She squeals as she peeks inside, her pupils widening at what she finds. Instead of reaching in, she dumps the contents on the table, inspecting each piece of wrapped goodness. Her tongue sneaks out of her mouth, licking the corner. It's enough to make me crazy with lust, an emotion I can't act on.

"This is quite the haul." Maple candies, chocolate truffles, honey-filled candies, among others I grabbed not knowing her favorites. "This one is calling my name. I won't ruin supper if I have just one, right?" She holds up one of my favorites—dark chocolate with a hazelnut in the center—and looks at me with a pleading expression I can't say no to. As if it's my place to tell her what she can and can't eat and when.

"One will not ruin your appetite."

She claps, her excitement tangible.

To distract myself, I go to the pantry for a bottle of red to share with Willa and Lenny. I choose a Merlot which pairs nicely with beef Wellington. As soon as she mentioned what she was serving, I hoped Willa agreed. It's been a while since I've had it.

For as many traditions as our family has, Christmas Eve dinner is one we've lost over the years. Giving it some thought, it was soon after Nana died, that first Christmas Eve. Though she died in the summer, we couldn't decide how to celebrate if she wasn't in charge. Or maybe it's because Mom does a huge dinner on December twenty-third, a Christmas Day brunch, and wants a meal off. Perhaps this one will stick, though with a baby on the way, next year will look different.

And Willa won't be here.

Nope, not thinking so negatively on a day reserved for celebration.

"Oh, I was hoping I'd get to try that one," Willa states when I emerge from the pantry, bottle in hand.

"One of my local favorites." The chemistry in the air changed, the atoms fizzle around us. I blame myself and quickly reprimand myself to do better. "How was the chocolate?"

Willa's eyes close, a smile eclipses her mouth. She sways on her feet, lost in her own world. When her eyes pop open, she divulges, "Oh my god, so delish. Creamy, not too bittersweet, even for dark chocolate. That seems like an oxymoron, but it's not."

"Agreed. Not sure how they make it not so bitter. Maybe the hazelnut?"

She shrugs. "Your guess is better than mine. I'm good at eating. You're the master chef."

I don't know if I'm supposed to take that as literally as I do.

"We should go back to the B and B. The sooner we eat, the sooner we can get back to more pressing matters. How sore are you?"

She shuffles from foot to foot, assessing something, I guess. "The kind of sore I've never been. Not sure how long it will last."

I can't help the pride exuding from me at her comment. *The kind of sore I've never been.* I shouldn't take such enjoyment from that, but hell if I can stop it.

Moving one foot closer, I snake my arms around her waist, pulling her into me. "Too sore for more later?"

She peers up, her eyes clouded with a vacant look. "No. We don't have much longer, and I won't waste the time we have. I can rest back at home."

Reminded of how transient we truly are, the familiar ache in my chest reappears. I hate how it's becoming a thing every time I recall she's not here to stay, she's only mine temporarily. All I can muster is a fake smile.

"Later it is." I swipe a kiss against her lips and let her out of my embrace. It's too soon, but if I don't let go now, I'm certain I may never. "Get ready for dinner."

Melancholy washes her expression, her smile sad. "Will do, Santa." With a half-hearted giggle, she escapes the kitchen, leaving more in her wake than a dead Christmas tree in January.

27
willa

WHEN I FIRST PLANNED MY trip, had someone told me the plans would go awry and I'd be celebrating Christmas Eve dinner—and enjoying myself—I would have laughed in their face. Yet, here I am, surrounded by people who were strangers a week ago, having the time of my life. Like old friends, Heidi and Lenny have fit me into their fold, sharing stories of growing up in Winterberry and showing me what Christmas can be. Even if I had the inkling to write about the holiday in my books, it wouldn't have been like this. I didn't know it could be this good.

Growing up, we barely celebrated Christmas Eve. Mom would attempt some kind of beef dish—you never knew what it would be or taste like—and after dinner, we'd maybe watch a Christmas movie, while Mom and Dad would pass out from their wine. Clem and I would often stay up late into the night, wishing and hoping for whatever gift was the "it" gift that year, only to be disappointed when there were so few presents under the tree, the one gift we wanted always absent.

Things changed when Elias came into the picture, but even then, he didn't have any family left, so he joined ours. When my nephews were born, Clem wanted a different celebration for them. Until last year, I'd say it contrasted ours growing up, but it's still unlike anything I've witnessed with the Nicholas family.

So, yeah. I haven't always hated Christmas, but I never dared to imagine celebrations like this. Now that I have, Gibson holidays will be even more lackluster.

The beef Wellington practically melts in my mouth, an explosion of the perfectly paired flavors popping on my tongue. I'd say it's delicious, but that wouldn't do it justice. I don't have the words to describe the awesomeness of the dish, though I bet Beckett could. When it's something he's passionate about, the words ooze from him. In his raspy tone, I could listen for hours and get high on the sound.

Throughout dinner, my eyes drift to him, watching him interact with his sister and brother-in-law, invested in their conversation, obsessed with the way he devours the food on his plate, offering compliments to the chef repeatedly. Genuine praise. As much as my sister and I are close, there's a dynamic between Becket and Heidi on another level. Perhaps it's the opposite genders, but their closeness is something to strive for.

Dessert is a pecan bourbon cake, another thing lacking from my life. It's moist and nutty, and though I shouldn't, I consume two slices. Culinary expertise runs rampant in the Nicholas family.

For Beckett's part, his hand is always touching me. My back, my thigh, our fingers entwined.

The man is everything I never thought to ask for, anticipating my needs without me voicing them, often before they register as thoughts. I'm pushing away every notion of saying goodbye to him, living in the present, soaking up these last two days I get to call him mine.

He's not mine in any sense of the word. Once I leave here, we'll be a blip on each other's radars, someone we used to know when.

I'm saved from my emotional turmoil by Beckett's voice. "Should we call it a night, Bundy?"

Damn him and his nickname.

Damn him for sharing it with his family.

Damn him for being a man I could love, a man I could see spending forever with.

"Yep." I push the word out of my mouth, afraid to say more for fear I'll let him in on my thoughts. Addressing Heidi, I start, "Thank you for this mouthwatering meal. Between Beckett and the rest of your family, I'm screwed for when I'm back home eating ramen noodles and takeout for every meal." I don't mean for the comment to sound so dire, but Heidi's mood shifts.

"If Mom hears that, she'll send you home with a dozen meals." I can't decipher the underlying tone. Is she suggesting I do that? Or is it merely a statement she's making?

A giggle wiggles free, but I don't know how to respond. Thankfully, Beckett's got me.

"I won't send her home empty-handed," he assures, his hand splayed across the small of my back. There's a wistfulness present, his voice more guttural than normal, emotions weighing heavy. When he leans down and leaves a kiss on the top of my head, it's all I can do to stay upright and not fall into him.

I have to shake these emotions off. How will I handle brunch with his family if I'm on the verge of a breakdown? And for once, it has nothing to do with the Christmas holiday.

Hugs are shared, tears are shoved down, and we're back in the car, heading to his cabin. It doesn't escape my notice he turns the opposite way out of the driveway.

"You were quiet tonight," he muses.

"You should drive down Main Street." The words tumble out of my mouth, no regard for what I'm saying. Beckett disguises his gasp as a cough.

"Will it be a repeat of last time?" A hint of humor hides in his words.

"No."

My idea is a gamble. Much as I want to see the lights, a residual fear resides inside. I'm not sure I'll be able to conceal it from Beckett if it's overwhelming. But I want to try, and who better than him?

"You're sure?"

"Yes," I confirm with conviction. I can do this. Perhaps white-knuckling it the whole way, squeezing my eyes if it gets too overwhelming, but I can do this.

Content with my decision, he drives down a street we've yet to explore, somehow circling back to Main Street. He slips his hand in mine, laying both on his thigh. "It's easy enough to turn around. We don't have to do the entire street. You'll let me know if it's too much?"

"How are you single?" The question arises, and I can't keep it inside. But seriously. Here's this man who has been nothing but kind to me, taking care of me from the moment we met, going above and beyond the role of a friend, let alone a stranger.

He blows out a breath, and I wonder if he's going to respond to my—mostly—rhetorical question.

"I have high standards. I like things certain ways. I haven't found anyone compatible." Honesty pours from him, but there's a tinge of sadness, too. He's going to make the best husband one day. For the right woman, she's going to be his world.

Too bad it's not you, my brain reminds.

After Elias died, I would have said I don't deserve a guy like Beckett. Because I had Elias, so why should I have two loves? However, spending the last several days with him, I wish that weren't true. I wish I was deserving of Beckett Nicholas. Even if it won't ever work, between the distance and every other complication, I'd like the chance to see how good it could be.

"Gotcha." There's so much I want to say, but I keep it simple, not wanting to get into more tonight. Not when we only have a limited time.

He'll find his woman. He's too great of a catch not to.

We reach the beginning of Main Street, and Beckett idles at the stop sign. "Last chance to back out."

"Don't tempt me," I joke. Inside, nerves threaten, but I tamp them down. "I can do this." The words are whispered with little conviction behind them, but I'm here. I'm not going to let Beckett or myself down. I scrunch my eyes shut, count to five, and let go of the breath I'm holding. "Do it." He's still holding my hand, his fingers gripping tighter.

"I'm proud of you. I'm here."

No doubt in my mind, if I backed out, he wouldn't give me a hard time. He'd continue on the way to the cabin, dropping the subject and letting me have the space and time I needed to conquer the fear.

Even in my mind, it's stupid to consider this a "fear." Because there are so many more scary things in the world than Christmas lights. I suppose that's why my therapist calls it an irrational fear. It's not the lights I'm scared of, but what they represent.

The loss, the joy, the what should have been.

If I don't do this now, I never will. I'll never have the nonjudgemental support of anyone like Beckett at another time.

"Okay." I nod, signaling I'm ready.

He turns right, the lights blinding ahead. At a crawl, he drives down the street, allowing me to take in the multi-colored lights on the different buildings. Every building is decked out in a plethora of colored lights, some blinking, others static. They're bright because they have to be. To showcase the beauty of the colors, the luminescence of the hues.

As Beckett drives along the road, my eyes scan both sides of the street, absorbing it all. Awe doesn't do it justice. It's beautiful, the lights strung in a way to highlight the patterns and also the building itself. I can't believe I would have missed this had I continued not to confront my demons.

"It's stunning, breathtaking," I marvel, my sight not able to concentrate on one area for too long. I want to soak it all up, catalog every bulb, every design, to commit it to memory.

"Not so blinding anymore?" He chuckles, repeating my words from last week.

"Oh, it's still blinding, but in the best way. Not sure how I'll be able to see anything once we leave here." The car accelerates, but I demand, "Go slower." I glance in the side mirror, making sure we aren't holding anyone up.

I can't decide which building is my favorite. Beckett's a good sport and turns around at the end of the strip and travels back the other way, my oohs and aahs spurring him on.

"When do they shut them down for the night?"

"Midnight."

"And when do they take them down for the season? Must be a sad day."

"January second, the most dreaded day on Winterberry's calendar." Again with the chuckle, this one deeper than the last, the timbre becoming familiar and comforting.

"I can see why. This display is brilliant. Is it the same every year?" Questions flood my brain, like when I'm researching a topic for a book and need to know every detail before I can write.

"It's similar, but the visual changes. Some buildings get different colors. Some years, there are more white lights than colored ones, more of a theme. Depends on who's in charge."

I tear my eyes away from the magnificence and stare him down. "What kind of person gets to be in charge?"

A twinkle fills his right eye. "There's an election in July. Anyone can submit a proposal, and then the town committee selects a top five and the citizens vote. It's highly competitive, as you can probably imagine."

I let the information soak in, my brain working on follow-up queries. But first. "You ever win?" He waves his arm in front of him, and the gasp jumps from my throat. "This was yours?" I squeak, barely able to speak over my excitement. My gaze volleys between the decorations and Beckett, the magnitude of what he's telling me staggering. "Beckett. This is amazing. How long have you been planning it?"

A flash of red crosses his cheeks, illuminated by the outdoor lights. "Too long to admit."

I go to force him to answer, but I think better of it and shut my mouth. "Fair." I wonder, "Is this your first victory?"

"Yes. Town rules. You're only allowed one win. You can submit every year, but once you're deemed the winner, you're done. For life." He punctuates the last word, like it's a life sentence in a penitentiary instead of not being allowed to enter a holiday lights contest. His smile and enthusiasm haven't dimmed, triumph wafting off.

"That's so cool. I love how it's fair for everyone." I look out the windshield, taking in the display with a fresh perspective.

The way the lights around the candy shop blink in a pattern, almost as if they're dancing to an inaudible tune.

Oversized plastic candy canes attached to each streetlamp.

The strands of lights strung from one side of the street to the other.

It's breathtaking and simply fascinating, a spectacle to admire. Knowing the man behind the design elevates my already heightened emotions.

"I think it's later," I whisper, and I've never seen Beckett react so quickly.

28
beckett

THE LAST TWENTY-FOUR hours have flown by in a whirlwind.

Sex with Willa last night differed from all the other times. A slower pace, less frantic, more . . . lovemaking. I won't admit that to anyone else, but yeah. Last night was not two people having casual sex. It wasn't one-sided, either. She felt it, too.

In the way her eyes shone with affection, the kaleidoscope of colors breaking through.

In the way her expression was softer, yet full of intensity.

In the way she clung to me. Not in desperation but comfort. Familiar. Loving.

If I have my way, it won't be the last time we come together, but there was definitely a "goodbye" vibe.

This morning, we went to Mom and Dad's for brunch. I couldn't help but observe how she seamlessly fit in, what a great addition she'd make to our family, especially when Mom surprised her with a gift. Willa accepted it graciously, not letting the fact she had nothing in return make her feel guilty.

These thoughts have to stop.

She's not currently mine, nor will she ever be. We're too

different. She's not from here. The holiday break isn't "real life" but a fantasy.

Temporary.

The weather was warm enough for a stroll down Main Street at dusk when the lights come on. If I thought she came alive last night during our drive, it was nothing compared to her reaction to seeing them up close, walking among the brilliance. An air of wistfulness wafted off her, and she shed a few tears in Elias's memory, but she wasn't upset. Her hatred of all things Christmas seems to have dissipated with her breakthrough in coming to terms with her feelings. I'm not sad about it at all, and my ego is plenty full of itself about being the one to change her tune.

As if I should take full credit for it. In no way is it all because of me, but I like to think I had a large part to do with it.

We ate leftover chili as an early dinner and dessert will be later.

Now, we're cozied up on the couch, a movie playing in the background, the only lights those of the tree. Willa was the one who plugged them in and doused the room with light, smiling as she did it. She's tucked into my side, our legs tangled under the blanket, neither one of us taking it further than cuddling. Not that I don't want to, but this is also nice. Something I didn't think I'd enjoy as much as I do with her.

A phone rings faintly from the other room, and Willa groans. "It's Clem. I can't not talk to her." She skirts out of my hold, leaving a cool breeze in her wake. When I think she's going to take the call in my bedroom, she reappears, her phone held out in front of her, snuggling back into position. "Merry Christmas, Atlas. Did Santa bring you everything on your list?"

I peek to see the boy, his expression jubilant as one should be on Christmas.

"Yep. I got a new Creator Lego set, an A-Z mysteries box set, and a new bike." He must be a reader like his aunt. Bet she loves how he's into mysteries, too. Wonder if he knows what she does.

"Awesome. And what about Jace?"

"He got some blocks, a new puzzle, and a tablet to play on."
He seems less enthused about his brother's gifts.

"That's amazing," Willa coos, her excitement palpable. I try
to remove myself from under her to give her space, but she's not
having it. "Stay," she murmurs, her eyes never leaving the
screen.

So I do and listen as she chats with her nephews and her
sister, getting my first look at Clem, noting the contradictions
between them.

Clem's fiery red hair is pin straight to Willa's wild locks. Her
eyes are a sparkling emerald green. She has more of an oval face,
her lips less plump and more heart-shaped.

"Are you finally letting her leave tomorrow?"

Clem's question catches me off guard, and I'm sure it shows
on my face. "Uh, as soon as I can get her car fixed, she'll be on
her way. She's itching to leave." I try for joviality, but the
cadence falls flat.

Clem laughs, but it's short-lived, and a serious expression
coats her face. "Thanks for taking care of her, for giving her back
her spark. Even over the phone and FaceTime, the differences are
obvious."

"It's been my pleasure."

Which isn't a lie. It has been a pleasure getting to know Willa
this past week, but it's so much more than that, too. Things I'm
not prepared to deal with now. Maybe even later, after she's
gone. After her scent vanishes, fading without a trace.

"I'm excited to sleep in flannel sheets," Willa declares, a
yawn stretching her lips and gives me her attention. "How about
coffee with dessert?"

"Regular or decaf?"

"Depends on how long you plan to keep me awake tonight."

"On that note, I'll say good night. Enjoy your last night in
Winterberry. Call me when you're on the road if you want
company. Love you. Merry Christmas, Beckett."

"Merry Christmas, Clem. Thanks for sharing your sister with me for the holiday."

"As if I had a choice. I'm glad she celebrated the holiday. Her plans sounded so bleak—"

"And good night, Clementine. Merry Christmas to you and the boys. Call you tomorrow. Love you." Willa's finger taps the red button a ridiculous number of times.

"So, that's Clem."

"That's Clem." She sinks against the cushions, trying to become one with the couch. "How about dessert and spiked coffee? Maybe start the movie over again or choose a different one. I'm lost."

"Spiked with what?"

"Whatever's in your liquor cabinet. Today, I'm not feeling too picky, just a little . . ."

I wait for her to finish the sentence. When she doesn't, I prod, "A little . . ."

"Edgy? Unsettled? Restless. Yep, that's it. Restless. You should build a fire. A fire, dessert, spiked coffee, and a movie. Perfect way to end the best Christmas I can remember."

Her words elicit contradictory feelings, things I'm not prepared to tackle tonight.

And don't get me started on the way she peers at me, challenging me to disagree with any of her suggestions.

As if I could.

This girl's got my balls in a chokehold. I never thought I'd be the pussy-whipped guy. Sure, I'll go out of my way to help strangers, but my behavior for the last several days is uncharacteristic. Uncharted territory. A conundrum.

"Do you work early in the morning?"

Her question is out of the blue, but maybe that's because I'm too focused on trying to rationalize my actions toward Willa.

"Most years I'm there by eight because our Christmas celebration is never late, so no use wasting the day. The piece to your car should be delivered by nine. Figured I could get a jump on fixing it to get you on the road before daylight ends."

"I'm not looking forward to driving for several hours," she complains.

Stay.

I bite my tongue to keep the word from spilling out.

The idea is ridiculous, for all the reasons I've convinced myself of, the biggest one being we hardly know each other. Except, as my mind likes to argue, Willa's gotten a side of me I've shown no one else. For that reason alone, it would be worth her staying, seeing if this instant chemistry between us had staying power or would fizzle at the first sign of incongruence.

It's not like she has a job she has to get back to. She can write from anywhere, including my kitchen table. Hell, I'll build her an office of her own. I'll give her two if she wants.

Ludicrous. I've gone mad. Willa's officially pushed me to the brink of insanity.

"Beckett?"

I snap out of the trance I'm in. "Hmm?"

"What's wrong? Your body's here, but your mind's elsewhere. I recognize the vacancy in your eyes." She shifts on the couch, planting her feet on the ground, her expression one of concern.

"I'm fine. It's nothing. Coffee?"

She thwarts my attempt to stand. "Some things aren't meant to be. Much as we want them to work out, it's often better not to force it, you know?"

"No." I shake my head, not believing I voiced the word. Her shoulders slump, the repercussion of my action clear. "Shit. I mean, yeah. I get it."

Are we even talking about the same thing? How did she decipher my innermost thoughts? Or is she feeling something similar?

No, Beckett. Do not go there.

My head's a tangled mess. I should go out to the workshop

and hit something. My punching bag or the car I'm restoring. Pounding out the dents should set me straight.

Even as I think the words, I won't do it. She leaves tomorrow. I can feign I'm fine, pretend I'm not jumbled chaos for twenty-four more hours, and then once she's a memory, I'll get back to my real life, and I'll laugh about what a pussy I'm being.

For now, I'll make her spiked coffee, build her a fire, and curl up on the couch with a woman I wasn't ever supposed to meet, but one who unlocked the key to my heart.

Wonder what'll happen when she takes it with her tomorrow.

"You're up early." Willa stumbles into the kitchen around six, her hair falling out of the messy bun, her glasses askew on her face hiding tired eyes, and her fingers toying with her ear.

"The bed was too cold. How long have you been up?"

"Too long."

All night, I don't say aloud. Perhaps there was one hour I drifted to sleep, but other than that, I didn't catch a wink. My mind wouldn't quit.

Other than Nana, all the other grandparents died when I was too little to remember them. The only person I've said a permanent goodbye to was my grandmother. As much as I loved her, I knew she wouldn't be around forever.

It's different with Willa. I can't explain it, can't find the right words to express what her leaving means, how much I'll be devastated.

"I think I'll take one last soak in your tub before I pack up." She wraps her arms around her middle, leaving so much unsaid.

Or maybe there's no more. I'm so in my head, I'm assuming she's feeling the same as me, but I could be completely off base and out of touch. Maybe I'm hoping she feels the same way so I'm not the only schmuck reeling from our interaction.

"Good plan. I'll be out of your hair in an hour or so. I'm

going to work out and then head to the shop. I've got this one client who needs her car today, and she's not letting me forget it." I try for levity, and by Willa's small, shy smile, I've somewhat achieved it.

"Yep, gotta be on my way home . . ." she trails off, a melancholy lilt front and center. Maybe I'm not wrong about how she feels.

"Coffee will be ready in ten minutes, pancakes are warming in the oven, fruit's in the fridge. I take it you're capable of washing and cutting it up?"

"You know it." Another simper, smaller than the last. "Do you have time to eat with me or is that pushing your timeframe? Or we could do lunch before I leave. But you probably don't have time for that either since you mentioned you'll be busy today. Never mind. Forget I said anything. Don't mind me. I'm a bit inundated this morning. Words, the holiday, going home, leaving." Her voice wavers, and moisture pools in her eyes.

Despite what I told myself this morning—don't drag out the goodbye, let her leave with clean ties—I'm around the island, yanking her flush against me, my hand on the back of her head. My heart rattles, but it doesn't stop me from pushing her head against my chest, needing her to hear and feel the way the organ thunders.

I'm such a selfish bastard, needing her to know what I'm feeling when I should be offering her the comfort I'm stealing from her.

For however long, we stand in my kitchen, Willa crying silently against my chest, me trying to hold on to every shard of willpower I possess to not lose it. To not let even one tear fall.

I'm a man, damn it. Grown men don't cry. Grown men don't give their hearts away so easily, especially not to women they barely know.

Like a parent narrowly avoiding getting caught by their kids on Christmas morning, I pull away, schooling my features to not let her see how affected I am. Her forlorn expression about does me in, but I stay strong, battling forces I didn't know I had the strength to face, erecting concrete walls around my heart to hold back the emotions from springing free.

"I'll drive your car back here, we'll pack it up, and we'll do lunch on your way out of town. I'll text you later when I have a better estimate on timing."

For one of the last times, I lean in and kiss the top of Willa's head. Much as I want to, I don't linger, escaping to the garage.

Is this what it feels like to have a broken heart? No wonder I've avoided them until now.

29
willa

THE DOOR SLAMS BEHIND BECKETT, and the tears tracking down my cheeks come faster.

This shouldn't be difficult. Saying goodbye to a man I've spent less than a week with. Elias and I were together over three years, and while I've grieved him and his death for a while, this somehow hurts more. I didn't know an already broken—but healing—heart could ache like this. I didn't know I could hurt like this. But god does it hurt.

I throw myself on the couch, surrounded by Beckett's scent, tears gushing from my eyes. I have to pull myself together, get over this and myself, and follow Beckett's lead. He's not all weepy and devastated by my leaving. Which makes me cry harder.

How can he not be affected by what we've shared? Is his heart made of steel?

As much as I shouldn't, I let myself wallow in agony for a solid fifteen minutes. When the timer I set goes off, I brush away the tears, pick myself off the couch, march into the kitchen, pour myself a cup of coffee, and plate a few pancakes for breakfast. I don't bother with the fruit—who has the time to wash and cut it —and eat breakfast in silence. AJ is screaming inside my head, demanding me to get her story told, but I'm ignoring her. I'm ignoring everything, my focus solely on drinking the coffee and eating the pancakes.

Once breakfast is done, I go into Beckett's bedroom and block out everything but my next task: pack up my belongings.

One by one, I toss everything into my suitcase, holding my resolve and stoicism, not letting it crack.

"You're strong. You're a warrior. You've got this," I repeat as a mantra over and over. Until it's Elias's voice in my ear.

"You can walk away. Pick yourself up and start again. You've done this before. You're stronger now. You're a warrior."

I don't allow the tears to fall, but I hug myself tightly, imagining they're the arms of a strong male.

Problem is, I'm not sure whose arms they are.

True to his word, Beckett's gone a little after seven. He whisked in, changed his clothes, and blew back out the door, the sound of the truck's engine louder than ever.

A final nail in the coffin.

Dramatic Willa is out in full force today. To get rid of her, I drown her in a bath. Over forty-five minutes I soak, my mind listing everything I have to do once I'm home.

Grocery store.

Write chapters.

Email my editor.

Unpack.

Miss Beckett.

"No." I shout the word in the empty bathroom, emphasizing it, erasing it from the list.

I try again.

Plan a book launch.

Meet with PA about new graphics and merch.

Research the workings of middle schools.

Miss Beckett.

"STOP IT WILLA! Get a grip."

I drain the water but not ready to face reality, I stand under the showerhead, my tears mixing with the falling water. When the water runs cold, I shut it off, sheathing myself with Beckett's fluffiest towel. It's clean from the closet, but hell if it doesn't smell like him.

I'm not helping the situation but perpetuating it.

Snapping out of it, I dry off, walking to his bedroom. There's a text from him on my phone.

> I'll be back around twelve. Car will be ready.
> Have everything packed.

I read the words too many times, the finality in them settling like a rock.

I press on, getting dressed in the laundered lingerie he bought me because apparently, I'm a sadist now, set to torture myself at every turn. I'll think of him every time I wear them, which defeats the purpose of letting him go. But it's not like I'm good at letting things go . . .

Dressed and all packed, the clock shows I have fifteen minutes until noon. I sneak on social media but am too overwhelmed by the notifications of not checking it for a few days. Instead, I rummage through Beckett's pantry, stealing a few snacks for my road trip, laughing at the package of hot cocoa Oreos still hiding. I'm half-tempted to move it, so he doesn't get frustrated with me, but in the end, I leave it where it is. I'll never know the repercussions of my actions. I don't let the intensity of that filter in.

The back door opens as I'm sliding the snacks into my backpack.

"Willafred, your chariot awaits."

Ugh. His use of my full name doesn't help lessen any of the emotions swirling through me. He seems more upbeat now, less trodden like when he scurried away earlier.

"It's all fixed?" The tiny bubble of hope forming that he wouldn't be able to fix it bursts.

"The bumper is like brand-spanking new. My finest work, if I say so myself. And I picked out the perfect place for a farewell lunch. You're going to love it."

My heart skips because of his kindness, the glee lighting him up, but also because of the way he's not bothered by me leaving. Like we didn't just share the most intense week ever, as if I'm truly a stranger.

I turn away, not wanting him to see the threatening tears in my eyes. It's stupid to be so emotional, so attached to him, so fearful of leaving, but still, a panic attack tries to claw into me.

Burly arms assail me from behind. Like a lifeline, I grasp on tightly.

"We weren't supposed to meet. Revel in the time we got together, even if it was way too short. You've got stories to tell. I've got cars to fix. We'd be in each other's way. It's better like this."

Though the evidence is in his saddened tone, the question begs to be asked. "Is it?"

"I'm telling myself it is. It has to be enough."

"I get to say goodbye this time, but it's hard. It's difficult to form the words, to say what I need to before I get on the road back home. To tell you how appreciative I am for everything, Beckett. To express my gratitude for what you gave me back this week. I'm a writer, I should have the words, but I'm not sure the right words exist to convey what I feel in my heart, what I owe you."

"You don't owe me a thing, Willa. You've given me more than I could have ever wanted, and that's enough."

I twist in his arms, adjusting to peer up at him. My eyes glisten with tears, an exact match to his. It could be my undoing if I let it.

I can't let it.

"It feels like it's been more than a week. Like I've known you for years. That's insane, right?"

I giggle, the watery sound the only noise in the room. "Guess that makes me insane, too."

"You're exquisite. I can't wait to find your newest masterpiece in the bookstores. I'll smile and think how proud I am of you, and then promptly forget I know you."

It's a horrible thing to say, but I laugh, knowing exactly what he means.

"Every time I see anything related to Christmas, I'll wonder what you're doing, and then pretend you don't exist."

"Perfect coping strategy."

"I'd like to think so." I won't be successful in the slightest, but with time, the pain will fade. I learned that with Elias. It won't ever go away, but it won't be a raw hurt forever.

"We should go. You have a drive ahead of you."

"But first lunch."

"And a coffee for the road." He brushes his arm across his eyes, erasing the emotion. "Are you all packed?"

I nod. "Are we driving one car or two?"

"I chose a place on your way out of town, so I'll take mine so you don't have to backtrack."

More of the elation deflates, knowing our time is limited.

"Okay. Help me load my car?"

"If I must." His tone is playful, contrasting his words. "Lead the way."

We each compose ourselves, a silent agreement on how the other feels.

Outside, my car looks great, with not even a hint of a dent. Beckett loads up my bags and instructs me to follow him. With nothing else left to do, I have no choice.

Twenty minutes later, he pulls into the lot of a small tavern just outside the Winterberry Junction town limits.

It's straight out of a fairy tale with a brick exterior, a large chimney on the front wall, a red door, and complete with a thatch roof. Strings of white lights line the exterior. It's fitting for what I've learned about Winterberry.

"Are you ready to have your taste buds wowed?"

"They've been pretty impressed lately. You sure this place has what it takes?"

Beckett wraps his arm around my shoulder. One more thing I'm going to miss about this guy—the way he's always unabashedly touching me. "Have I not proven my trustworthiness?"

"Repeatedly. It amazes me how many times you've proved it. So maybe this is the time I'm let down."

"Never, Bundy."

Add his nickname for me to the list of things I'll miss. I've lost count of how many items are on the mental file. It's probably for the best.

"Let's hope you're not wrong."

Once inside, he leads me to a booth, following the "Seat Yourself" sign. A waitress comes over to take our drink order, openly flirting with Beckett. He does his best to ignore it. Whether it's for my sake or he doesn't want to encourage her, I don't question it.

A glance at the menu, and I choose a burger, asking Beckett to order fish and chips so we can share. After ordering, he grabs my hand, interlacing our fingers.

"So, a three-hour drive home?"

"Give or take, barring any stops for gas or to pee. I already checked the weather for the entire route, and it's clear skies. No storms to contend with."

"No more rescues for you."

"That's the plan." We share a smile. His is pained, and mine most likely mirrors it. It shouldn't be this difficult to part ways.

Try telling that to my heart.

"Will you write today?"

My head shakes, the action more dramatic than it needs to be. "I'll get everything unpacked and ready to start bright and early tomorrow. I'll order groceries to be delivered so I have food. But, I'm excited about the ideas for scenes and chapters. All thanks to you."

It was always my plan to get back to writing this week, no matter what. Having Beckett's help breaking the writer's block was much better than my original idea. If left to my own devices, even with nothing but my laptop, Wi-Fi, and phone at the cabin, I would have found excuses. Not only did he give me my writing mojo back, he did it without bribery and me making excuses.

Perhaps there was a little bribery . . .

"You're welcome."

The waitress drops off our plates, winking at Beckett. So rude when I'm sitting right here. She doesn't know this is our last meal and whatever started between us is over.

"Don't be surprised when she leaves her number on the receipt," I joke.

"Hasn't worked the first five times. Odds aren't in her favor." He pours ketchup on the burger and fries.

I don't stifle the chuckle. "Good for her for going after what she wants even if you're clearly not interested."

As we consume the meal, there's more idle chitchat, his plans for the rest of the week, our New Year's plans, stuff we haven't yet talked about. About halfway through, Shania and Autumn stroll through the door, Shania's eyes lighting up when she spots us.

"Willa. You didn't leave yet. I was so sad I didn't get to see you at Christmas brunch, but my mom made me go to my other grandparents' house." Her nose scrunches in disgust, making her opinion known.

"I'm on the road as soon as lunch is over, but I have something for you in my car. Are you guys eating here or taking it to go?"

"We usually take it to go, but I bet Mom will let us stay. If that's okay with you." She looks between us, giving Beckett pouty lips, which he most definitely can't say no to.

He waves at the empty spots next to us, making room for his sister on his side when Shania slides next to me.

"Wait. Let me grab your gift from the car to open while you wait for your food."

"She got enough gifts at Christmas, the girl doesn't need anything else."

"Way to make a girl feel good about giving your kid a gift, sis," Beckett chides. Autumn's cheeks flush pink.

I'm too excited to share my secret that I don't let it bother me. "Be right back." To Beckett, with a pointed finger, I say, "Do not eat the rest of the zucchini fries." I rush outside, grab the gift for Shania, and return, handing it over. "It's all I had with me."

"Willa, this is so kind of you. At the risk of more derision from my brother, you did not have to get her a gift. Not because she doesn't need anything else, but because you don't owe her anything."

I shrug. "Ah, I kinda do."

Shania digs into the wrapping paper I stole from Beckett's stash. I chose the one most fitting for the teen from his collection. "Collection" is the only way to describe how many rolls of paper he had in the basement. She squeals when she rips the first gift open, a hardcover copy of *The Puzzle Problem*, book one in the Hidden Clues series.

"Willa! You had this with you? This is amazing. I only have the paperbacks." Pure joy infiltrates her expression and her voice, confirming she deserves this gift.

The box of hardcovers has been in my car for over two years. I could never bring myself to take them out after Elias put them in.

"I love this edition, but want to know my favorite part?"

"Duh." Shania rolls her eyes at my ridiculous question.

I take it from her hands, flipping to the page where I signed it, personalized to her.

Shania does a double take at her name and the signature, the pieces not falling into place. "I don't understand. How does it have my name in it?"

I grab a napkin and a pen and sign my pen name. The moment it clicks, she jumps from the booth, her hands waving wildly, her mouth open but no sounds emerging.

It's Autumn who speaks first. "You're Evelyn Ravenhurst? *The* Evelyn Ravenhurst?" she shrieks. Thankfully, the few other patrons aren't paying us any attention, nor do I think AJ Hart books are their jam. "You've been here all this time, and we didn't even know? How did we not know? How are you here? Are you bullshitting us?"

I don't take offense to her surprise. "I wouldn't do such a thing. I promise you I'm Evelyn Ravenhurst."

Shania finds her voice. "Willa . . . whatever your last name is, you are freaking Evelyn Ravenhurst? I am meeting Evelyn Ravenhurst? Is this real life?"

"Yep."

"Pretty cool, huh?" Beckett exclaims.

When Autumn clues into what he's saying, she swats his arm. "You knew all this time and said nothing? You're no longer my favorite brother."

He holds up his hands. "Not my secret to tell. Heck, you're lucky Willa likes your kid enough to share it. She could have left here, and you'd never have been the wiser."

His voice stumbles on the word "left," and all the feelings I've tamped down try to reemerge.

"Can I hug you?" Shania asks, her voice watery with unshed emotion.

"Bring it in, girl." I open my arms wide but am not quite prepared for her onslaught.

She whispers in my ear so no one else can hear, "You're my favorite author. And I'm not saying that because you're here."

"I'd be okay if it were the reason, but I know you're not saying it because you know. That's why it was okay to tell you."

A tear drips from her eye as she pulls away. "I don't know why I'm crying. I've always wanted to meet her. You," she corrects with a snort. "I'm a bit overwhelmed."

"I get it. The first time I met an author I admire, I pretty much told her I wanted to have her babies." I can't believe the words came out of my mouth. Both then and now.

"Will you take a selfie with me? With the book? Can I tell my friends? Is that okay? I know you're not big about sharing pictures on social media, but I promise I won't send them the picture. I'll show it to them and that's all. They won't think it's as cool as I do because they don't read much."

"Tell whoever you want."

"Wait until Alanna gets wind you were here. She's going to go bananas she didn't get to meet you."

"Beckett has books to drop off at the book store. I'm sure glad I never took them out of my trunk after all this time." I point to Shania's other gifts. "Books two and three. I'll send the others when I get home. Anything else you might want?"

"A Hidden Clues bookshop hoodie like the one you were wearing. Oh, and some stickers or bookmarks. If it's not too much."

"For my biggest fan? Never." I bring her to my side, giving her another hug, her excitement bleeding into me.

The waitress interrupts our soiree, taking Autumn's and Shania's order while Beckett and I order dessert. Over the shared meal, Autumn and Shania ask me all kinds of questions, most of which I can answer. Some I can't because even I don't know the answers, but some I'm not at liberty to say.

When the food is gone, our stomachs full, and my bladder empty, as much as I don't want to leave, it's time to get on the road to guarantee I'm home before it's too dark.

"I should probably head out."

Beckett drops his card on the table. "Lunch is on me. Give us a few minutes." He doesn't wait for their response but drags me outside to the side of the building.

"I want to say goodbye to them."

"You will. Stupid or not, I can't let you leave without kissing you one last time."

The word "kiss" out of his mouth has me pushing up to tiptoes and bringing my lips to his. He reaches under my thighs, lifting me into the air.

Our tongues duel, a last dance, a last goodbye. Neither of us rush it nor hurry. As much as I want to take it further, hell, have it last forever, I don't. Beckett doesn't push it either, but too soon, he's lowering me back down to the ground, my lips swollen, my eyes wet.

"This is it."

"Yeah." He pushes a hand through his hair. "The only thing I regret is not having enough time, Willa."

"Same. This week was exactly the opposite of what I thought it would be, but exactly what I needed. Imagine that."

He trails his finger up the side of my chin. "I'm gonna miss you."

"Me too. So much." I want to tell him so much more, but I leave it all unsaid. "Back to reality." I want to tell him not to forget me, but that's selfish. Of course, he needs to forget me to move on, to find someone to spend his life with. Just as I need to do the same.

"There's a disposable cooler in your car with snacks and a few meals, a little parting gift from me and the town of Winterberry. So you don't forget us." His expression is vulnerable, like he's embarrassed about the gift when it's the sweetest ever.

"Like I ever could," I deadpan. "Nothing about this week is easily forgettable, especially you, Beckett."

"There you are." Autumn's voice crests the corner before she does. "Car looks good. Guess you were able to hammer out the dents after all, huh? Didn't even need the new part?"

Her comments don't sink in right away, but by the way Beckett's eyes close and he mutters something under his breath, I'm missing something. I rewind what she said, especially the part about "new."

Something clicks.

"You didn't need to wait for a part?" I accuse, my voice shaking. "I could have left before now? Like days ago?"

Beckett says nothing, but his expression gives away his answer. Guilt and shame encroach his handsome face, his eyes darting to the ground, not meeting mine.

The news hits me like a load of bricks.

On the one hand, I'm grateful for the time with him, for the breakthrough I had, for the closure I needed.

On the other, he lied to me.

That hurts. It hurts more than leaving did a few minutes ago.

I try again, hoping for his words this time, his explanation of why he did it. "Beckett?"

He blows out a breath, his vision going everywhere but on me. "In my defense, I didn't know if I could get it done at first."

"But when you realized?" I prod when he doesn't continue.

"I didn't want you to leave." His answer is so nonchalant, so matter-of-fact, so honest. There's not a trace of deceit in it. "Scratch that. I *couldn't* let you leave. Not then. Not without more." He finally meets my gaze, his full of remorse and sadness.

As much as I would have liked him to have been completely truthful, would it have mattered? Would I have left earlier? Depending on when, I can't say I would have.

"Why didn't you tell me? I would have understood."

He laughs humorlessly. "Tell you I was falling for you after knowing you for a few days? Scare you off? Make you think I was crazier than the serial killer you pegged me as from the start? That wouldn't have gone over well."

Everything after "falling for you" lands on deaf ears. "Because it's crazy, absurd, insane. And yet, I get it. Because I was feeling the same."

His eyebrow raises. "Was feeling?"

"Am," I amend. "Am falling for you. Fell for you." I throw my hands in the air. "I don't even know at this point. But I don't like how you lied," I rush out, needing him to know how I feel.

He steps closer, eliminating the distance between us. "I swear my intentions were only because I wanted to see what this was between us. They weren't to keep you here against your will."

"Weren't they though? I was prepared to leave, but you took the option away from me."

My emotions are all over the place. I want to be upset with him, but I'm not sure I can. Nor does it matter. Regardless of why he did it, I'm leaving today. Now.

"I have to go." I push the words from my mouth, but as I say them, they're not the truth. I don't *have* to go. What's waiting at home for me? Nothing that can't be accomplished here.

"I know. And this time, I won't keep you here. Not even for selfish reasons. Not even because I fell for you harder than when I told you I couldn't fix your car without a new part. Not even to see what could develop between us. Your life is there, mine is here. We'd never work, anyway."

"Right," I agree. "For all of those reasons, I need to go."

I don't consider telling him to ask me to stay. Because in the long run, I'll only get hurt again if what I think this is doesn't work out. I can't put myself in that spot. I can't expose my already battered heart to more heartache if either of us decides this won't work. Better to cut ties now. I can get over a week of knowing Beckett.

I can do it.

Rather than draw out the inevitable, I fall into his arms, stealing more comfort than I should. If there's one thing I can't do right now is be selfless.

"Thanks for a great week, Beckett Nicholas. My world is

forever changed by knowing you. I hope you find a woman who's going to live up to your incredibly high standards, and she makes you happier than you could ever imagine." I stop myself from saying: *I wish it were me.* As much as I wish it, it can't be.

He cups my chin in his hands. "It's been my pleasure, Willafred Gibson. My absolute pleasure. Go home, write all the books, and now and again, think of me, k?"

"Absolutely. Every time I watch a Hallmark movie, it's only you I'll think of."

He leans down, pressing his lips to the top of my head. I hold back the dam of tears knowing it's the last time he'll ever do it. I have to be strong.

I give him a final squeeze, understanding I have to be the one to walk away.

After quick hugs to Shania and Autumn, I scramble to my car, my heart fracturing after just being sewn up, leaving behind a piece that will always belong to Beckett Nicholas.

30
beckett

NEW YEAR'S DAY

Six days ago, Willa walked away, leaving me brokenhearted and alone.

She sent a brusque text message letting me know she had arrived home safely. Three words.

> Home. Thanks again

I wanted to do so much more than text back, **Thanks for letting me know. You're welcome,** but I didn't. I can't let myself be pulled under her spell any more than I already am. She made her choice, and we both have to live with it.

It's stupid to think she would have made a different choice. She didn't *have* a different choice to make. I didn't give her another option. To ask her to stay would have been asinine. She couldn't stay. I don't even know if she would have stayed. Or come back had she needed to go home and get some stuff and return.

Six days I've been miserable. I've tried to work her from my head—with physical labor at the shop and in the gym. No matter what I do, she won't leave. Her memory's here to stay for the foreseeable future, which makes it hard to move on.

Because that's exactly what I need to do—move on. Let her go. Banish her from my life. Pretend we never met.

I don't want the last one. Not even a little. As much as life sucks this week without her, not having met her would be worse. I loved the time we spent together, am glad I got to experience the week with her, help her get out of her funk. I wouldn't trade the time with her for any amount of money in the world.

As if that's an option.

"Uncle Beck! Are you even listening to me?" Shania's face fills my hazy vision.

"Ever hear of personal space?" She steps back, and I chug the last half of my beer. "What do you want?" The question is laced with frustration. It's not fair to take my bad mood out on her.

"Just wanted to show you my new sweatshirt. Jeez. Who set your Christmas tree on fire?"

Any other day, I'd commend her retort, but I'm not in the mood. Even more so when my eyes spy the image on her sweatshirt. The logo for Hidden Clues bookshop stares back at me. My stomach roils. I'd blame the beer, but it's heartache.

"I like it."

Shania beams, missing the indifference in my tone. "It's the best. Willa's the best. She sent all the books in the series, some stickers, Vellum pages, and cool fan art." I don't know what half those things are, but the way she's carrying on about them, I'm guessing they're good. Of course, Willa followed through with sending stuff.

"That's cool."

"The coolest. The kids in my English class are going to be so jealous I met Evelyn Ravenhurst. I can't wait to rub it in."

I go to correct her, but I don't have the energy. It's not Shania's nature to make other people jealous, so for this one time, I'll allow it. She deserves the best things in life, and this tops the list for her.

Wish I could say the same for myself.

Because I wasn't miserable enough, I read all the books. Twice. I wrote questions in the margins, wanting to know how she came up with some things. When it hit me I'd never be able to ask her the questions and get the answers, the stupid cycle of depression started again.

"Want to go to the bar?" my brother prods.

"Not particularly."

"Get a bite to eat at the diner?"

"No."

"Go for a drive?" he tries.

"We're not a couple."

"Hit the strip club?"

"Is it even open on the holiday?"

Dax takes my question as interest, looking up the info on his phone. "No. Rats. You need to get laid, my friend."

"Language, Dax," our mother chides. "Little ears."

"It's okay, Gram. Uncle Beck does need to get laid. Though with the way he hasn't shaved or taken a shower in however many days, no women will be lining up to do the deed." Seven pairs of eyes swing Shania's way. She holds up her hands and shrugs, like she's an adult and speaks this way every day. "Tell me I'm wrong."

Except no one does.

Fuckers. All of them.

"I do not need to get laid."

"Yeah, brother, you do. Willa did a number on you. You gotta fuck that girl out of your system."

Now it's Dad's turn to reprimand Dax. "This isn't appropriate language for Shania's ears. Nor for New Year's. Be respectful."

"Uh, sorry, Shania."

"No worse than what I watch on *Outer Banks*."

This conversation is going nowhere fast. Standing from the couch, I'm a little unsteady on my feet. I lost track of how much alcohol I consumed since I arrived. "I'm going to take off. Early morning at the shop tomorrow."

Dad stands up. "I'll drive you home. Come back for your truck tomorrow."

"Solid plan." I swipe the half-empty bottle of wine from the counter for later. I haven't tried drowning my sorrows in wine. Perhaps that's the solution.

ONE WEEK LATER

Drowning in alcohol isn't the solution. Unless my goal is alcohol poisoning, then I'm achieving it. But trying to banish Willafred Gibson from my head isn't being accomplished.

She's there when I wake up, when I'm working, when I'm cooking dinner, and as I drift off to sleep. The term "invading my waking hours" doesn't do how often I think about her justice. She's constantly on my mind. I don't know how to get her out of it.

Alcohol isn't working.

Going out to the bar to pick up a woman isn't working. Wouldn't you know the first woman I talked to was named AJ? Yeah, because that's not a sign or anything.

Getting myself off a few times a day is only making my hand chafed.

Nothing is helping. Not even a little.

I refuse to disturb her, though I'm now following all her social media pages.

Stalking. I'm stalking her. It's mostly stuff about her books, no personal life updates, but it's something. If memory serves, she might not even write the posts, but my wounded heart doesn't care. It needs a Willa fix and if this is the only way to get it, then so be it.

The decorations are down, and now Main Street looks pitiful. It happens every year when the lights disappear, but this year hits harder. Between watching them dismantle my design and sharing the holiday with Willa, they might have well cut off a limb with how much life sucks right now.

Did I mention I'm dramatic when I'm sad? This is why I don't do sad. I'm pathetic.

"Call her." That's Autumn's advice. "Stop being a miserable fuck. Grow a pair of balls, tell her you miss her, and go see her."

"Ha. Like it's that easy."

The comment earns me a harsh stare.

When she left, it was understood we were cutting ties. I won't be the one to break the unspoken vow.

"Then at least be a miserable fuck at your own house."

She earns a finger, but ten minutes later, I walk home. I hoped the frigid air might take away some of the miserableness, but alas, it does not.

There's no place in my cabin that doesn't hold a recollection of Willa, which makes it hard to be home, too. Work isn't tainted with her memory, and neither is the cabin's garage, so I spend a lot of my time in those two places. Even when I should sleep, I'm out in the garage, tinkering on the car. Restoring my granddad's Mustang is a passion project Dax and I have been working on for years. Whether it's tracking down the right parts or trying my hand at rebuilding the engine, it's consumed many hours of my life. Last night I thought it would be wise to sleep out there, hoping I could get rest. I'm not planning on that again. The cement floor is way too unforgiving on my back.

"Have you showered today?" Heidi wonders, stirring something on the stove. She's got her hand on her stomach like I've seen pregnant women with a belly do. It's weird because she's not showing at all.

"Does last night count?"

She studies me, looking for a clue or something. "If it's true."

I flip through the last few days. "It was last night or the night before. Can't be one hundred percent certain."

"I could understand your behavior if she broke your heart."

"She did," I exclaim, meaning it. My heart cracked in the parking lot of the tavern. Even gorilla glue can't mend this tear.

"It was a week. You went out with Luna for years and carried on like business as usual when she up and moved across the country, leaving you for another man."

"I didn't love her."

If I had given prior thought to what I was saying, I wouldn't admit that. But can't take it back now.

Heidi's brow raises, but that's her only reaction. If she's surprised by my comment, she hides it. "I repeat. A week. You can't fall in love with someone that fast."

"You can when she's Willa. Besides, love at first sight is a real thing. Lenny, back me up."

"Hated Heidi's guts when I met her." He laughs, cut off by his wife's glare.

"Dad knows. Ask him. He'll tell you it's a thing." I sound like I'm nine, arguing with her about the best way to string lights.

Heidi contemplates my statement. It will be hard to refute. We've memorized the story of how Mom and Dad met in high school when Dad's family moved to Winterberry. Mom's family practically founded the town, and Dad wanted to make a name for himself here while trying to impress her. To do so, he entered the town's holiday lights contest. It was the first year a transplant to the town had won. Mom's been smitten ever since. As she tells it, it wasn't so much the win as his tenacity to design something majestic enough to dazzle the judges.

"What makes you so sure it's love?" she asks.

I wave my arm over myself. "Why would I look like this? Why else would I be, in Autumn's words, 'a miserable fuck'?"

"Dude's got a point. On Christmas Eve, he couldn't keep his eyes off her. And he had the look. Like he would do anything for her."

"Thanks?" I muse. Is that a compliment?

"Then call her. You have her number. Use it. Maybe she's miserable, too. You can be miserable together instead of apart."

"If we were together, I wouldn't be miserable."

She points a wooden spoon in my direction. "Even better."

"What if she's not miserable? What if she's destined to find someone better than me?"

"You're a pretty good catch, Becks. She'd be lucky to be on the receiving end of your affection."

I'd like to think that's true, and she's not one to blow smoke up people's asses.

"What if what we had wasn't real? It's not like our time together was 'real life.' She was on vacation, it was Christmas, I was on my best behavior, wanting to impress her."

"Valid points."

I wish she'd elaborate more, but she goes silent. I retreat into my head, thinking about Willa and how much I miss her.

"What if this is fate? Like you were destined to be on call that day she crashed?"

"Uh, I'm usually on call. Doesn't seem very fateful to me." Dax is supposed to share the duties, but nine times out of ten, calls default to me.

"What if it was fate that made her crash her car in Winterberry?" she tries.

It's a theory I've worked through in my mind. She ended up here for a reason.

"What if it was only to give her the closure she needed?"

"What if you stop playing the 'what if' game and Call. Her?"

"I don't like your tone of voice, young lady."

"My tone of voice has nothing on your appearance, Elfie."

I cringe at the nickname Autumn bestowed on me when I was a baby. Despite not wanting to go home, I stand up. "I'm not hungry anymore. I'll see myself out."

"Make yourself useful and take the trash out, would ya?" Heidi taunts.

"Bring me a plate later. I'll be hungry then." Not letting her argue, I pop a kiss on her cheek and take the bag out of the can, depositing it in the bin outside before getting into my truck.

Could it be as simple as "call her"?

What if she doesn't answer?

What if she's already forgotten about me?

What if . . .

I shake out of my stupor. "This is getting you nowhere. Man up and call her or let her go. What'll it be, Beckett?"

Can't wait to find out myself.

31
willa

GETTING over a broken heart is for the birds.

By the end of January, I've written over fifty thousand words, enough for one book and some of the next. The words bleed out of me. Some days, I fell into old habits, forgetting to eat and drink, never mind showering. A few nights, I was up until after three, not wanting to stop in fear I'd hit writer's block again.

And throughout it all, visions of Beckett loomed in the forefront.

When my eyes opened, I'd think of waking up in his arms.

When I poured coffee, I'd remember the taste of the cups he brewed.

When I laid down to sleep, it was his face behind my closed lids.

He's everywhere. He wasn't even in my space, yet I can't eradicate him. It's a problem.

I had hoped he'd be in touch, but other than his reply to my "I'm home" text message, he's been radio silent. Which was stupid since we both knew our relationship wasn't there. He and I are over. It'd be best to remember that.

Shania called when the package was delivered, her enthusiasm both a balm to my soul and a reminder of what I was missing. She didn't mention Beckett, but his spirit somehow joined our conversation.

I set a tentative deadline with my editor, and even though the first draft is finished, I'm not sure the final copy will be done in time. That's the self-doubt talking, the "it's going to flop because it's been so long since I released a book and no one wants to hear from me." It's utter crap because my social media following continues to grow, thanks mostly to my PA who continues to post engaging content. Occasionally, I'll pop on and interact. Shania tagged me in a post after the new year, but she didn't share our picture and her location is private, so it's not like people can figure out where I was.

Alanna, the bookstore owner, emailed me, thanking me profusely for the donations and swag. She ended with, "If you ever find yourself back in Winterberry, please, please, please stop in." I ignored that part of her email in my response.

I won't be back in Winterberry.

I stalked Beckett online, typing his name into Google to see what came up. I hit the mother lode because the guy's name is mentioned like every month on one Winterberry site or another. I smiled and cried my way through the articles, staring at his face from decades past and then the most recent one announcing him as the winner of the Main Street Lights Spectacular. I didn't know it had an official name. There were pictures of every year since the competition began, and I'm probably biased, but Beckett's was by far superior.

It sucks how much I miss him.

I wouldn't have thought this much misery was possible, to miss someone I knew for a week. It's absurd the amount of agony I feel. Even my therapist agrees. She did credit Beckett with giving me the closure I needed. For that alone, I'll be eternally grateful for the man.

Clem convinced me it was time to set up a dating profile and "get back on the horse." I let her do it all, including talking to one guy and setting up the date. Unfortunately, since we aren't identical—and she's married and lives hundreds of miles away —I couldn't send her on the date. He was a nice guy, but there was no spark. Even if Beckett hadn't been on my mind, I didn't see a future with this guy. Even as friends.

I've since logged out of the app and have no plans to try again.

I'll get there someday. I don't want to be alone forever, but someday isn't here yet.

I booked a week-long vacation to North Carolina to visit my family. We celebrated a late Christmas and New Year's, and Clem and I spent the rest of the week working out, drinking coffee, and discussing my week with Beckett. She convinced me his "fabrication" about my car not being able to be fixed was romantic and showed how much he cared for me. I can't say she was wrong.

I even spent time at my parents' house for dinner twice. It was tolerable, but only because it's annoying enough to help get my mind off Beckett. Of course, as soon as I left, he was front and center again.

Clem's ringtone pulls me out of my head.

"Hello?"

"You home?"

"It's eight at night. Where else would I be?"

"You dressed?"

"Does a baggy sweatshirt and flannel PJ pants count as being dressed?"

"Are you wearing a bra?"

I've been a little lax about wearing one lately. Mostly because every time I go to put one on, even if he hasn't seen it, Beckett comes to mind. Mainly, what he'd say if he saw it. How much he would worship my breasts. To combat this, I stopped wearing fancy ones and only wear a sports bra to leave the house.

I peek inside my shirt. "It's old, but it's there. Why the sudden fascination with my undergarments?"

A rustling comes across the line, but I can't make out what she's saying or who she's talking to.

"Did you eat dinner yet?"

I reflect on earlier. "Uh, nope. Definitely didn't do that. That must be why I'm starving." I chuckle. I get up off the couch and head into the kitchen, pulling open the tall cabinet door. "Let's see. Cereal or pasta. What sounds most appealing?"

My doorbell rings. Seriously? Who is here at eight p.m. on a Thursday evening?

"Clem, can I call you back? Someone's at my door."

"No!" she yells. "I mean, stay on the line. Because what if it's an axe murderer or a serial killer or a robber? I need to know you're safe."

I roll my eyes. "Don't be dramatic."

Her laugh sounds in my ear. "Me, dramatic. Funny coming from you."

The peephole reveals no one standing on the porch, but there's a white paper bag on the table. "There's a takeout bag on the porch. Did you order me food?"

"Nope."

"Why do I get the sense you know more than you're saying?"

"I'm not saying anything."

"I noticed." I unlatch the deadbolt and pry the door open. An eerie chill washes over me. "Is someone going to jump out at me? Is this a prank?"

Clem giggles on the other side of the line. "No prank. No jumping. Just look in the bag."

I put the phone on speaker and rest it beside the bag. Peering inside, it's not hot food. It's a, "What in the ever love?" I bring out the package of hot cocoa Oreos, the one I hid in Beckett's pantry--evidenced by the red heart I drew in the corner—and never told him about. But how did it end up here? "Uh, Clem?"

"Call me later. I want all the details. Well, maybe not *all* the details. And tomorrow is fine, too. But call me!" she screams into the phone before the call drops.

"She hung up on me. Rude."

I put on my best AJ Hart detective hat, trying to figure out what's going on and how Clem got involved.

"It took me a month to find, but I found it." At the sound of the male voice at my back, I spin around, the cookies flying from my hands in surprise. Beckett easily catches them.

"Beckett! You freaking scared me." I put my hand to my chest, willing my heart rate to regulate. It's a losing battle. Between being nearly scared to death and Beckett standing on my porch, no chance in hell I'll calm down soon.

"Sorry, but you were taking too long to figure this out. I couldn't wait any longer."

"How are you here? How did you get Clem's number?"

"Facebook Messenger," he states nonchalantly, as if it's obvious.

"What are you doing here?"

"Are you a miserable fuck?"

His words make no sense and are kinda rude. "Huh?"

He takes a step closer. His stubble's a little longer than it was when we spent time together, like he's decidedly not shaven on purpose. Purple circles under his eyes signify he hasn't been sleeping. He's no less handsome than the last day I saw him. Despite my initial shock, it's damn good to see him.

"Autumn tells me daily I'm a miserable fuck. Are you?"

"A miserable fuck? Care to elaborate so I can confirm or deny whether I am?"

He points behind me to my apartment. "Can I explain in there? It's kinda chilly out here."

Until he mentions it, I didn't feel cold, even without a coat and shoes. The wind chooses that moment to whip around the building.

"Oh, yeah. Sure. Come in." He holds the outer door with his empty hand, following me. Inside, he toes out of his boots and looks around.

"Love your blanket fort."

I glance at the pile of fleece blankets on the couch. "It's a cocoon."

He holds up a hand and chuckles. "My bad." Without waiting for an invitation, he sits on a cushion, pushing the blankets to the side, making room for me. Or I assume that's what he's doing. Maybe I'm hoping he's making a spot for me. Maybe he simply wants the blankets out of his way.

"So, a miserable fuck," I prod.

"It's not self-explanatory?"

"If I had to guess, someone who is miserable. Why does she call you that?"

"If I had to guess, because I am. Fucking miserable. Know anything about that?"

I could lie. I could tell him it's been sunshine and rainbows. That my life is so great now, and I'm not miserable.

"For the past month, Clem might have called my days 'les miserables.'" I shrug. My fingers curl into a fist so I don't touch him. I force my feet to stay planted so I don't maul him.

"Want to know why I'm miserable, Willa?"

"If you want to tell me, Beckett."

"I miss you." He lays it out so simply, so astute, so casual.

My shoulders sag with the weight of the past month. "Same. So much."

He lets out an audible breath, his chest rising and falling with the motion. "Then what are you doing over there?"

I practically leap to the couch and onto his lap, crashing my mouth to his. He anticipates my action, grabbing the back of my head to be in charge of the kiss.

Our mouths meet familiarly, our tongues dueling for control, his the victor, as always.

It's a kiss of remembrance, of missed connections, of needing more.

What does his being here mean?

Where do we go from here?

Is there an us to fight for?

Beckett pulls away, his bottom lip swollen from where I tugged it into my mouth. "Out of your head, in the present. We'll question it later."

His use of "we'll" sets my heart into motion.

But I can't help myself. "What if—"

He cuts me off. "Later we'll play the 'what if' game. After you feed me. Your vagina or food, I'm not picky."

Said vagina somersaults.

I pinch myself to make sure this isn't a dream or some fictional world. I fall into those pretty easily, especially these days.

"You're really here?"

"I'm really here." A smile so big, his dimple breaks through.

"For how long?"

"For as long as it takes to convince you to come home."

His words give me pause. I regard my apartment, hella confused. "I am home. You're the one who's not."

"Come home with me," he clarifies.

"Oh." A smile spreads quickly across my lips. "Might take a while. I'm kinda stubborn."

"I have skills in my arsenal you haven't seen yet and enough sick days to wait you out."

"Is that so?"

"Guess we'll wait and see." He cups my chin in his hands. "Can we get back to the kissing now?"

"You came all this way for kisses?"

"I came all this way for you, Bundy. The kisses are bonus."

Is it any wonder why this man stole my heart?

Two days.

It takes Beckett two days to convince me I belong with him in Winterberry.

I tried to last longer, to find out what other skills he'd use against me, but forty-eight hours after he arrived, it was torture to not tell him.

Wherever he is, I want to be there with him.

I didn't even have an argument for him to move in with me. Winterberry's in the man's blood, and I love him enough not to deny him that.

Yep, I love him. He got that one out of me the first night. Right about the time he coerced me to a second orgasm in ten minutes.

But soon after, he echoed my sentiments. In his sex-induced, raspy voice, the man professed his love, and the words "I love you" never sounded so sweet. So tender. So phenomenal.

I don't care that it's fast, that we still have so much to learn about each other, or that I'm uprooting my life for a man I met less than two months ago. When it's right, you know. It's not worth fighting.

He offered the option of staying in his investment property. I swear it was fake, that he made it up that first night to not seem like such a creeper. But he showed me pictures—with him in them—of the progress he's still yet to make on it. The cabin seems like a much better solution. If I hate it, I can find a place in town.

I'm not going to hate it.

Since he's been in my space, he made it his mission to learn what else makes me tick, including asking me all kinds of questions about Evelyn—how I decided on the name, needing to see the glasses and the entire look, collecting knowledge about my process. It launched a dynamic discussion about the two sides of my personality: Willa and Evelyn. He made it clear he loves them both.

Now, it's the third day of him staying with me, and he's cooking breakfast in my kitchen. He came prepared with a list and forced me to the grocery store the morning after he arrived. This isn't the first meal he's cooked.

"Should I get used to you cooking every meal for us? Because I don't want to be let down if this isn't something you plan to do."

He lays the wooden spoon on the spoon rest. "*Every* meal might be a stretch, especially during the winter months when there's decorating and plowing to do, but I'll cook you one meal per day at the minimum."

I'm going to be so spoiled and well-fed. No more cereal or pasta nights for me.

"And you'll let me help clean up in exchange?"

The man visibly twitches. "If I must."

"You must. We'll hire a cleaning service for the cabin."

He quirks a brow. "We will, will we?"

"It's my contribution. I'll pay rent, too." I punctuate my statement with a nod. I won't be a freeloader if we're living there together.

"Cabin's paid off."

"Utilities, then. Cable, Wi-Fi, your car loans and insurance," I try.

He raises his right hand in the air. "I'm not having this discussion now."

"Why not?"

"Because I'm not in the mood to argue." His tone leaves no room to challenge him. Not that I obey.

"Who says it will be an argument?"

"Don't couples always fight about money?"

"Are we a couple?" I don't need confirmation for something I already know, but I can't take it back after asking.

"Do you think I invite just anyone to live with me?"

"After you asked me, I sure hope not. The cabin's not big enough for more than two people."

"So you're saying it's not our forever home?"

My belly twinges at the thought of what he means. "What? You got that out of what I said?"

"We'll save the kids discussion for later, too. Still not in the mood to argue."

"So you're saying there will be times you will be in the mood to argue?"

"A plethora, I'm sure. If you let me. You'll see."

"Whoa. I didn't sign up for this crazy persona you've inhabited the past few days."

"Didn't you?"

"No. Certainly not. I don't do crazy." I can't even get the words out with a straight face. Because of the two of us, he's the less crazy.

"You do the best kind of crazy, Willa. I love your brand of crazy. Serial killers, girl detectives, split personalities, hating my favorite holiday . . . shall I keep going?"

I've joined him in the kitchen, my hip leaning against the counter. "Plenty certain of my type of crazy. But hey, when it comes down to it, remember I was born this way. You're choosing to love me."

I get all in my feels every time I hear him say anything with the word "love" in it as it relates to me or our relationship. Call me crazy—ha—but this man gets me, down to my core. Fast or not, when I picture my future, it's Beckett I see. Maybe a couple of kids, a pet or two, but always Beckett.

"How long will you need to pack up your apartment and things here before you move home?"

He keeps saying "home," and every time, I fall deeper. Ironically, none of my places of residence has ever felt as much like "home" as being with Beckett at the cabin.

"Other than figuring out the lease, packing and hiring movers should about do it. Lucky we don't have to cross state lines. Don't even need to get a new license."

His brow dips. "You'll have a new address. Hence, a new license."

"I suppose that's true."

He turns off the burner, pushing the pan of eggs to a back one that's not on. "You didn't answer my question."

"A month?" I propose.

"Too long. I'll give you a week."

"A week? You ask me how long and then give me a timeline that fits your needs?"

He shakes his head, looping his arms around my waist, tugging me toward him. "My timeline would be today."

"Eep," I squeal. I can't help it. Today! The man wants me to move today. To pack up my life and be on the road today. Hardly seems feasible.

"Which is why a week gives you plenty of time."

"Are you staying to help me pack and get my affairs in order?"

"Told you I have the sick days for as long as needed."

"Yeah, but won't they miss you? The boss? The best tow truck driver in town?"

"Dax's got it covered." A flash of concern washes over his face, gone as quickly as it came. "He's got it covered," he repeats, to reassure himself as much as me.

"One week." I look around my space, the place I've called home for the last two years. "Think we could do it in two days? Then I won't have to worry about breaking the lease since it's the last day of the month."

He scans my space. The whole one thousand square feet of it. "You don't have that much stuff to pack. We'll rent a moving truck, load it up, and bring the big stuff, then come back here and pack our cars with what's left and be on our way. Two days. I think we can do it."

"You've got yourself a deal." We seal it with a kiss, embarking on something epic. "For the record, I don't hate Christmas. Not anymore." Because of him.

"Yeah, I know." He smirks, the action landing straight in my gut.

What started as a rescue in the snow led to more. Beckett Nicholas saved me in all the ways, and I'll never be more grateful for him being on the other end of that phone call.

It also helps he's not a serial killer, but what a story we've got to tell.

epilogue

BECKETT

ONE YEAR LATER CHRISTMAS EVE

"'The stockings were hung by the chimney with care . . .'" Willa stops reading, her glasses sliding down her nose. Her gaze swings to our fireplace, back to me, back to the fireplace. "Next year, we need matching stockings." She readjusts her glasses, getting back to the book.

She's reading me *'Twas the Night Before Christmas*, stopping at certain points to share her thoughts about the story or as it relates to our life. So far, she's mentioned the stockings and the not-so-stirring mouse. Or in our case, mice. Willa's not a fan. It's a cabin in the woods. She's lucky we don't have larger rodent guests.

A fire roars in the fireplace, and the Christmas tree illuminates the corner of the room. When it was time to decorate the cabin for the holiday, it was Willa who broached the subject, letting me know she'd be in charge of interior decorations and I would do the yard. Letting her have this, I was amazed at the lengths she went to, making sure to put her stamp on it. It's perfectly imperfect, and I couldn't love it more.

Before she can start again, I ask, "Will we need three matching stockings next year?"

"As of this moment, no," she's quick to reply, "but with the way you can't keep your hands off me, it's not out of the question."

"I'll see what I can do later tonight."

I watched my sister struggle with a baby at twenty and knew I never wanted that for myself. As Shania grew and she wasn't so fragile and scary as a toddler and then a kid, my desire for having kids in the future expanded. With the birth of Isla and having Willa in my life, I've become a little obsessed. We're not getting younger, and she wants kids, too. As much as I'm enjoying her and our relationship, I want to be a dad.

"Don't forget our deal."

"Our deal?"

She peers over her glasses at me. "This cabin isn't made for three. The bedroom will be too crowded for even a cradle."

I love this cabin and am not prepared to give it up, but she's not wrong. It's too small for the two of us, let alone a kid. It just so happens I have an investment property willing and waiting for us, along with a surprise for Willa tomorrow.

"Even if you get pregnant tonight, we have nine months to figure out a new living situation."

"Just so long as you're aware. I'm also okay with us living in a bigger place just the two of us. If you catch my drift. In case your plan of getting me pregnant takes longer than tonight."

"Loud and clear, Bundy. Get back to the story because we still have to watch a movie before bed."

She wanted to recreate our first Christmas Eve together, complete with a meal at the B and B. And because my family is all about traditions, Heidi was on board immediately, right down to the beef Wellington, which may have been better this year than last.

Once we were home, Willa informed me of a new tradition she wanted to start, and being so in love with her and her embracing my favorite holiday, I couldn't deny her request.

Hence, the reading of the book. I could listen to her read all day long, so it's not quite a hardship.

What is hard is my cock. It's willing and waiting to get inside her. I'm hoping she'll agree to my plan of during the movie instead of after.

I'm betting it won't be a problem.

CHRISTMAS MORNING

Gotta love the power of persuasion.

Or in my case, letting her think it was her idea to have sex while we watched the Hallmark movie of my choosing. I didn't even have to plant the seed. She's the one who stuck her hand down my pants. With the fire roaring and the movie playing low in the background, we made love on the couch.

And then again in the bedroom before we fell asleep.

And once more this morning before we had to get ready for brunch at my parents' house.

Surely one of those times got her pregnant.

With the addition of Isla, Christmas brunch looks a little different this year. Unlike last year, Willa's a permanent addition to our table.

Excited to attend this year's brunch, Shania wowed her with a hand-drawn picture of the bookshop in Willa's books. My girl cried. Hard. Which led to all the women crying about the sweet gift.

I only wasn't jealous because I have my own sweet surprise planned for her later.

Mom outdid herself today with the meal comprising of eggs Florentine, eggnog bread pudding, and a tater tot breakfast casserole. I offered multiple times to come early and help, all of which she refused, telling me to enjoy Christmas morning with Willa.

Once we're stuffed and say our goodbyes, I lead Willa to the SUV. It doesn't get driven much because if we're going somewhere and not driving the truck, we usually take Willa's car. It's newer and nicer than mine, and she even lets me drive it. With the stipulation it's not allowed to crash again. Once was enough.

"Where are we going? Isn't the cabin the other way?"

Despite living here for almost a year, she doesn't get out much except to Main Street and my family's houses, and she's bad with directions. Too busy in her head most days, she barely leaves the kitchen table or the couch. Building her an office in the garage is on our list, but once I realized the house was a better option, I pushed it to the bottom.

Maybe one day.

"One last Christmas gift."

"Beckett. That wasn't our agreement."

Her and her "deals" and "agreements" can shove it some days. It makes it hard to spoil her when I have to abide by her wishes, most of which are her putting stipulations on our relationship. In eleven months, I've already broken nearly all of them. Wouldn't you know it, I never hear her complaining.

"Consider it a New Year's gift then."

"Yeah, 'cause those are things."

"They are if you let them be."

Out of the corner of my eye, I watch her harrumph and cross her arms across her chest in mock frustration. She has pretty much abandoned all coats and jackets in favor of my fleece hoodies. No matter what she's wearing—like a festive red and green dress and leggings currently—if the weather calls for something heavier, she usually chooses the one I offered her last year. Thankfully for her, she doesn't have to brace the elements too often. She's an indoor girl.

Or as I like to refer to her, my indoor black cat.

I love riling her up, pushing her to the limit, finding new ways for her "grumpy" side to appear. It's the side I first fell in love with last year before I knew who else was hiding under the facade.

She doesn't know I've had a construction team working on the house. She doesn't ask about it, so I don't tell her the details. I'm prepared to have her tell me she hates everything and have to start again. Everyone told me I should let her make some decisions if this is our home, but I didn't want to ruin the surprise. Besides, I've subtly been asking her questions for months, gauging what she likes and doesn't like. I think she'll be okay with the eventual design.

And if not, the ring box burning a hole in my pocket will smooth things over.

I turn down the street—Reindeer Road—and drive to the house at the end of the block, the one that years ago belonged to my grandparents on my mother's side. I only ended up with it because none of my other siblings wanted it after Nana died. As much as I didn't have use for it then, I'm hella glad I didn't sell it.

The former house has been torn down and the one currently standing in its place is brand-new. Bigger than its replacement, but with elements the original contained. Like the front porch, black shutters, and two fireplaces.

"Wait. I know this location," Willa admits as I park the car in front of the two-car garage. Like at the cabin, the plan is to build a three-car garage behind it, which will become my new workshop. There are some nights I wake up with too much on my mind and need the outlet, but I'm not prepared to drive to the cabin when the urge hits. Besides, I have ideas for the garage at the cabin. "This is your investment property?"

"Yes."

It's not so much an "investment" now as "home." Instead, the cabin will become the investment property, one I have no intention of renting out. It's already paid off, so I don't need the income from it. I can't say what will happen in the future to the cabin, if we'll use it as much as I hope we will, but the option will always be there.

"Wow. I didn't realize you'd been working on it. It looks almost completed."

"A few finishing touches and it'll be ready for occupancy. Want to see it?"

"Yep."

I unbuckle and climb out of the car, rounding the hood to stand next to her as she takes it all in.

Instead of the white of the original house, I chose gray clapboard siding, hoping it will stand out more when it's decorated for the holidays. The front boasts five windows lining the top floor. Below, the porch wraps around to the left, and the black front door welcomes visitors.

Or in our case, welcoming us home.

I'm still waiting for the driveway to be paved, but part of me is digging the dirt pathway. Though it might be a pain to plow with bigger storms.

"It's gorgeous, Beckett. Almost too good for an Airbnb rental."

I'm glad she thinks so.

Latching on to her wrist, I tug her behind me. "Come on. Let me show you the inside."

We start downstairs, with the living room and half bathroom, making our way to the kitchen.

"It's like the one at the B and B," she notes, her eyes lighting up. The woman can't cook to save her life, but she's in love with kitchens. Go figure. She trails her hand along the marble island. "One of these days, when I'm on a hiatus from writing books, you're going to teach me to cook."

"Yeah, sure." I'll believe it when it happens. She says it once a month at minimum, yet when I offer to teach her, she claims she's too busy. Good thing I love making meals for her.

After the kitchen, we climb the stairs to the second floor. I debated about three or four extra bedrooms beyond the primary, finally settling on three larger ones rather four smaller. Even if we have more kids than bedrooms, they're big enough to share.

Willa explores the primary bedroom, oohing and aahing as she absorbs it all. "His and her closets. And this bathroom. This bathtub. Oh my gosh." She peeks her head out the door. "Are you sure you want to rent this place out?"

"What else would I do with it?" I keep my tone neutral, not letting the giddiness out. Mentally, I pat myself on the back for knowing my girl so well.

She joins me in the room. "I could think of one thing."

I laugh. "Only one?" It's never "one" thing with her.

"Yes," she claims, punctuating it with a nod of her head. "One thing."

"Lay it on me."

She rubs her ear. It's only gotten even more adorable the longer I'm with her. "Promise you won't be mad?"

"Depends."

"Beckett," she whines, stomping her foot. "It's Christmas. We don't argue on your favorite holiday."

"I never agreed to that." The words fall out of my mouth without thinking. After hearing them, she's right. We haven't talked about it, but I have no intention of arguing with her on my favorite holiday. "I promise not to be mad."

Slowly, she spins around the room, her eyes darting around. "What if we lived here?" she murmurs, almost inaudibly, I can barely make it out.

"You haven't even seen the entire house yet."

Willa faces me, her expression a mask of indignation. "I've seen enough. And there are a plethora of bedrooms for all the kids you're going to impregnate me with. Plenty of land in the yard for a workshop. A huge front yard for your lights extravaganza. I could even use one room as an office until it's needed for a bedroom. *If* it's needed for a bedroom," she corrects.

"What about the cabin?"

"Oh, we're keeping it. Heck, maybe I can use that as my writing studio." She shrugs. "We'll figure it out."

"Before you officially decide, let me show you the rest of the house."

Not waiting for her answer, I take her hand, letting her poke her head in the bedrooms before leading her back downstairs to the office. The French doors are closed, but I push inside the empty room, having left this room up for her to design since it'll be the place she'll spend most of her time.

"This is the last room left to do. Any ideas?"

"It would make the perfect office. A desk there." She points to a side wall. "A couch or chair there." She points to the opposite side. "A bookshelf there." Another wall. "Think of all the books I could write here."

"So many," I confirm, happy she's so ecstatic about it. "What do you say you write the books as a Nicholas instead of a Gibson?"

I drop to one knee, holding out the box with the sparkling diamond.

"Beckett," she croons, her fingers covering her lips. She steps closer, her eyes trained on the ring. "It's exquisite, magnificent, radiant." She raises her sight to meet mine, tears in her eyes. "So pretty."

"Glad you think so." I clear my throat. I drafted a proposal, but in the moment, I'm tossing it out the window and speaking from my heart. "Willafred Gibson, we were never supposed to meet, but am I elated that we did. You're the other half of my heart, the missing piece in my life. When you crashed—literally —into my life last year, I admired your beauty, your quick wit, your grumpiness, but most of all, your abhor of my favorite holiday." I can't help the way my body quivers, but Willa's giggles spur me on. "Being stuck with you that week was torture, in the best and worst ways, but I wouldn't trade it for anything. I wouldn't change anything about how we met, how we fell in love, how we got here. I hope you agree our story is one for the books." I pause long enough for her to nod before I continue. "What do you say we do life together every day from here on out? Be my wife?" I almost forget to add the question mark at the end, though I'm not opposed to telling her what to do.

"Yes."

"Yeah?"

"Duh, Beckett. Yes, of course, I'll be your wife. Thanks for asking."

I leap from the ground, enveloping her in my embrace, basking in the joy of her saying yes. I had no doubts she'd turn me down, but it feels damn good to hear her confirm what I've known for a while.

Slipping the ring on her finger, I rest my forehead against hers. "I like your idea of living here. I'm not good at sharing my space with strangers."

"It's not really my idea, is it?"

"Not even a little, Bundy. But I'll let you take twenty-five percent of the credit. 'Cause I'm generous like that."

"Extremely. You're the most generous person I've ever known. It will be my pleasure to be your wife, but even more to call you my husband. Even at my worst, you saw through to what's underneath, made me face my demons, and didn't even balk when I insinuated you might be a serial killer."

"Not any of the plethora of times you said it," I interject.

"I love you. For the rest of my life, I will love you every day. Even when you make me crazier than I am."

"I do no such thing." She balks at my insinuation, but I can't blame her. I tend to push her beyond her limits of crazy but in a good way. Because I love her.

She studies the room again, seeing it from a different perspective of making it hers. Her gaze meets mine. "When can we move in?" Her phone rings, interrupting our conversation. "It's

Clem. I'll call her back." She returns it to her pocket, but it rings again.

"Answer her. She must need something."

"Merry Christmas!"

"Where are you?" Clem's worried voice fills the room.

"Presently standing in my soon-to-be office, ogling my fiancé. You?"

"The cabin."

"What cabin?"

"Your cabin," she screeches. "I left Keith. I didn't know where else to go." Her voice cracks.

I grab the phone from Willa. "There's a key under the mat by the side door of the garage. Make yourself comfortable. We might be a little while, but I'll send Dax over in case you need something. Are you okay?"

"No, not really. Thank you. I'm sorry to ruin your holiday—"

I cut her off. "Nonsense." I look over at Willa, a woman who crashed into my life at the most unexpected time, tilting my life on its axis, only righting itself when I realized she's the one I'm meant to do life with. "It's not a Christmas holiday if a Gibson doesn't need my help. We'll be there soon. Hold tight."

Her relief is palpable, even over the phone. "Thank you, Beckett."

Willa stands next to me. "I hope you don't mind I'm going to revel in my Christmas gifts before we tackle your issues," she admits with a laugh, the concern for her sister shining through.

"Yeah, sure, Willafred. Go be happy with your man while my life crumbles to shit. Take your time," she deadpans.

"Love you too, Clementine," Willa calls out, hanging up the phone before any rebuttal from Clem. "Where were we?"

"You were asking when we can move in," I remind.

"Oh, right. So, when can we?" Her sister's issues temporarily forgotten, she hooks her arms around my waist.

"It's move-in ready. We'll need to order some furniture and bring over what we're keeping from the cabin, if anything."

"We should start fresh. New everything, so it's ours instead of mine or yours. Maybe we hit up the stores this week, move in by New Year's?"

I chuckle. "It might take longer than a week to get everything delivered."

Her enthusiasm falls. "Hmm, good point. We should still go shopping, see what we can find, and get a better timeline."

"I thought I'd have a harder time convincing you this was a good idea."

"No, you didn't." She calls me on my bullshit. "But if you're in the mood to argue . . ."

"What I'm in the mood for is to take you upstairs to our new bedroom and christen it and our upgraded relationship status."

Willa pushes to her toes, swiping her lips across mine. "That's a start. While you're at it, work on putting a baby in me."

"If you insist . . ."

She finagles out of my grasp, pausing in the doorway to peer at me over her shoulder. "It would be fitting, knocking me up on your favorite holiday."

"It would be the jingle bells on Santa's sleigh."

Cheesy as the line is, Willa smiles brighter than the extravagant holiday display at the cabin.

Perhaps it wasn't fate that led Willa to crash in Winterberry Junction.

Perhaps it was truly the magic of Christmas.

Wait! Willa and Beckett's story isn't over quite yet. Read this bonus scene and find out what happens when Beckett finally knocks Willa up . . .

Want more swoony small town romance? For more in Havenwood, start the Aspenridge College Hockey series with *Pucked Up Plans*. Or if you want to meet Willa's cousins, the Murrthams, check out *The Magic of Us*.

pucked up plans

My top three priorities:
    my daughter
    playing hockey
    a college education

Add in a few hours working a part-time job, and my days are pretty packed. But does that stop me from pursuing Tate Winchester?

Nope, not even a little.

Until she turns me down for a date.

To her credit, she has a lot on her plate. She's new to our small town, she works a full-time job, and she's a single mom to my daughter's new friend. Our relationship initially stems from playdates for the kids, but I'll take time with her any way I can. However, the more time we spend together, the more I want that date.

Pucked Up Plans

A plan forms in my mind, and though life never goes according to how I envision, I'm determined to make this happen.

If–*when*–she finally agrees, I hope I don't puck up the plans…

author's note

Thank you for choosing to read *A Not So Merry Rescue*. I hope you enjoyed reading it as much as I loved writing it. And I LOVED writing it (more on that later).

This book was born from the idea of repeatedly seeing "I'm looking for holiday romances" last year. Because who doesn't love a holiday romance, right? I wanted to be able to say here's mine, even if the window for them is short. However, this year, I noticed people in earlier months looking for holiday romances, which only heightened my excitement for the possibility of the book.

As usual, I went into this book with almost nothing planned. A few of my friends encouraged me to tie it to the Murrtham's Tree Farm series ("You have the perfect setting already"), but that didn't feel right. What felt right was a standalone, a new setting, with unfamiliar characters. Somewhere that has the feel of a Taylor Delong book but was still uncharted territory. And so, Winterberry Junction evolved. (Fun fact, during edits, the town's name changed because it was too similar to another fictional place). I truly hope you've enjoyed your visit. Come back anytime. The Nicholas family will love to have you!

What I love about writing the discovery draft of a book is meeting the characters, learning their quirks, their occupations (did I know Willa was a children's mystery book author? Nope, not until she told me lol), and their backstories. I'm sure this sounds crazy to some of you, but I don't know everything that happens in the story until I write it. I didn't know Willa had such a tragic past with Elias. I didn't know how much she needed Beckett in her life, beyond him rescuing her from the accident. But you know what? It makes the story more fun to write. It makes me want to keep writing to find out what other secrets the characters haven't yet told me. It's not always easy getting them to spill their secrets (I'm looking at you, ETHAN), but eventually it all—mostly—gets revealed.

Willa—who went through three or four name changes, I can't even remember at this point—is high on my list for favorite heroines. Maybe it's her quirkiness, maybe it's the way she's quick with a comeback, or how she's a bit obsessed with Beckett being a serial killer. Maybe it's everything about her. Whatever it is, I loved writing her side of the story, finding out her *reasons* for not liking Christmas (I mean, who can blame her when you find out), and watching her fall in love with this man who basically embodied everything Christmas has to offer. Man, he is so good to her. Which is definitely something I love about Beckett. From the first moment, when she implied he was a serial killer, he didn't back down. In fact, he pushed back. He was smitten from the start. And yes, *smitten* is the only way to describe him. He fell for her almost immediately, even if he didn't want to admit it to himself. Despite their differences, they are perfect for each other. Like Willa, I never thought of him as "Beck"; in my mind, he was always Beckett. Either she influenced me or I influenced her. Guess we'll never know.

I love how this story takes place in such a short timeframe, yet so much gets revealed about both characters, and hopefully the setting, too. It was so much fun to create a town where everyone loves the holidays, but also where Beckett was so involved. I definitely loved turning that trope upside down where *he's* the one who loves Christmas and Hallmark movies, yet it fits him so well.

When I first wrote the story, I didn't have a firm state location in mind. The actual location for Winterberry Junction went through a few edits until I landed on Vermont. Or maybe I didn't "land" on it so much as the characters told me where they lived. I had to do a lot of rearranging in the second and third drafts to make sure it made sense of where everyone lived. But hey. The most important thing now is Willa is "home" to live in Winterberry Junction, right where she belongs.

I hope you found the nods to other Taylor Delong books (two series if I counted correctly). This book stands alone, but it wouldn't be a true Taylor Delong book without some mention of other characters, right? (And, Willa has already made it clear she has an idea for an upcoming book. Who am I to deny her?). Time will tell if this is the last time we're in Winterberry Junction, but I have a high suspicion it won't be . . . If you want to see more of any of these characters, be sure to let me know! I love receiving email from readers and fans.

As much as I do the heavy lifting of this business on my own, I'd be remiss not to mention the people on my team and behind the scenes who help make this book a reality.

With deepest gratitude and appreciation, thank you:

Denise: for your detailed notes and making sure I keep track of locations of where the characters live. For this text message: "This was like the quickest "notes" read! I ate it up." Seriously, the best message ever! Also, for being the best assistant at Rain City Author Signing. I couldn't have cleared that table without you!

Missy: for finding the mistakes I miss during my read-throughs and for loving all these characters I keep throwing your way. For the never ending and unwavering support.

Arell, Libby, Mary Ellen and Nicole: I've said this before, but thank you never seems appropriate enough for the joy, guidance, and support you bring into my life. I love our daily sprints, even when we're all forced to actually work. I often wonder how I got so blessed to find the *best* author tribe. I don't know where I'd be without you. Well, maybe I do, and it wouldn't be anywhere good! Thank you for putting up my antics and for all the support with blurbs, plots, titles, covers, and everything else that comes along with this business. Can't wait for next February for our retreat!

Kitty: for being the last set of eyes on the book before it goes to ARC readers and for finding mistakes that only we'd care about. Or for mistakes that aren't really mistakes. "It's dialogue. I'll allow it." LOL Also for our walks keeping me sane!

Jillian: for being the kind of friend where it never felt like we were ever strangers. For your support and encouragement. Let's make the Rhode Island retreat a yearly thing. Pretty sure my bestie invited us back! **Heidi,** thank you for being my bestie, for the TT chats, and every bit of encouragement. Here's to working smarter, not harder!

Megan: for taking my ramblings of notes and turning it into the BEST ILLUSTRATED COVER EVER! When I found out you did illustrated covers, I couldn't reach out fast enough to get on your schedule. I love every little clue/element that represents the story in the pages between the covers. I can't wait to get it in my hands and put it on my shelf. It is simply adorable, and I'm so thankful to you for taking the time to tweak it until it was just right. You are so talented and do amazing work!

My enthusiastic **cheerleaders** who've believed in me from the start and never stop encouraging me. I'm putting it into the universe about jet-setting to Spain and Iceland on my private jet. Hey, stranger things have happened, and no we're one book closer to this happening!

Members of the ARC team: All the thank yous in the world! For those who have been here from the beginning or who have come along the way, I'm so thankful for you. Thank you for being a part of my team when they're are so many amazing books to read. Thanks for helping to spread the early word of this book and for loving these characters.

Readers/influencers: For choosing my books of the millions available, from the bottom of my heart, thank you! I'm always amazed at how strangers take my words to heart and fall in love with the characters who live in my head. It's definitely a lot surreal.

Author friends: This business isn't for the faint of heart, and I appreciate every friend I've met along the way. I'm grateful for the pleasure of knowing you and hope we get to meet in real life at some point. I have to keep saying that because even though I keep meeting people IRL, I keep stacking up the friends who I still have to meet.

Mom (and Dad): thanks for showing me what true love is. Thanks for showing all of us how great family can be. Dad, still not ready to take you off this list. I know you're here in spirit.

Last, but not least, **E and A**: for helping me make this dream a reality. Whether that's helping me manifest things, talking plot and characters, telling me how much you don't like something (HA HA HA), and everything else. I'm doing this. For you as much as me. Because how else are we going to get the lake cabin, right? Love you forever and always! You'll always be the two best characters I've ever created.

also by taylor delong

Aspenridge College Hockey Series

Pucked Up Plans

It's Pucking Complicated

Sweet as Puck

Summer Puckin'

Creek Valley Creamery Series

Rocky Road

After Eight

Tin Roof Sunday

Cold Brew

Zero Visibility

Forever in Laketon Series

Waiting on Forever

Forever Squared

Forever and a Day

Laketon 2.0

Love Unscripted

Life Unscripted

Brew Play Love

Rocky Water Series

Defining Us

The Breaking Point

Murrtham's Tree Farm Series

The Magic of Us

The Magic of Her

The Magic of Baseball

Love on the Tree Farm (Box Set)

Standalones

A Not so Merry Rescue (Christmas romance)

The Highway Ride

Up to Fate part of the Steamy Shorts anthology

Opposing Fate part of A Kiss at Midnight

Loving Rebel

Whiskey Tears

Can't Buy My Love (Girl Power Romance)

Where Forever Leads (Falls Village)

The Lawn Boy (All American Boy)

about the author

Taylor Delong writes small-town, contemporary romances full of heart and heat. Her cinnamon roll heroes protect the ones they love and will leave you swooning. She has been reading and writing for as long as she can remember. It's always been her dream to be a published author. She spends her days chasing after toddlers and her nights scribbling down stories and ideas the characters in her head dictate to her. She lives in CT with her two children.

Check out her website for more.

www.ingramcontent.com/pod-product-compliance
Lightning Source LLC
Chambersburg PA
CBHW071732150726
47998CB00005B/1604